THE LONDON PUNK TAPES since 1976

Jordi Valls

BARCELONA 2010

EDICIÓ CATALÀ / CASTELLÀ / ANGLÈS
EDICIÓN CATALÁN / CASTELLANO / INGLÉS
CATALAN / SPANISH / ENGLISH EDITION

_RTS S_NT_ MÒNIC_

ACTAR

EDICIÓ / EDICIÓN / EDITION: Arts Santa Mònica i Actar. | © dels textos, els autors. | © de les imatges i les fotografies, els fotògrafs. | © de les traduccions, els traductors. | © d'aquesta edició, Arts Santa Mònica/ Actar – Departament de Cultura i Mitjans de Comunicació de la Generalitat de Catalunya. | ISBN: 978-84-393-8389-5 (Arts Santa Mònica). ISBN: 978-84-92861-51-4 (Actar). | Dipòsit Legal: B-29837-2010 | Arts Santa Mònica. La Rambla, 7. 08002 Barcelona. Tel.: +34 93 316 28 10. www.artssantamonica.cat | Actar. Barcelona / New York. Part of ActarBirkhäuser. www.actar.com.

GENERALITAT DE CATALUNYA DEPARTAMENT DE CULTURA I MITJANS DE COMUNICACIÓ. Conseller de Cultura i Mitjans de Comunicació: Joan Manuel Tresserras. | Secretari General: Lluís Noguera. | Secretari de Cultura: Eduard Voltas. | Secretari de Comunicació: Carles Mundó. | Entitat Autònoma de Difusió Cultural. Gerent: Conxita Oliver. | ARTS SANTA MÒNICA. Direcció: Vicenç Altaió. | Àmbit d'Arts: Manuel Guerrero. | Àmbit de Ciència: Josep Perelló. | Àmbit de Comunicació: David Vidal. | Coordinació General: Marta Garcia, Fina Duran. | Administració: Cristina Güell. | Relacions externes: Alicia Gonzalez. | Edicions: Cinta Massip. | Comunicació i premsa: Neus Purtí, Cristina Suau. | Producció i coordinació: Lurdes Ibarz, Ester Martínez, Arantza Morlius. | Àrea Tècnica: Xavier Roca, Eulàlia Garcia. | Secretaria: Pep Xaus, Carles Ferry. | L'Arts Santa Mònica compta amb el suport de la Corporació Catalana de Mitjans Audiovisuals, i amb *La Vanguardia*, *Vilaweb* i *Mau Mau* com a mitjans de comunicació col·laboradors. I amb la Fundació Bosch i Gimpera, de la Universitat de Barcelona, i l'INCOM, de la Universitat Autònoma de Barcelona, com a institucions acadèmiques col·laboradores.

EXPOSICIÓ / EXPOSICIÓN / EXHIBITION. Concepte / Concepto / Concept: Jordi Valls, amb Franc Aleu, Pedro de Cos, Marc Valls i Marc Viaplana. | Coordinació / Coordinación / Coordination: Fina Duran i Ester Martinez. | Vídeo: Franc Aleu / Urano [inclou imatges filmades per Erika Lust / Lust Films; i el vídeo *Orsini* de Marc Viaplana]. | Enginyer de so / Ingeniero de sonido / Sound engineer: Pedro de Cos. | Digitalització / Digitalización / Digitalisation: Jordi Bonet / Oido. | Equip tècnic / Equipo técnico / Technical team: Xavier Roca, Eulàlia Garcia, Marc Ases, Luis Bisbe, Juan Carlos Escudero, David Garcia, Juande Jarillo, Pere Joval, Xesco Muñoz.

Agraïments / Agradecimientos / Acknowledgements: Paco Alvarado, Rosa Arruti, Monte Cazazza, Ester Cutillas, Toni Fortuny, Morfi Grei, Irene Guga, Eliseu Huertas i Cos, Mike Ibañez, Charles Malson, Memi March, Antoni Mateu, Jordi Mustieles, Albert Pijuan, Genesis P-Orridge, Magda Redondo, Pau Riba, Cecília Soler, Oriol Soler, Guim Valls, Roc Valls, Dana Vilà, Arturo Xalabarder.

Agraïments especials / Agradecimientos especiales / Special acknowledgements: Ben Browton, Ray Burns, Hannah Collins, Paul Cook, Salvador Costa i Montse Ferré, Martin Costello, Xavi Cot, Rich Defame, Raf Edmonds, Jean Genet, Vic Godard, Daisy Hugh, Jeff Jacquin, Tony James, Erika Lust / Lust Films, Shane MacGowan, Malcolm McLaren i Vivienne Westwood, Shreen El Masry, Julius Name, Mercedes Padilla, Mark Perry, Jamie Reid, Silvia Resorte, Tricia Ronane, Nils Stevenson, Ray Stevenson, Katie Szolnoki, Rosa Tharrats i Carolina Caralt / CROMMORC, Lucy Toothpaste, Ari Up, Zeus Valls, Zoë Valls i Marc Folch, Katy Vives Phipps –lefreak– i Rai Escalé, Hellen Wellington-Lloyd. THE SEX PISTOLS, THE CLASH, SUBWAY SECT, THE SLITS, THE DAMNED, THE BUZZCOCKS, GENERATION X, THE BROMLEY CONTINGENT, *SNIFFIN' GLUE*...

LLIBRE / LIBRO / BOOK. Edició / Edición / Edition: Cinta Massip, Jordi Valls i Marc Valls. | Fotografies / Fotografías / Photographs: Ben Browton, Salvador Costa, Getty images (Hulton Archive; Michael Ochs Archives; Homer Sykes), Harry T. Murlowsky, Silvia Resorte, Subway Sect, Paul Trevor. | Grafisme / Grafismo / Graphics: Marc Valls. | English translation: Andrew Stacey. | Traducción al castellano: Marc Viaplana. | Producció/ Producción/ Production: ActarBirkhäuserPro | Distribució / Distribución / Distribution: ActarBirkhäuserD, Barcelona - Basel - New York, www.actarbirkhauser.com. Roca i Batlle 2, E-08023 Barcelona. T +34 93 417 49 43, F +34 93 418 67 07, office@actar-d.com. Viaduktstrasse 42, CH -4051 Basel. T +41 61 2050 777, F +41 61 2050 792, sales@birkhauser.ch. 151 Grand Street, 5th floor New York, NY 10013, USA. T +1 212 966 2207, F +1 212 966 2214, officeusa@actar-d.com. | Llibreries de la Generalitat de Catalunya. www.gencat. cat/publicacions.

"The London Punk Tapes", de Jordi Valls, és una producció d'Arts Santa Mònica – Departament de Cultura i Mitjans de Comunicació de la Generalitat de Catalunya.

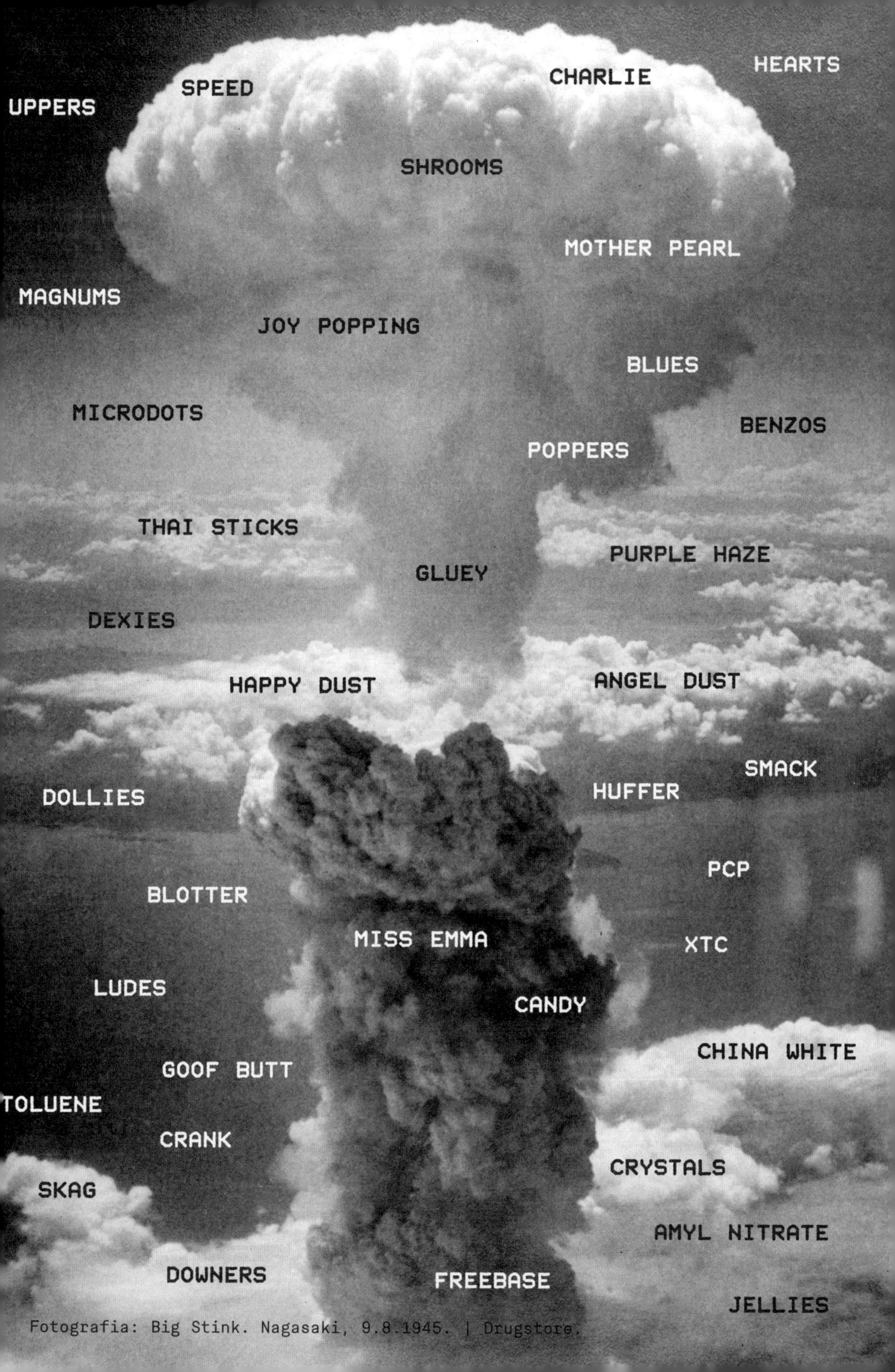

Fotografia: Big Stink. Nagasaki, 9.8.1945. | Drugstore.

"THE LONDON PUNK TAPES"

Arts Santa Mónica, per obra de Vagina Dentata Organ, presenta l'original i inèdit "The London Punk Tapes", l'arxiu de cassets amb música original dels grups punk The Clash, The Damned, Subway Sect, The Sex Pistols, Generation X, The Slits i The Buzzcoks, que Jordi Valls enregistrà en directe, gravadora al coll —abans que aquests grups fossin gravats en estudi—, en els antres urbans i dels barris suburbials de Londres en l'explosió punk del 1976 i 1977. A la vegada l'arxiu documental personal d'aquella explosió (cartells, fulls volants, programes, fanzines, revistes, retalls de diari, fotografies, entrades dels concerts,etc.) ha servit perquè, conjuntament amb l'artista multimèdia Franc Aleu, es produís un vídeo d'art, collage d'imatges, que es projecta en 7 pantalles al mateix temps que s'emet la música enregistrada amb la qualitat tècnica del directe del moment; i, a la vegada, amb el material documental, s'ha fet, amb el grafista Marc Valls, germà d'en Jordi, el llibre-catàleg de mateix títol: THE LONDON PUNK TAPES.

L'artista català franctirador Jordi Valls (1945), d'exili voluntari del franquisme, residí a Londres del 1969 fins el 2007 i, com tants altres joves del moment, visqué la revolta a través de la música i l'art. A partir de la música electrònica i industrial de grups com Throbbing Gristle i Whitehouse s'introduí a l'underground anglès i tot seguint l'actitud punk del "fes-t'ho tu mateix", que permetia que tothom es llancés al carrer, inicià les edicions de Vagina Dentata Organ amb sons de no-música trobada. Són obres audibles, més que sonores, on els sons són transformats en sons metafísics i, a la vegada, en escultures o objecte-disc amb iconografies fetitxistes reelaborades visualment per Marc Valls. Discos penjats a la paret o audicions adreçades a l'inconscient automàtic irracional. L'escassa obra d'aquest artista fill dels punks es redueix als impactants cants als instints bàsics de sexe i violència a *Music for the Hashishins*; als precs per al famós suïcidi col·lectiu de la secta del reverend Jones *The Last Supper*; a l'exercici rítmic físic dels tambors de Calanda a *The Triumph of the Flesh*; a la ranera i els gemecs de l'orgasme per a una necrofília envers Marylin i Elvis a *Cold meat / Eros & Thanatos*; i el so d'una Harley Davidson a *Un Chien Catalan*, entre d'altres. També va exposar una sola vegada a Grenoble (2000) en el marc de "Coup de grâce, la poésie comme connaissance objective", un conjunt de teles de retrats metamòrfics de "top-models", pintades amb la pròpia sang de l'artista i tirades pel terra al mig de la galeria. L'obra de Valls, un nihilista fascinat per la destrucció per la destrucció, manifesta un desig de "castrar" una societat uniformada, avorrida i pedant amb la realitat de la realitat.

Els punks, Vagina Dentata Organ i els dos germans Valls són l'altra cara del "cal ser radicalment moderns" per a una utopia il·lustrada quan arribaria al dia (on som) que tothom i qualsevol podria crear i editar en la cosmòpolis. A l'anvers de la "il·luminació" dels joves *rimbaud*, "l'infern"; al costat del "vident" amb rostre "d'àngel en exili" (de Verlaine), "el meu contemporani, el meu castrador" (de Pasolini). Drogues, sexe i violència que s'escapaven de les sinestèsies vocàliques de la bohèmia simbolista al dinovè per anar esclatant, de nou, en la nit dadà, l'antipintura surrealista i la respiració de la música punk.

La fatiga pre-post-moderna que tota revolta acaba en "isme", propiciarà un art radical que, a les acaballes de l'art mateix, abandona el concepte per gemegar i insultar sense proposició. El punk fou el "grau zero" de la música i l'art que es constituïen com una antimatèria, feta de fàstics i podridures, enfront de les radicalitats formals seriades. El punk obrí la politització ni a la dreta ni a l'esquerra, sinó en batalles campals contra l'extrema dreta que és tot sistema. El dolor s'exhibia en fotocòpia cremada, un sadomaso adolorit per l'estretor del marxisme. Les lletres punk són proclames polítiques de ràbia.

En aquell marc d'agonia de les ciutats postindustrials, de falta de perspectiva per als joves i de revolta juvenil, els sintonitzadors permetien l'autonomia electropunk sense acadèmia i corrien les caràtules d'autoedició i l'intercanvi de cintes sense mercat. La música no mor. I la societat industrial moribunda fou ocupada per independents, autodidactes i amateurs, salvatges i gossos de ciutat, que al cap de poc convertirien la merda i la podridura en or, com Rimbaud. A Catalunya, el dictador acabava de morir i els festivals de música (Canet rock), més psicodèlics, laietans i massius —amb proclames a favor de l'amnistia, l'autonomia i la llibertat—, contrarestaven amb el nihilisme polític dels partidaris de la ruptura i els seqüenciadors i audiogeneradors de primera generació de canvi de sistema. La merda també es convertí, sense alquímia, en or. / **Vicenç Altaió. ARTS SANTA MÒNICA**

the london punk tapes.

Punk? El 1976 els joves londinencs cridaven: "A la merda!" Els filòsofs, sociòlegs i psicòlegs, que sempre busquen una llarga explicació intel·lectual, cercaven un pretext per definir un nou moviment amb paraules sofisticades escrites des de la seguretat i el confort de les seves cases. Punk és el carrer dels suburbis amb excrements i pixats de gos. Rostres sense futur, guerrilles urbanes amb guitarres i navalles. Havia de passar per trencar l'estat apàtic en què es trobava el rock, juntament amb la violència i la monotonia de tota metròpoli. L'actitud i el so del punk són agressius, amfetamínics, més que una orgia és una massacre. Es va canviar la serra mecànica per la guitarra elèctrica com a instrument de destrucció. La simbiosi dels fans i els conjunts de música era perfecta, nihilista, amb un desig ocult de cremar la ciutat. El punk vol esgarrapar amb ungles el fons de la nafra i arrencar i escopir el pus per llençar-lo sense cap escrúpol contra tota autoritat i institució estatal.

Entusiasmat per aquesta explosió urbana, em vaig llençar al carrer a enregistrar en viu les actuacions d'aquests conjunts:

The Sex Pistols. 20.9.1976, 100 Club Oxford Street, London (festival punk).
The Clash. 20.9.1976, 100 Club Oxford Street, London (festival punk).
The Clash. 16.10.1976, University of London.
The Clash. 29.10.1976, Fulham Old Town Hall, London.
The Damned. 2.11.1976, Hope & Anchor, Islington, London.
Subway Sect. 5.11.1976, Royal College of Art, London.
The Clash. 5.11.1976, Royal College of Art, London.
The Sex Pistols. 15.11.1976, Notre Dame Hall, Soho, London.
Generation X. 21.12.1976, The Roxy, Covent Garden, London (inauguració del local).
The Clash. 11.3.1977, The Coliseum, Harlesden, London.
The Slits. 11.3.1977, The Coliseum, Harlesden, London (primera actuació).
The Buzzcocks. 11.3.1977, The Coliseum, Harlesden, London.
Subway Sect. 11.3.1977, The Coliseum, Harlesden, London.
The Clash. 1.5.1977, Civic Hall, Guildford.
Subway Sect. 1.5.1977, Civic Hall, Guildford.

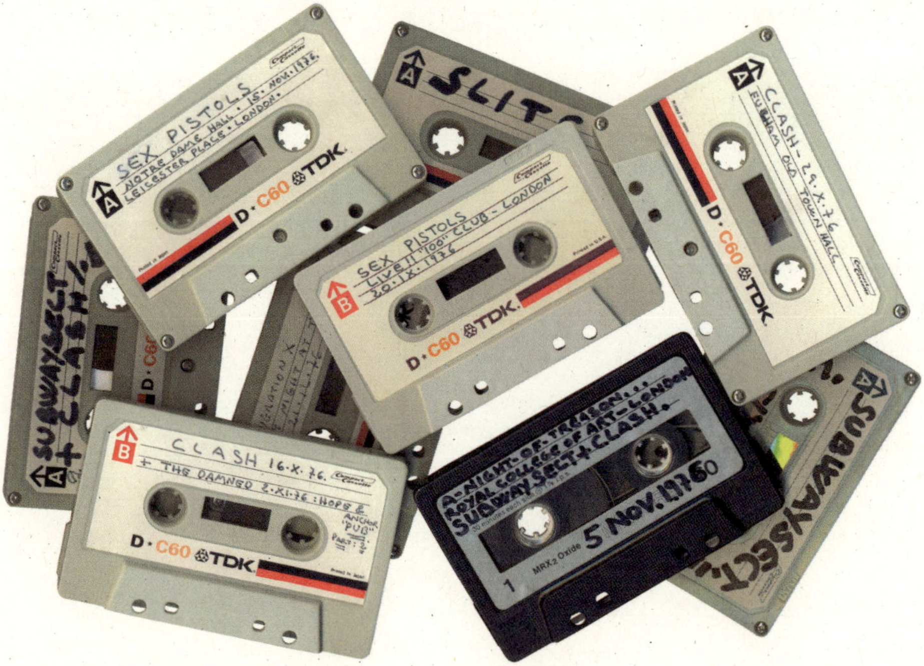

Aquestes gravacions, inèdites fins ara, mai no havien estat escoltades en públic.

Altrament, de la mà de l'enyorat Malcolm McLaren i de la Vivienne Westwood era fàcil preveure el gran màrqueting comercial que en un futur proper ens queia a sobre, fins i tot arribant a la "high fashion" més extraordinària.

Tanmateix, el punk és un fenomen amb fort impacte radical dins el rock, amb el resultat extrem dels Sex Pistols. El nom d'aquest conjunt de música ens parla de sexe i violència, embolcallat d'anarquia. Era el temps en què la gent de la Baader-Meinhof era assassinada "per suicidi" a la presó.

A Londres, l'estiu de 1976, esclaten els "riots", uns forts disturbis urbans contra la policia durant el carnaval del barri de Notting Hill. Un any després, les festes al carrer per tot el Regne Unit per celebrar el vint-i-cinquè aniversari d'Isabel II, reina d'Anglaterra, coincideixen amb les revoltes antifeixistes del barri de població negra de Lewisham, al sud de Londres, i amb la mort inesperada d'Elvis Presley. Una gran metàfora.

El més enriquidor del punk és la seva energia vital, visceral i, alhora, la demostració que qualsevol persona, encara que manqui de talent ortodox, pot agafar una guitarra, un pinzell, un martell, una escarpra, una càmera fotogràfica o de cinema i fer el que es proposi fer. L'únic que és important és la intenció, la força de la imaginació. Res més. Gràcies Malcolm McLaren. / Jordi Valls

SEX PISTOLS

Teenagers from Londons Shepherds Bush and Finsbury Park:
'We hate everything.'
The Sex Pistols are....

John Rotten	Vocals
Steve Jones	Guitar
Glenn Matlock	Bass
Paul Cook	Drums

The boys met at the shop 'SEX' in Chelsea's Worlds End in October '75. Enthused and spurred on by the shop owner, Malcolm Mclaren, they became the Sex Pistols.

November found them gatecrashing college gigs throughout London and it's suburbs, causing a furore wherever they went.

After being banned from the Marquee club in February '76 and sell-outs at other gigs, the group created a precedent by starting their own rock venue at the El Paradise club in Soho on April 4th.

Their own numbers include:

Pretty Vacant
Submission
Only Seventeen
Problems
No feelings

Along with their own versions of 'The Who's' 'Substitute' and some lesser known Small Faces songs. The Sex Pistols spontaneity and honesty threatens all the highly packaged pop of the past.

Sole representation and management:
Malcolm McLaren,

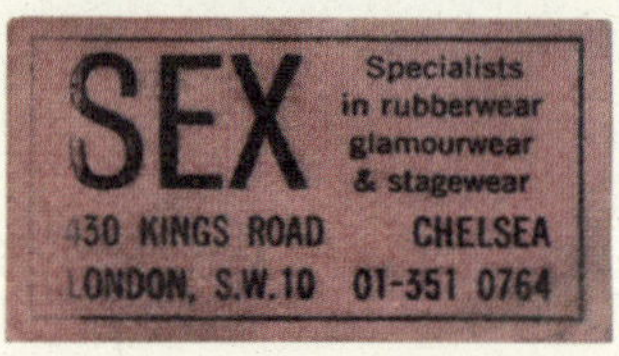

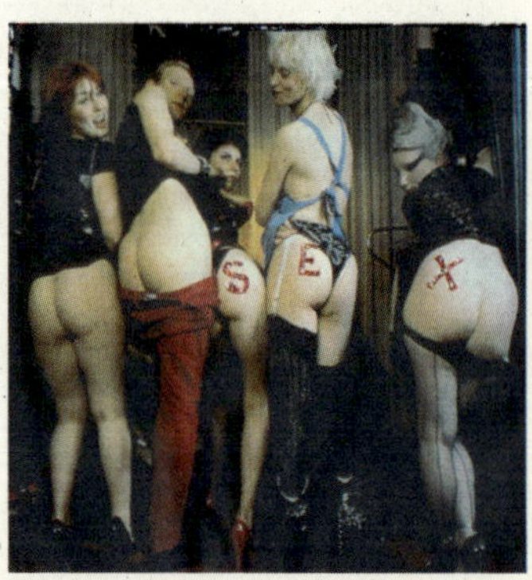

Nota de Malcolm McLaren. | Tarja i fotografia promocional de la botiga SEX, 1976.

I'm going to change the face of music scene! All the music at the moment is by and for thirty year old hippies. Boring. The Sex Pistols are fresh and young. They are kids playing music for the kids. Not some property tycoon singing "My Generation". The Sex Pistols are from the street and the dole queues, they're representative of most of the kids in this country. They can't play very well yet but that's not what's important. It's their attitude! Yes, we are going to change the scene but we've got to make it big before everyone else jumps on the band wagon, and we get left behind.

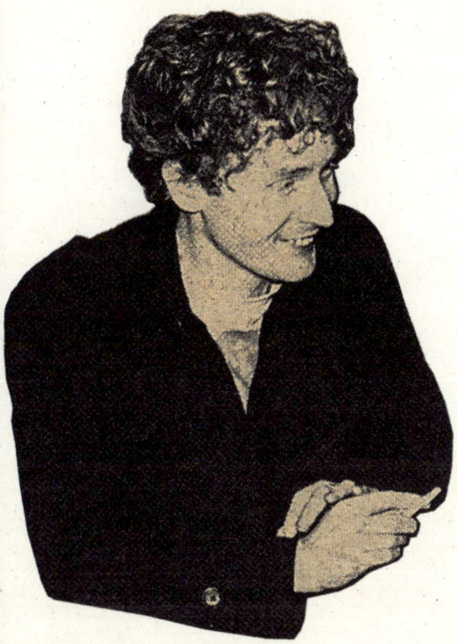

Paraules de Malcolm McLaren a Ray Stevenson, gener del 1976. | Retall de diari amb la imatge impresa de Malcolm McLaren, 1976.

6.11.75 St Martin's School Of Art, London
7.11.75 Central School Of Art, Holborn, London
21.11.75 Westfield College, Frognal, London
28.11.75 Queen Elizabeth College, Kensington, London
5.12.75 Chelsea School Of Art, Chelsea, London
9.12.75 Ravensbourne College, Chistlehurst, London
23.1.76 Watford College, Watford, Herts
12.2.76 Marquee Club, Soho, London
14.2.76 (Andrew Logan's Party), Butlers Wharf, London
19.2.76 Hertfordshire College Of Art, St Albans
20.2.76 College Of Higher Education, High Wycombe
21.2.76 Welwyn, Garden City
25.3.76 Hertfordshire College Of Art, St Albans
30.3.76 100 Club, Oxford St, London
3.4.76 The Nashville, West Kensington, London
4.4.76 El Paradise Strip Club, Soho, London
23.4.76 Nashville, West Kensington, London
29.4.76 Nashville, West Kensington, London
5.5.76 Babalu Disco, Finchley Rd, London
11.5.76 100 Club, Oxford St, London
17.5.76 Screen On The Green, Islington, London - CANCELLED
18.5.76 100 Club, Oxford St, London
19.5.76 Northallerton, Yorkshire
20.5.76 Penthouse, Scarborough
21.5.76 Middlesborough Town Hall, Middlesborough
25.5.76 100 Club, Oxford St, London
30.5.76 Reading University, Reading
4.6.76 Lesser Free Trade Hall, Manchester
15.6.76 100 Club, Oxford St, London
17.6.76 Assembly Hall, Walthamstow, London
29.6.76 100 Club, Oxford St, London
3.7.76 Pier Pavilion, Hastings
4.7.76 Black Swan, Sheffield *
6.7.76 100 Club, Oxford St, London **
9.7.76 Lyceum Ballroom, The Strand, London
10.7.76 The Sundown, Charing Cross Rd, London
20.7.76 Lesser Free Trade Hall, Manchester ***

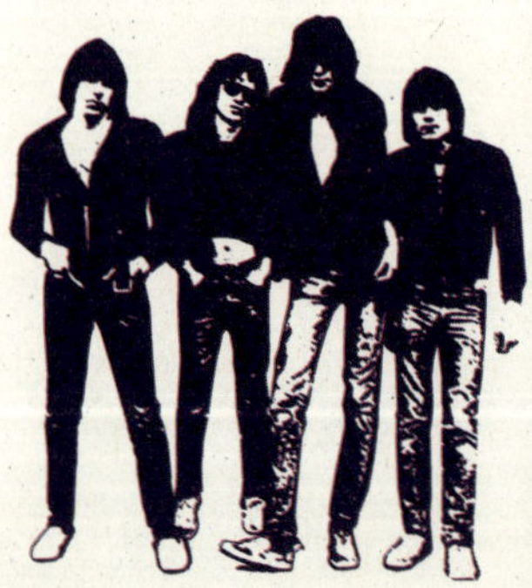

Primers concerts dels Sex Pistols. * Primer concert dels Clash. Els Ramones actuen a la London Roundhouse amb Flaming Groovies i The Stranglers. Imatge dels Ramones a partir de la foto de Roberta Bayley, 1976. ** Primer concert dels Damned. *** Primer concert de Buzzcocks. A Manchester, els Sex Pistols toquen "Anarchy in the U.K." per primera vegada. | El 13 de juliol surt el primer número del fanzine *Sniffin' Glue*... [50 exemplars fotocopiats] publicat per Mark Perry.

It's great the way all this is getting up the old fart's noses.

The Sex Pistols, led by a one-time sewage worker who styles himself Johnny Rotten, were launched last April by Malcolm McLaren, 29-year-old owner of a London clothes shop called "Sex."

Rotten—real name Lydon—and Glen Matlock, Steve Jones, and Paul Cook, are all 19 years old and were unemployed before Mr. McLaren gave them guitars and billed them as leaders of the teen craze "Punk Rock," described as anti-music music.

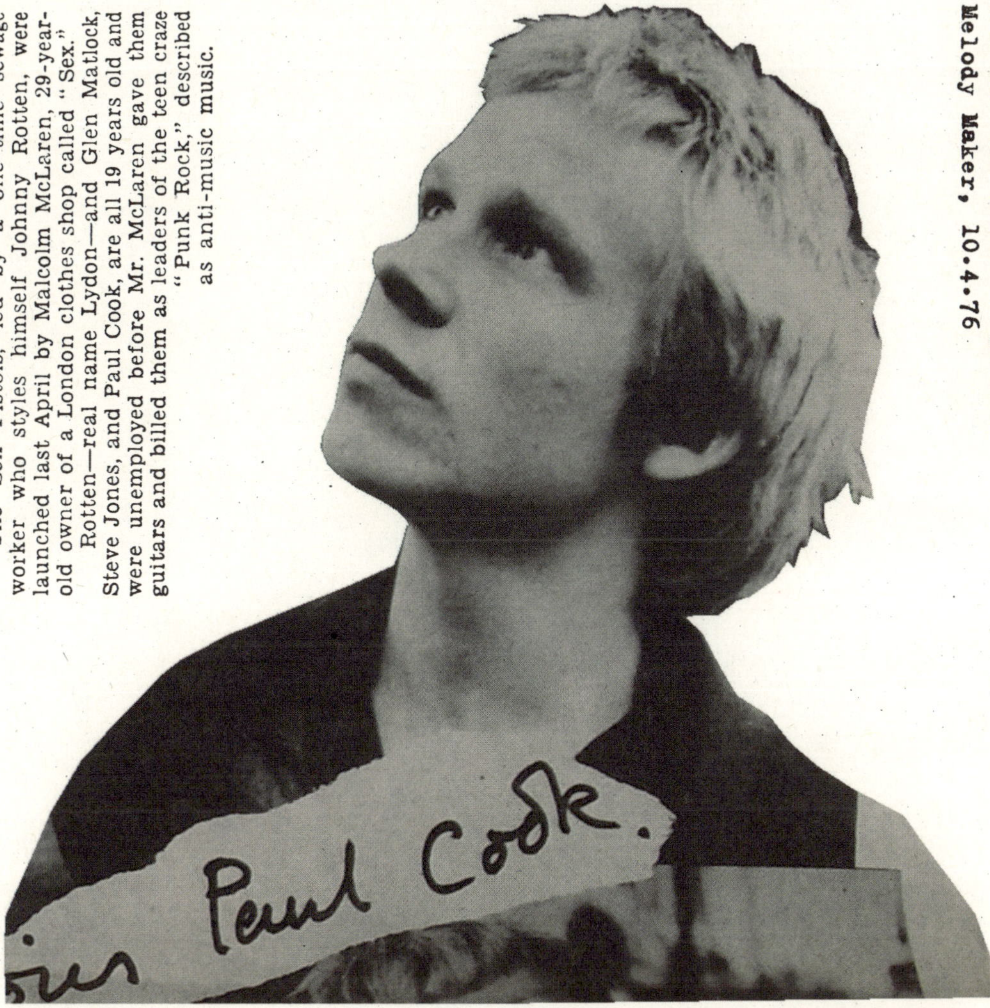

They do as much for music as World War Two did for the cause of peace.

Melody Maker, 10.4.76

NO FUTURE

Paraules de Paul Cook, 1976. | Notes de premsa, 1976. | Retall d'una fotografia de Ray Stevenson publicada al diari *Anarchy in the U.K.*, 1976. | "No future": text d'una entrada d'un concert dels Sex Pistols, 1976.

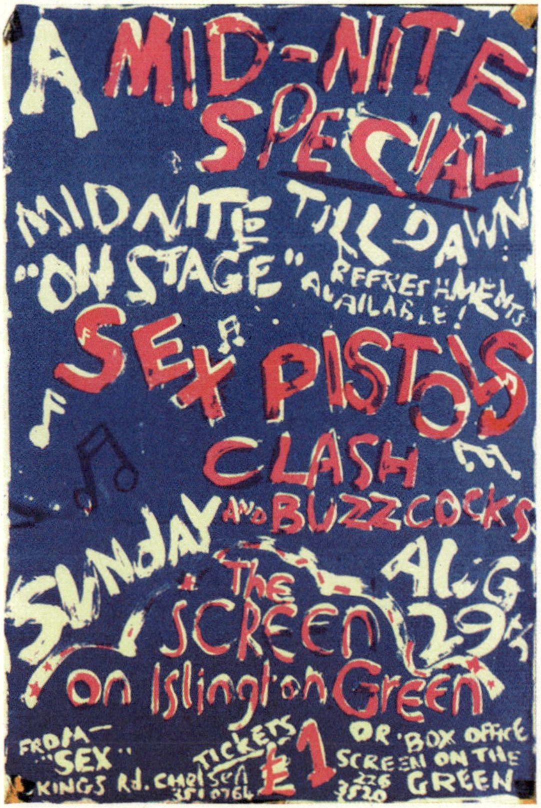
A MID-NITE SPECIAL
MIDNITE TILL DAWN
"ON STAGE" REFRESHMENTS AVAILABLE!
SEX PISTOLS
CLASH
AND BUZZCOCKS
SUNDAY AUG 29th
The SCREEN on Islington Green
FROM "SEX" KINGS Rd. CHELSEA 351 0764
TICKETS £1
OR BOX OFFICE SCREEN ON THE GREEN 226 3520

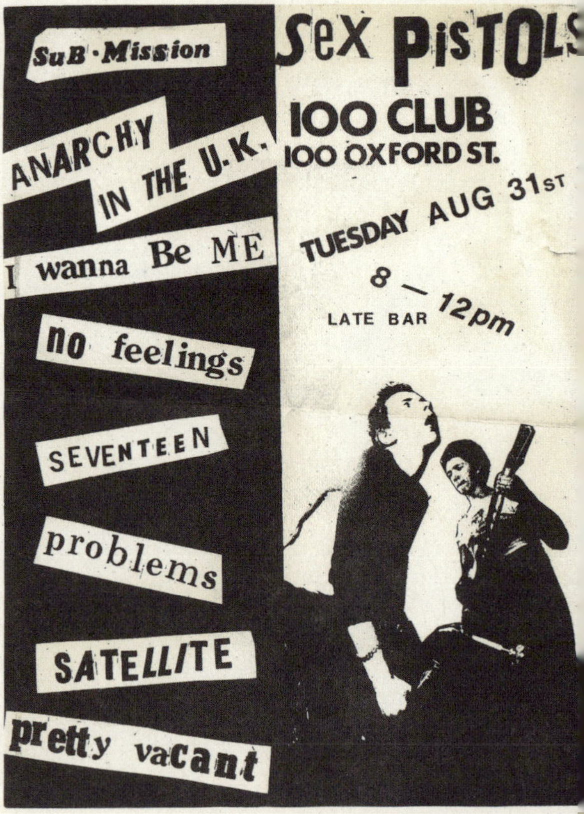
SuB·Mission
ANARCHY IN THE U.K.
I wanna Be ME
no feelings
SEVENTEEN
problems
SATELLITE
pretty vacant
SEX PISTOLS
100 CLUB
100 OXFORD ST.
TUESDAY AUG 31ST
8 — 12pm
LATE BAR

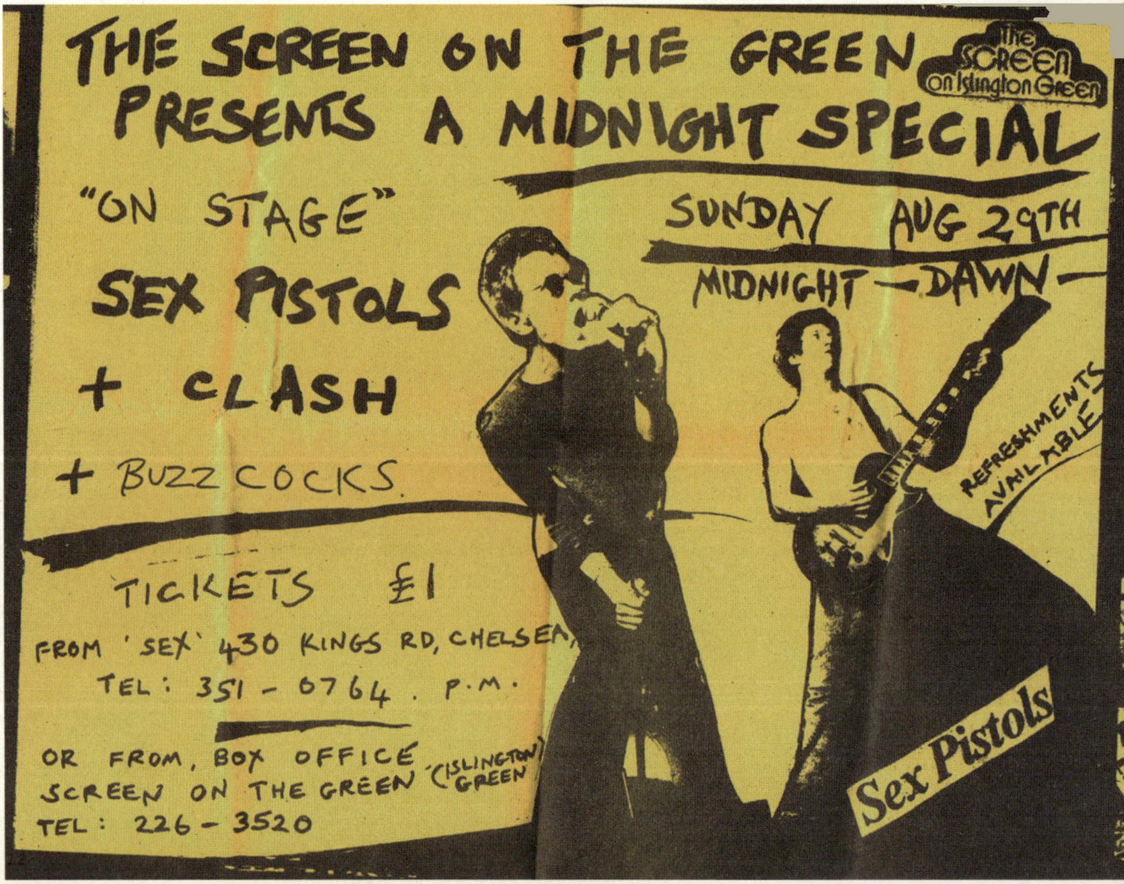
THE SCREEN ON THE GREEN
PRESENTS A MIDNIGHT SPECIAL
The SCREEN on Islington Green
"ON STAGE"
SEX PISTOLS
+ CLASH
+ BUZZCOCKS
SUNDAY AUG 29TH
MIDNIGHT — DAWN —
REFRESHMENTS AVAILABLE
TICKETS £1
FROM 'SEX' 430 KINGS RD, CHELSEA
TEL: 351 - 0764 . P.M.
OR FROM, BOX OFFICE
SCREEN ON THE GREEN (ISLINGTON GREEN)
TEL: 226 - 3520
Sex Pistols

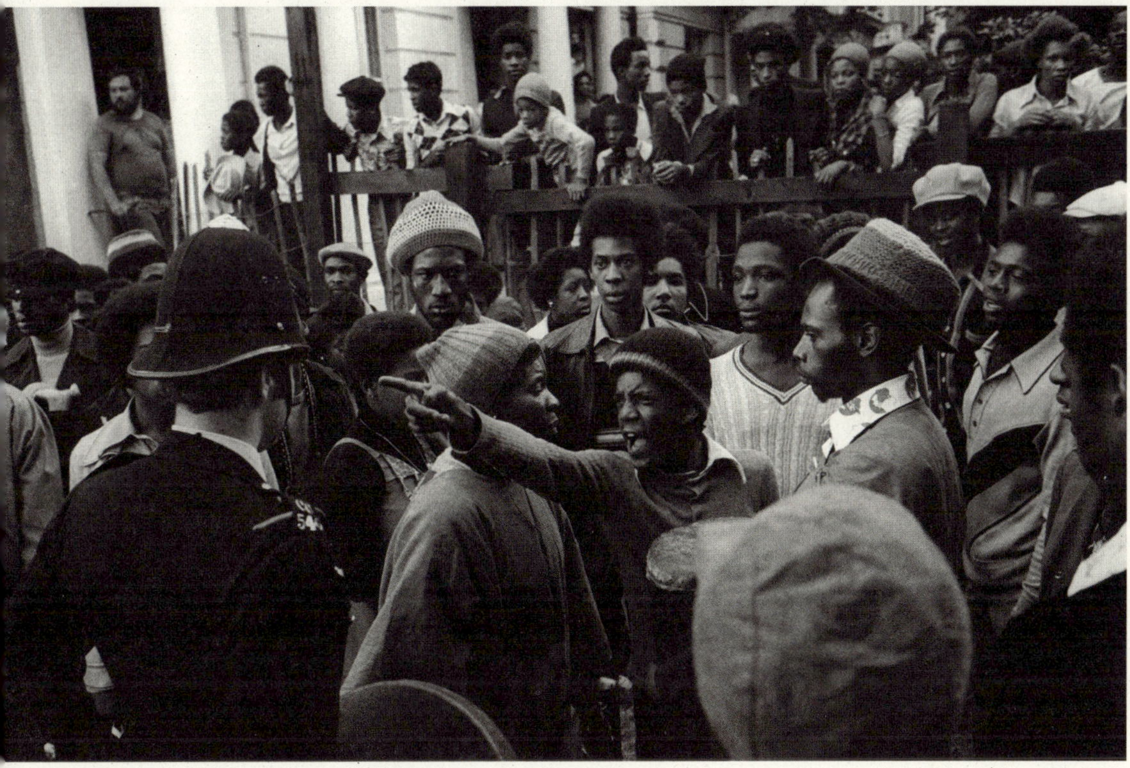

10.8.76 100 Club, Oxford St, London
14.8.76 Barbarellas, Birmingham
19.8.76 Village Inn, Runton, Norfolk
21.8.76 Boat Club, Nottingham *
29.8.76 Screen On The Green Cinema, Islington, London
31.8.76 100 Club, Oxford St, London
2.9.76 Nags Head, High Wycombe
3.9.76 Club De Chalet Du Lac, Paris, France
5.9.76 Club De Chalet Du Lac, Paris, France
11.9.76 The Royal Ballroom, Whitby
12.9.76 Fordgreen Ballroom, Leeds
13.9.76 Quaintways, Chester
15.9.76 Lodestar, Blackburn
17.9.76 H.M. Chelmsford Prison, Chelmsford
20.9.76 100 Club, Oxford St, London (Punk Festival) **

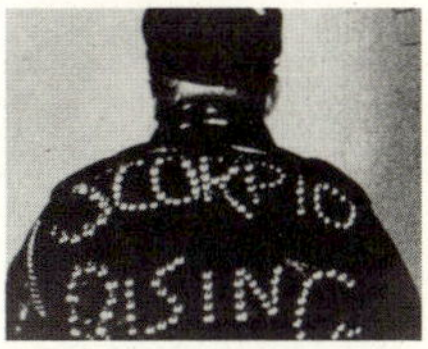

Cartell i fulls volants fets per Hellen Wellington-Lloyd, Nils Stevenson i Jamie Reid l'agost del 76. | Un jove percussionista rastafari escridassa un agent de policia durant la revolta del carnaval de Notting Hill, el 30 d'agost de 1976. La revolta es va produir a la conclusió del carnaval i va tenir una duríssima repressió policial. Entre els participants en la revolta es troben Joe Strummer i Paul Simonon, de The Clash. La seva cançó "White Riot", escrita poc després, s'inspira en aquests fets. Fotografia de Homer Sykes. | Fotograma del film *Scorpio Rising,* de Kenneth Anger, 1964. | Concerts dels Sex Pistols durant els mesos d'agost i setembre del 76. | * Festival Punk de Mont-de-Marsan, França, amb concerts d'Eddie and the Hot Rods, Doctor Feelgood, Roogalator, The Damned, Bijou... | ** Primer concert de Subway Sect; primer concert de Siouxsie and the Banshees amb Sid Vicious —l'inventor del "pogo"— a la bateria.

ron watts

THE

100 CLUB

LONDON'S PREMIER JAZZ CENTRE

100 OXFORD STREET, LONDON, W.1

Manager: ROGER HORTON Telephone: 01-636-0933

The average members' price is between 80p and £1.50 depending on the day of the week and the quality of the artiste performing. Admission for guests is usually 20p to 50p dearer. All British and Overseas Students and Nurses may attend any session at members' rates.

Club Calendar for September and October 1976

johnny rotten
malcolm mclaren
vivienne westwood
jamie reid
jonesy
steve jones
paul cook
alan jones
nils stevenson
kim
glen matlock
ray stevenson
celia
adam ant
jordan
hellen wellington-lloyd
chrissie hynde
sophie richmond
sally
jo faul
margret
ray burns
rat scabies
dave vanian
brian james
rob collins
vic godard
t.v.smith
paul smith
berlin
gaye advert
paul myers
phillip salon
linda
lorry driver
robert miller
soo catwoman
sharon
howard pick-up
simone
debbie juvenile
simon barker

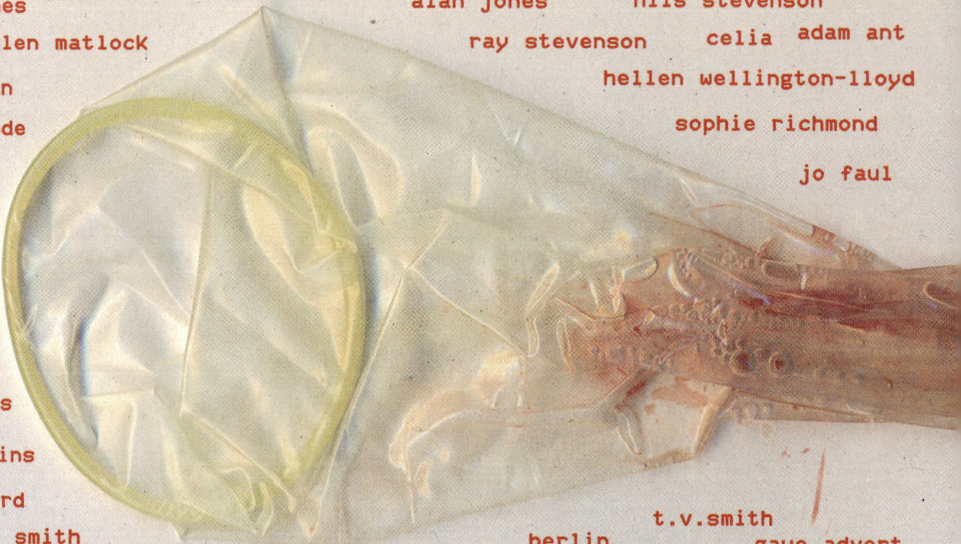

THE

100 CLUB

LONDON'S PREMIER JAZZ CENTRE

100 OXFORD STREET, LONDON, W.1

Manager: ROGER HORTON Telephone: 01-636-0933

The average members' price is between 80p and £1.50 depending on the day of the week and the quality of the artiste performing. Admission for guests is usually 20p to 50p dearer. All British and Overseas Students and Nurses may attend any session at members' rates.

Club Calendar for September and October 1976

Patrons do not require membership to attend the 100 club. Membership,(which costs £2 per year) is beneficial however in that substantial reductions in admittance prices are offered to members and a current programme is posted to each member every month. If therefore you intend to patronise us regularly (and we certainly hope that you will) membership becomes very worthwhile.

ALL SESSIONS TILL 11.00 p.m. unless otherwise stated.

SEPTEMBER

Wednesday	1st	7.30 to Midnight, Mr. ACKER BILK AND HIS PARAMOUNT JAZZ BAND.
Thursday	2nd	7.30 to 1 a.m. LIVE SOUL GROUPS plus STEREO DISCO
Friday	3rd	7.30 to Midnight. THE ORIGINAL CRANE RIVER JAZZ BAND with MONTY SUNSHINE, KEN COLYER, SONNY MORRIS, etc.
Saturday	4th	7.30 to 1 a.m. CHRIS BARBER'S JAZZ BAND plus STEVE LANE'S SOUTHERN STOMPERS
Sunday	5th	THE GENE ALLAN JAZZMEN (All members admitted free this evening. Others 80p)
Monday	6th	THE BLACK BOTTOM STOMPERS (All members 50p this evening. Others 80p)
Tuesday	7th	7.30 to Midnight. Rock Special. ROOGALATOR plus THE LEE KOSMIN BAND
Wednesday	8th	7.30 to Midnight. KEN COLYER'S ALL STAR JAZZ MEN
Thursday	9th	7.30 to 1 a.m. LIVE SOUL GROUPS plus STEREO DISCO
Friday	10th	7.30 to Midnight. THE NEW ERA JAZZ BAND
Saturday	11th	7.30 to 1 a.m. MAX COLLIE'S RHYTHM ACES plus THE SHEFFIELD BOTTOM STOMPERS
Sunday	12th	THE GENE ALLAN JAZZMEN (All members admitted free this evening. Others 80p)
Monday	13th	THE BLACK BOTTOM STOMPERS (All members 50p this evening. Others 80p)
Tuesday	14th	British Blues and Boogie Festival. JO ANN KELLY, THE BLIMPS, GORDON SMITH, GARENT WATKINS, THE TEQUILA BROWN BLUES BAND, etc.

If you wish to join the 100 Club fill in this form, detach from the calendar, and post it, together with a remittance of £2 and a stamped addressed envelope.

To MUSICAL ENTERPRISES LTD., 100 OXFORD ST., LONDON, W.1.

I wish to join the 100 Club and enclose the membership subscription of £2 for one year's membership from date of joining, together with a stamped addressed envelope.

Name ....

Address ....

....

Wednesday	15th	7.30 to Midnight. THE LONDON JAZZ BIG BAND with RAY CRANE, AL FAIRWEATHER, COLIN SMITH (Tpts), WILLIE GARNETT, MALCOLM EVERSON, AL GAY, PHIL DAY, BRUCE TURNER (Saxes), MIKE HOGH, TONY MILLINER, JOHN PICARD (Tbns), STAN GREIG (Pno), HARVEY WESTON (Bass) and LENNIE HASTINGS (Drs).
Thursday	16th	7.30 to 1 a.m. LIVE SOUL GROUPS plus STEREO DISCO.
Friday	17th	7.30 to 1 a.m. GEORGE MELLY AND THE FEETWARMERS
Saturday	18th	7.30 to 1 a.m. MAX COLLIE'S RHYTHM ACES plus BILL BRUNSKILL'S JAZZ MEN.
Sunday	19th	THE GENE ALLAN JAZZMEN (All members admitted free this evening. Others 80p)
Monday and Tuesday	20th 21st	7.30 to Midnight both days 2 day Punk Rock Festival featuring SEX PISTOLS CHRIS SPEDDING'S BAND CLASH THE VIBRATORS THE BUZZCOCKS and THE DAMNED
Wednesday	22nd	7.30 to Midnight KEN COLYER'S ALL STAR JAZZ MEN
Thursday	23rd	7.30 to 1 a.m. LIVE SOUL GROUPS plus STEREO DISCO.
Friday	24th	7.30 to 1 a.m. Music from the African Townships with JABULA, plus JOHN STEVEN'S AWAY.
Saturday	25th	7.30 to 1 a.m. THE AVON CITIES plus THE TOM COLLINS JAZZ BAND
Sunday	26th	LOUIS MOHOLO'S BAND with CHRIS McGREGOR, JOHNIE DIYANTI, DUDU PUKWANA
Monday	27th	7.30 to Midnight. THE JOHN PICARD BAND with TREVOR TOMPKINS, RON RUBIN, COLIN SMITH, DON WELLER and MATT MATTEWSON.
Tuesday	28th	7.30 to Midnight. The American Blues Singer DOCTOR ROSS plus THE TEQUILA BROWN BLUES BAND
Wednesday	29th	7.30 to Midnight. KEN COLYER'S ALL STAR JAZZ MEN.
Thursday	30th	7.30 to 1 a.m. LIVE SOUL GROUPS plus STEREO DISCO.

OCTOBER

Friday	1st	7.30 to Midnight. THE LONDON VINTAGE JAZZ ORCHESTRA.
Saturday	2nd	7.30 to 1 a.m. ROD MASON'S JASS BAND plus THE JOHN MADDOX JAZZ MANIACS
Sunday	3rd	THE GENE ALLAN JAZZMEN (All members admitted free this evening. Others 80p)
Monday	4th	THE BLACK BOTTOM STOMPERS (All members 50p this evening. Others 80p)
Tuesday	5th	Rock Special PLUMMET AIRLINES
Wednesday	6th	7.30 to Midnight. ALEX WELSH AND HIS BAND
Thursday	7th	7.30 to 1 a.m. LIVE SOUL GROUPS plus STEREO DISCO
Friday	8th	7.30 to Midnight. The Celebrated American Jazz Pianist TEDDY WILSON and his TRIO. (Teddy Wilson will be remembered as part of the renowned Benny Goodman Quartet. Don't lose this only London opportunity to hear this great Jazzman)
Saturday	9th	7.30 to 1 a.m. BILL KERR'S WHOOPEE BAND plus supporting programme.
Sunday	10th	LOUIS MOHOLO'S CULTURAL SHOCK
Monday and Tuesday	11th 12th	7.30 to Midnight both nights USA Rock and Roll LINK WRAY AND THE WRAYMEN
Wednesday	13th	7.30 to Midnight KEN COLYER'S ALL STAR JAZZ MEN
Thursday	14th	7.30 to 1 a.m. LIVE SOUL GROUPS plus STEREO DISCO
Friday	15th	7.30 to 1 a.m. THE PASADENA ROOF ORCHESTRA plus supporting programme
Saturday	16th	7.30 to 1 a.m. MONTY SUNSHINE'S JAZZ BAND plus BILL BRUNSKILL'S JAZZ MEN
Sunday	17th	GENE ALLAN'S JAZZMEN (All members admitted free this evening. Others 80p)
Monday	18th	THE BLACK BOTTOM STOMPERS (All members 50p this evening. Others 80p)
Tuesday	19th	Punk Rock Special. Bands to be announced.

paul simonon

mick jones

joe strummer

terry chimes

bernard rhodes

keith levine

micky foote

shane macgowan

steve diggle

pete shelley

howard devoto

garth smith

john maher

richard boon

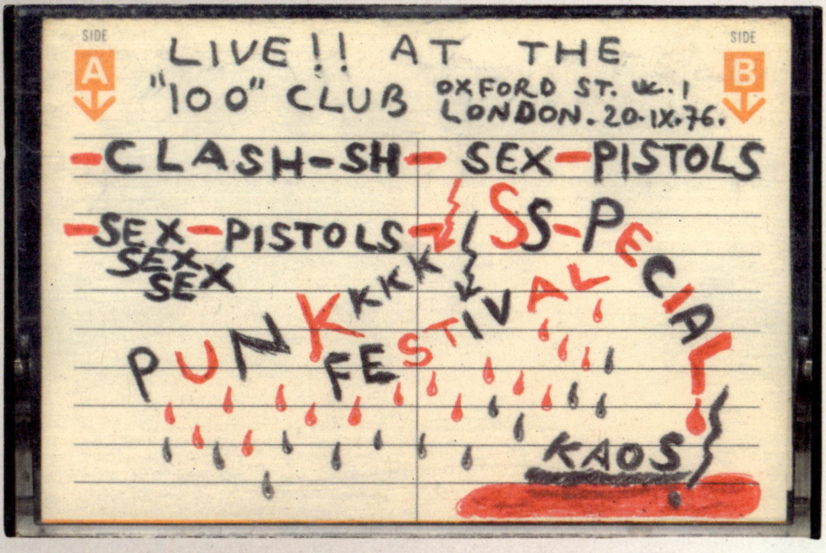

mark perry   tracey o'keefe   ian woodcock   jordi valls

rat rodent   henry daze   danny baker   alex fergusson   need a

ellie   carey fortune   steve walsh   sarah hall   tyrone thomas

social demise   brian chevette   james stevenson   bob andrews   billy idol   mark laff

dee generate   andy blade   john towe   gene october   simon vitesse

philip rowland   tony james

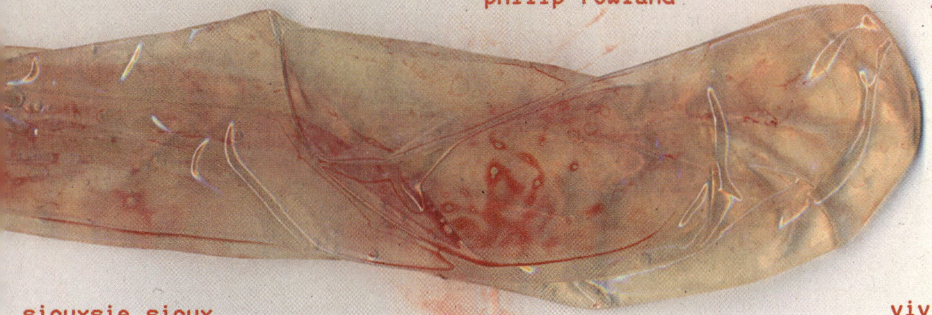

kate chorus

alan drake

johnny moped

slimey toad

chris speeding

don letts

ari up

siouxsie sioux   viv albertine

marco pirroni   tessa   john mackay   palmolive

steve severin   peter fenton   kenny morris   caroline coon   jon savage

sid vicious   fred burk   dave burk   poly styrene   jonh ingham

Monday	20th	7.30 to Midnight both days
		2 day Punk Rock Festival featuring SEX PISTOLS
and		CHRIS SPEDDING'S BAND
		CLASH
Tuesday	21st	THE VIBRATORS
		THE BUZZCOCKS and
		THE DAMNED

Capçalera i pàgines del programa editat pel 100 Club on s'anuncien els dos dies del Punk Festival. | Noms i malnoms. | Coberta de K7 amb les gravacions dels concerts dels Clash i els Sex Pistols al Punk Festival. Londres, 20.9.76. | Condó.

“We don’t necessarily think violence is a bad thing because you have to destroy to create.”

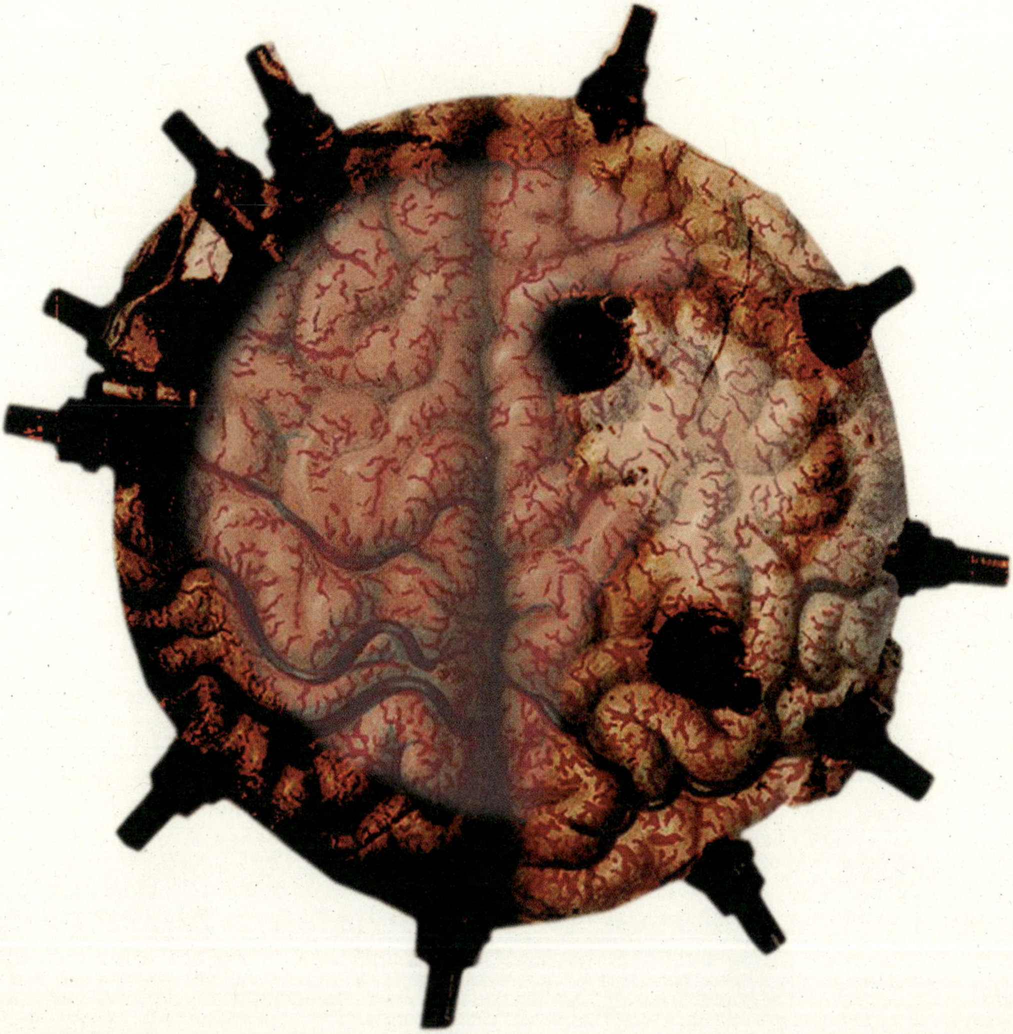

Paraules de Malcolm McLaren. | *Orsini* de Marc Viaplana.

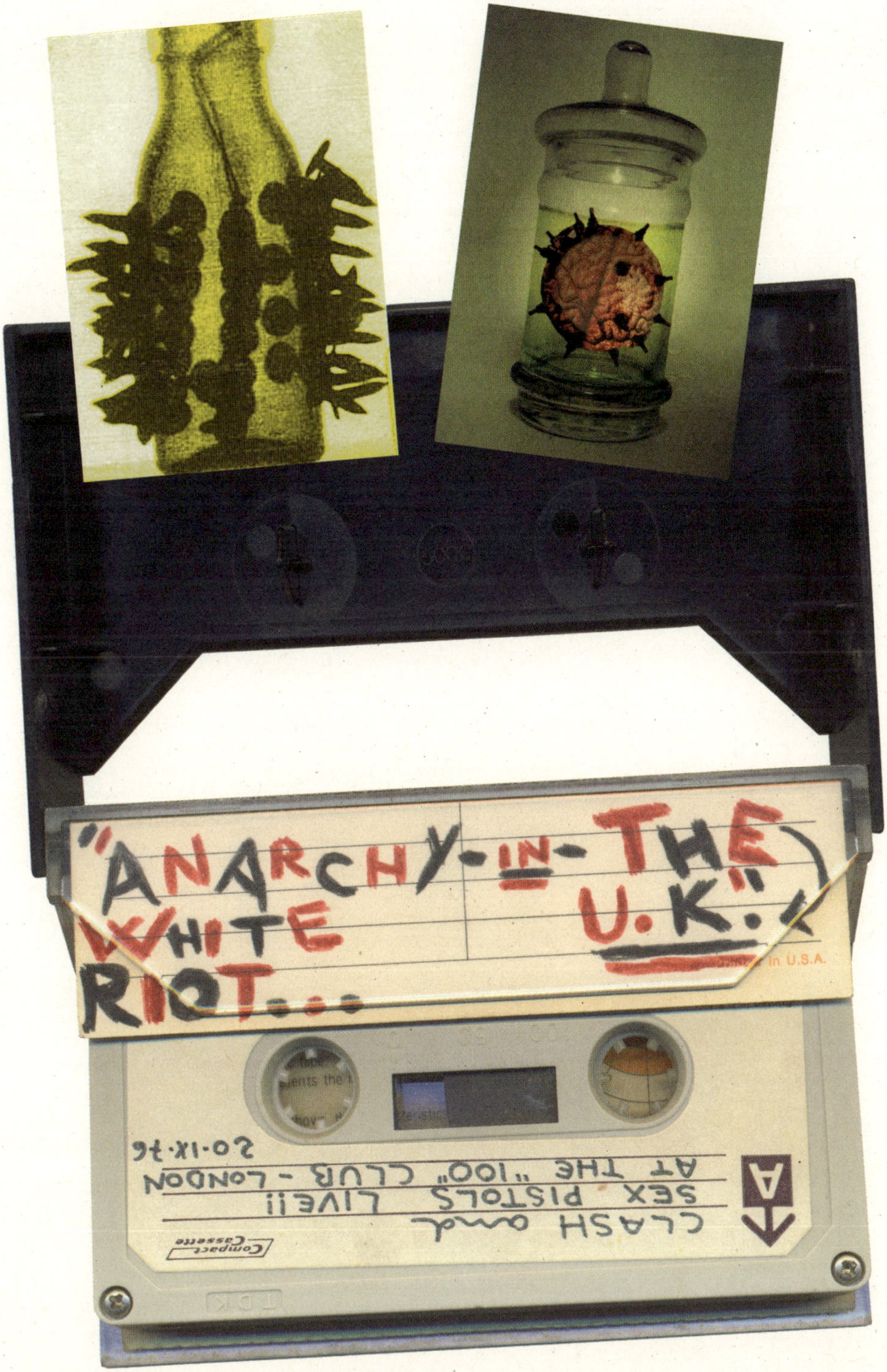

Escàner d'un còctel bomba i bomba orsini en suspensió. | K7 amb l'enregistrament dels concerts dels Sex Pistols i The Clash al 100 Club. Punk Rock Festival, Londres, 20.9.76.

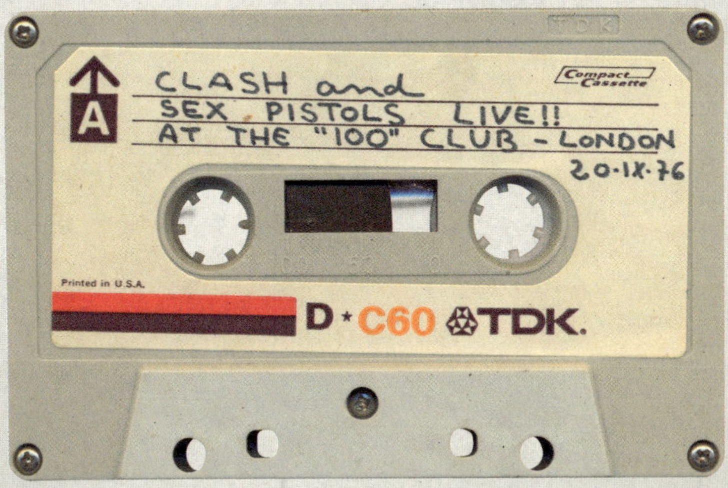
A
CLASH and
SEX PISTOLS LIVE!!
AT THE "100" CLUB - LONDON
20-IX-76
Compact Cassette
Printed in U.S.A.
D C60 TDK.

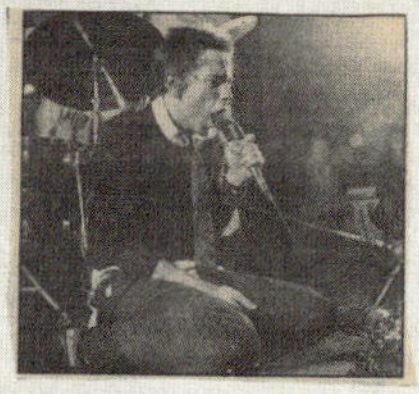

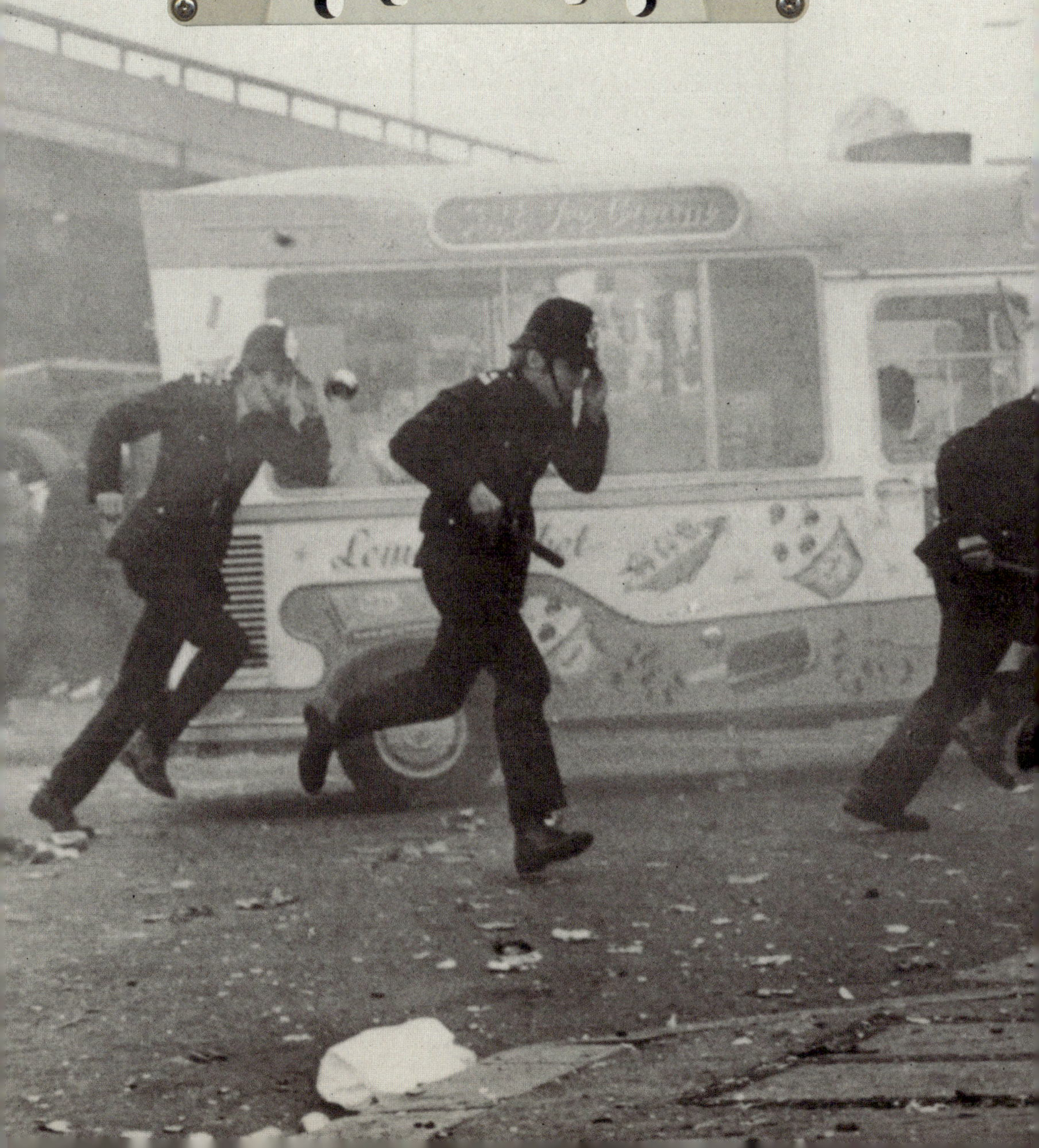

Cares A i B de la K7 amb els concerts de The Clash i Sex Pistols al Punk Festival, setembre del 76. | Retall de diari amb Johnny Rotten fotografiat per Ray Stevenson al Punk Festival. | La policia fuig durant la revolta del carnaval de Notting Hill, el 30 d'agost de 1976. *Evening Standard*, Hulton Archive.

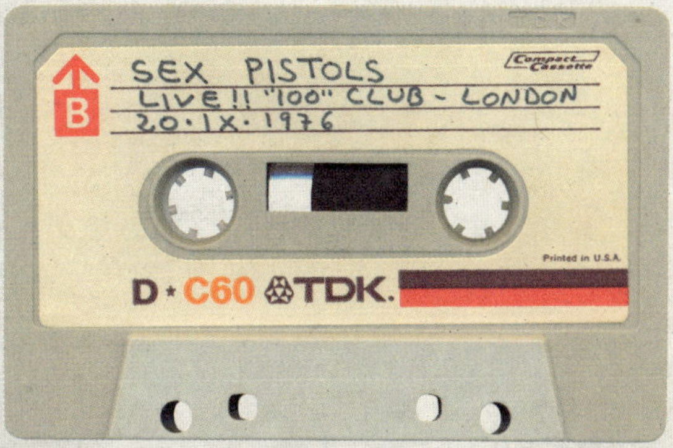

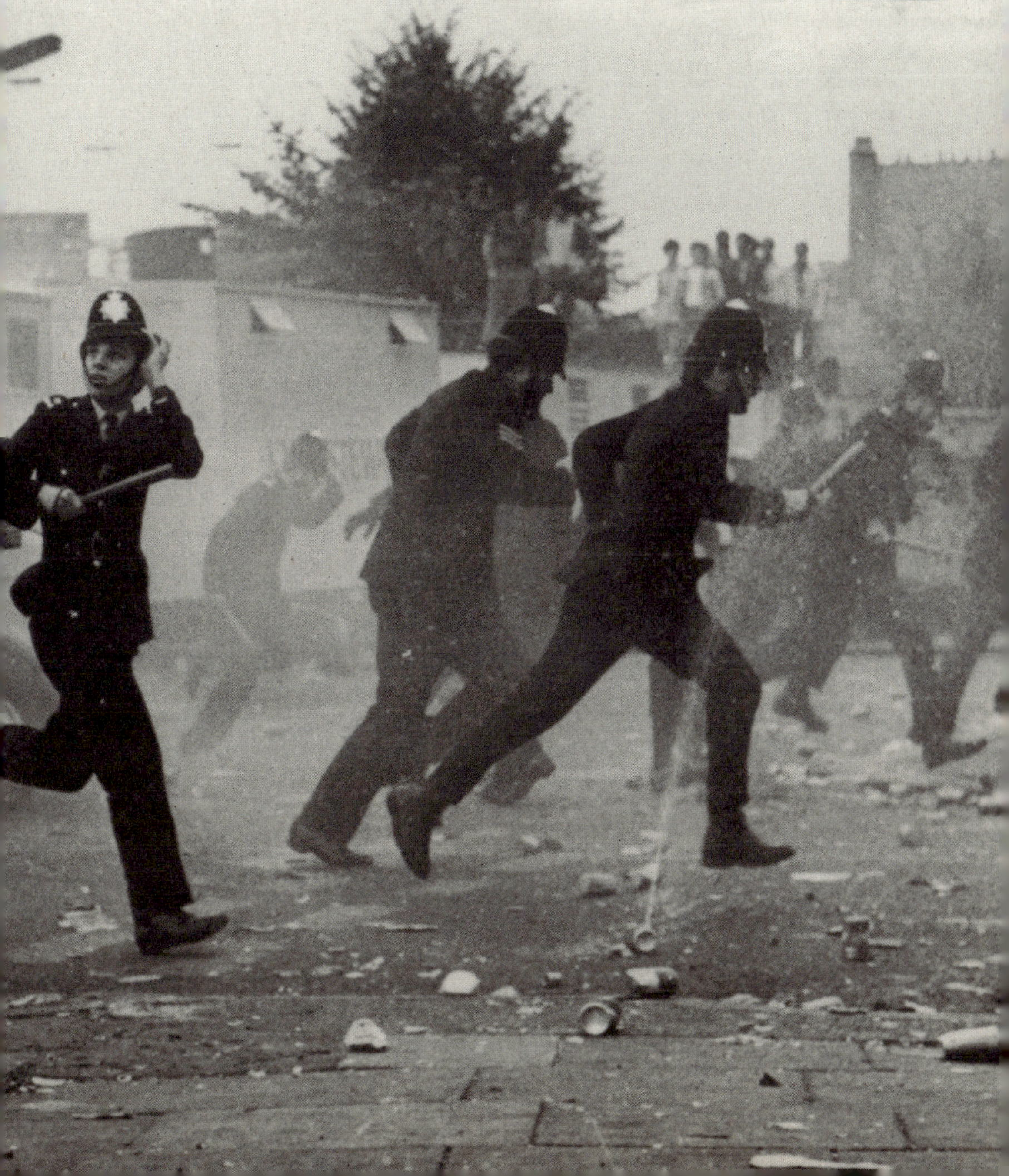

CLASH!

Steve Walsh (SW).
Mark Perry (MP).
Sniffin' Glue... núm. 4, octubre del 1976.

SW-What's the name about, why call yourselves Clash?

Paul-Well, it's a clash against things that are going on ... the music scene, and all that we're hoping to change quite a lot.

SW-Does this mean you're political?

Mick-Yes, we're definitely political!

Joe-We wanna be the apathy party of Great Britain, so that all the people who don't vote go out and don't vote for us!

Mick-We're really into encouraging creativity ... we ain't a bunch of raving facists!

SW-Are you a bunch of raving anarchists?

Joe-I don't believe in all that anarchy bollocks!

Mick-Yeah, anarchists believe in lawlessness ... look, the important thing is to encourage people to do things for themselves, think for themselves and stand up for what their rights are.

SW-You hate apathy?

Mick-Oh, I fuckin hate apathy but I hate ignorance more than anything.

SW-Do you try to put this over in your songs?

Mick-All our songa are about being honest, right? The situation as we see it, right?

SW-Right! So the songs relate directely to you and your enviroment?

Mick-Right, otherwise we'd be writing bullshit!

SW-So, what do you want to happen today?

Joe-What I'm most aware of at the moment, is that most people in London are going out every night to see groups or something and they're making do with rubbish and because everything else around is rubbish, it's not immediately apparant that it's rubbish. People are prepard to accept rubbish, anything that's going. I mean, every single LP anybody plays me in any flat I go to and they aay, "this is good" ... it's rubbish and they have got nuthin'else to play ... the thing is they've got to think it's good, otherwise they go insane ...

Mick- ... and it's all shit!

SW-What's shit?

Mick-All them records, right ... you know, you can't go out and buy a record 'cause you know it's just, like, fuckin' bollocks ... just a load of shit!

Joe-The only good one is that Ramones one.

Mick-Yer, the Ramones record is good.

HERITAGE.

Joe-It's our heritage ... "What are we livin' for, two-room apartment on the second floor". That's English, not what's goin'on now.

Mick-They're the most important English band. Like Mott the Hoople's Ian Hunter always spoke to the kids straight and even when they went to the States and they were getting a bit flash and a bit dopey he still used to sing about the dole and he had to translate for the Americans and say, "look, this is really the welfare". They don't know what the fuckin' dole is, where as we're all down the dole anyway, coppin'our money off Rod Stewart's taxes!

SW-What do you think is wrong with people today?

Mick-They're apathetic... boring ... boring music bores me! Boring 'cause it's not new, boring'cause it's not...

Joe-It's a lie ...

Mick-...they ain't pushin' themselves nowhere they ain't being creative.

Joe-Where's that picture of the George Hatcher Band?

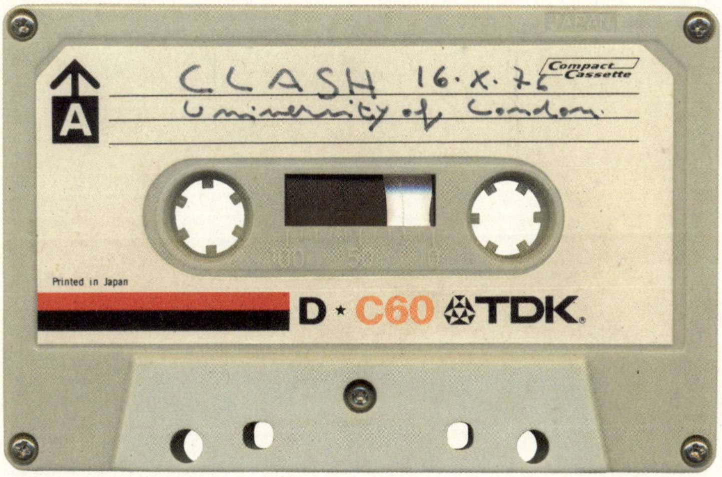

K7 amb el concert dels Clash a la University of London, 16.10.76.

Paul-oh yeah, that's a real joke, that is ...

Joe-We found this to be ...

Mick-Hilarious, have you seen it?

Joe-I mean, the whole thing is a lie, it means nothing.

Mick-Except that they're on tour with Dr.Feelgood.

Joe-All this crap like, oh yeah, they've got long hair and his got his arm up here ana look at his cowboy shirt and the trousers.

SW-What have clothes got to do' with it?

Mick-Well, this is what rock'n' roll's supposed to look like ...

Joe-It's a state of mind.

Mick-What's the differance between this ad. and the cover of last weeks NME, it's the same pose ain't it? I think that's the same pair of trousers, from 'Jean Machine'. (Mick was referring to the previous weeks' cover-pic of the Rod's Dave Higgs).

MP-But they're a pair of trousers!

Joe-No, you can't say that's clothes and this is music, it's a state of mind, a complete thing. If anything was going on in that blokes head he would do something about it.

Mick-To show he was a person, he would've done something to himself. Now, he's just showing that he's one of the many -a consumer, i.e.: I eat shit all the time!

SW-Everyone's a consumer, I mean, if you go down to 'Sex' and buy a pair of leather trousers you're still a consumer. That's the odd thing about the'70's, in order to change society you must first consume it. (You can tell he's been to art-school-Ed).

Mick-Yeah, but if it comes out of creativity. Some people change and some people stay as they are, bozos, and they don't try to change themselves in any way.

Joe-We deal in junk, you know, I just realised that the other day. We deal in junk. We deal in like, the rubbish bin. What we've got is what other people have put in the rubbish bin. Like Mick's shirt was gonna be put in the bin until he paid 10p for it. I mean, you ain't gonna go down to 'Sex' with yer ten quid stuffed in yer pocket and buy some stupid ... er ... I dunno, I've never even been down there.

Mick-I think it's a bit easy to go down there and look great, I mean, there stuff's pretty good. Looks good to me, but I think the way we do it is much more accesible to kids cos' anyone, at very little price and it encourages 'em to do something for themselves. It's to do with personnal freedom ... I don't think it's just the trousers though, I mean, the trousers reflect the mind.

Joe-Like trousers, like brain!

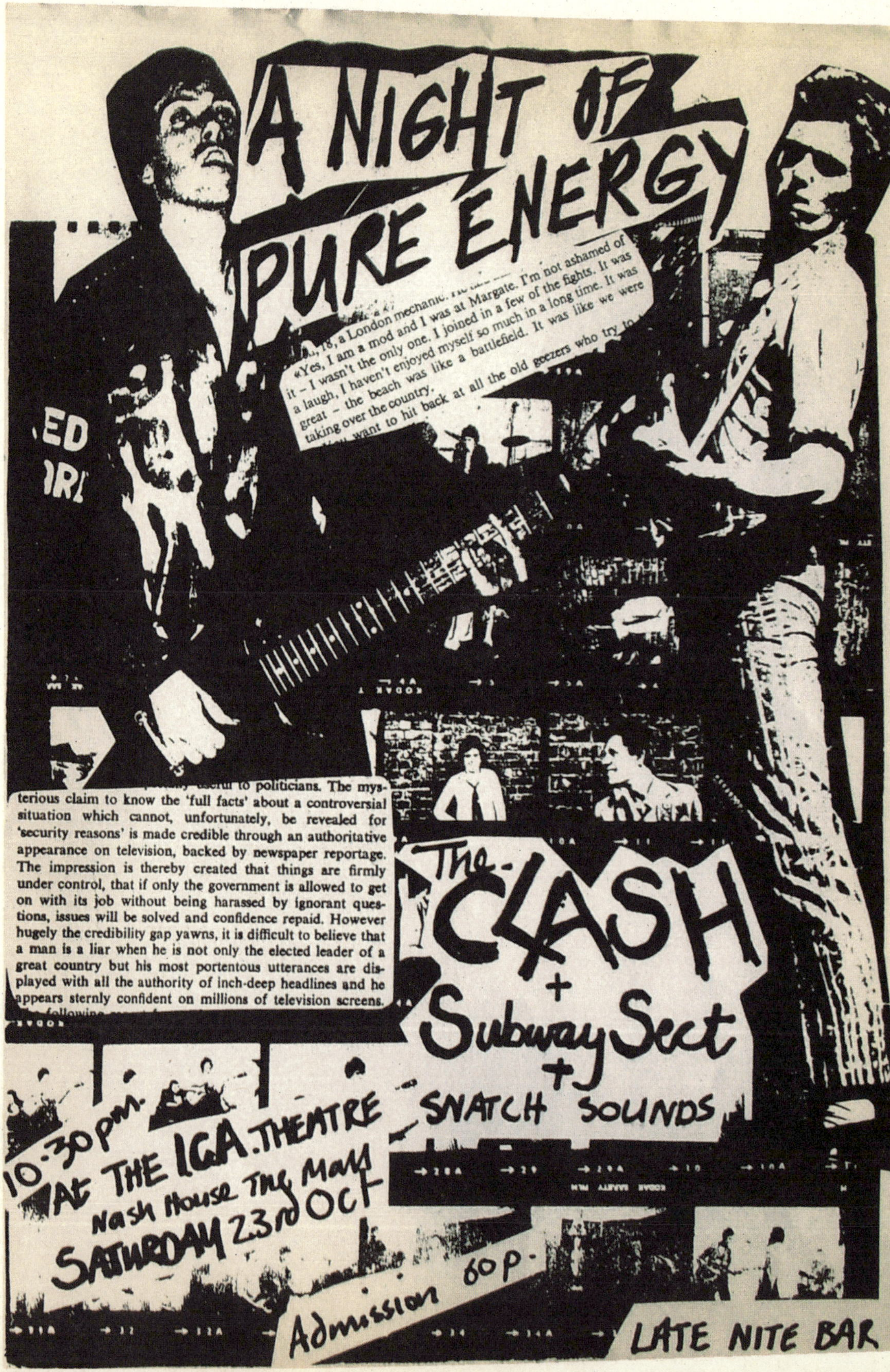
A NIGHT OF
PURE ENERGY
a London mechanic.
«Yes, I am a mod and I was at Margate. I'm not ashamed of it – I wasn't the only one. I joined in a few of the fights. It was a laugh, I haven't enjoyed myself so much in a long time. It was great – the beach was like a battlefield. It was like we were taking over the country.
want to hit back at all the old geezers who try to
to politicians. The mysterious claim to know the 'full facts' about a controversial situation which cannot, unfortunately, be revealed for 'security reasons' is made credible through an authoritative appearance on television, backed by newspaper reportage. The impression is thereby created that things are firmly under control, that if only the government is allowed to get on with its job without being harassed by ignorant questions, issues will be solved and confidence repaid. However hugely the credibility gap yawns, it is difficult to believe that a man is a liar when he is not only the elected leader of a great country but his most portentous utterances are displayed with all the authority of inch-deep headlines and he appears sternly confident on millions of television screens.
The CLASH
+
Subway Sect
+
SNATCH SOUNDS
10-30 pm.
At THE ICA. THEATRE
Nash House The Mall
SATURDAY 23rd OCT
Admission 60p.
LATE NITE BAR

WHITE RIOT, I WANNA RIOT!

SW-Would you say your image is violent or suggestive of violence?

Mick-It reflects our'no nonsense' attitude, an attitude of not takin' too much shit. I don't like violence tough.

SW-What do you think of the aura of violence that surrounds the Pistols, I mean, it can easily get out of hand.

Joe-I think it's a healthy sign that people arn't going to sleep in the back-row.

Mick-I think people have got to find out where their direction lies and channel their violence, into music or something creative.

SW-Thing is, you talk about being creative but say the thing got so popular that we had all those fuckin' footballs and discos and all that lot coming down to see Pistols gigs, They'd take the violence at face value and go fuckin' crazy!

Mick-So you think it can get out of hand?

SW-You bet it can ...

Mick-It got out of hand on Tuesday (100 Club fest-glass throwing incident).

SW-I reckon it could get worse.

Mick-I definitely think it could escalate but the alternative is for people to vent their frustrations through music, or be a painter or a poet or whatever you wanna be. Vent your frustrations, otherwise it's just like clocking in and clocking out ... clock in at the 100 Club, every one comes in, everyone clocks out, it ain't no differant.

SW-How much change do you want, do you want a revolution?

Joe-Well ... yeah!

SW-A bloodless one or do you want just total chaos?

Joe-No, I'm just not into chaos, and I don't believe it when people say they are 'cause you've got to be a special type ...

SW-of maniac?

Joe-Well, a Frenchman, about 100 years ago could be into chaos 'cause it was possible then, but nowdays, this is like sleepytown. So, when someone tells me they're into chaos I don't believe it. What I would like to see happen is, very much ... I realise a lot of people are quite happy, you know, at that market down the road from here. All them people, they're as'appy as sandboys and I'd just like to make loads of people realise what's goin'on. Like, all those secrets in the government and all that money changing hands and every now and then it comes to light and someone gets sacked and someone else comes in the back-door, know what I mean? I'd like to get all that out in the open and just see what's goin'on. I just feel like no one's telling me anything, even if I read every paper, watch TV and listen to the radio!

RADIO.

SW-What was that with the radio at the 100 Club gig?

Joe-Well, all that was ... I'd been lucky and bought a cheap transister in a junk-shop for ten-bob and it worked quite well. l'd been goin' around with it on my ear for a few days just tasee what it was like. When someone broke a string I got it out and it just happened to be something about Northern Ireland.

Mick-A state of emergency ...

SW-Yeah, bombs ... I thought it was interesting I thought maybe it was part of the way you approach your audience.

Mick-That was part of it, but we've tried other things since then, like at the Roundhouse ... er ... we 'talked' to the audienceo ...

Joe-But they were half asleep ...

Mick-The ones who were awake were pretty clever.

Joe-I didn't think so, I mean, you could hear them, I couldn't. How can I answer smartass jibes when I can't hear 'em? All I could hear was some girl sayin', "nyah, nyah, nyah!" and

Full volant anunciant una nit de pura energia a l'ICA Theatre, octubre del 76.

then every-one goes, "aha, ha, ha (bursts out laughing)". If you can't hear what they're saying, then you can't really get out your great wit!

Mick-Well, I'm sure they were funny 'cause everyone was laughing at 'em but when Joe said something like, you know, "Fuck off, fatso!", there was just complete silence! (More laughter).

SW-So, what do you wanna do to your audience?

Joe-Well, there's two ways, there's that confronting thing right! No ... three ways. Make'em feel a bit ... threaten'em, startle'em and second -I know it's hard when you see rock'n' roll bands, to hear the lyrics are but we're workin' on getting the words out and makin'em mean something and the third thing is rythmn. Rythmn is the thing 'cause if it ain't got rythmn then you can just sling it in the dustbin!

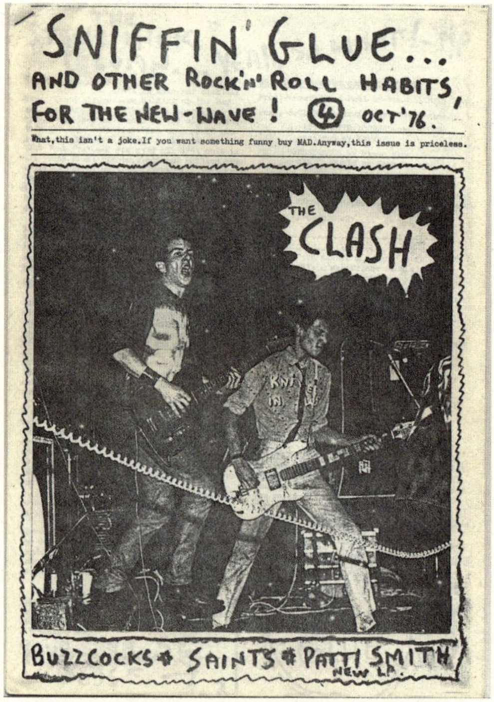

ANY INFLUENCES?

Joe-That's a tricky question ... Paul's are the Ethiopians and what's that other band?

Paul-The Rulers.

Joe-I've never heard of'em!

Mick-Up until now,I thought everything was the cat's knackers and every group was great. I used to go to all the concerts all the time and that's all I did. Until, somehow, I stopped believing in it all, I just couldn't face it. I supose the main influences are Mott the Hoople, the Kinks, the Stones but I just stopped believing. Now, what's out there (points out the window) that's my influence!

SW-What changed your way of looking at things?

Mick-I just found out it wern't true, I stopped reading all the music papers 'cause I used to believe every word. If they told me to go out and buy this record and that, then, I'd just go out and do it. You know, save up me paper round and go out and buy shit and now I'm in a position where I'm selling the records 'cause I don't have much money and they're showing me how much my shits' worth! 'Cause I paid 2 quid for them albums and they give me 10 pence down the record shop, that's how much they think you're worth!

Mick-I've played with so many arse-'oles and my whole career has been one long audition. Like, I was the last kid on my block to pick up a guitar 'cause all the others were repressing me and saying "no, you don't want to do that, you're too ugly, too spotty, you stink!" ... and I believed 'em. I was probably very gullible and then I realised that they wern't doing too well and I said, ah fuck, I can do just as well!

LONDON'S BURNING WITH BOREDOM!
LONDON'S BURNING, DIAL 999!

SW-What do you think of the scene so far?

Mick-Well, it's coming from us, the Pistols, Subway Sect and maybe the Buzzcocks, that's it, there are no other bands!

MP—What do you think of bands that just go out and enjoy themselves?

Mick—You know what l think, I think they're a bunch of ostriches, they're sticking their heads in the fuckin' sand! They're enjoying themselves at the audience's expense. They're takin' their audience for a ride, feeding the audience shit!

MP—What if the audience say they're enjoying themselves?

Joe—Look, the situation is far too serious for enjoyment, man. Maybe when we're 55 we can play tubas in the sun, that's alright then to enjoy yourselves, but now!

Mick—I think if you wanna fuckin' enjoy yourselves you sit in an armchair and watch TV but if you wanna get actively involved, 'cause rock'n' roll's about rebellion. Look, I had this out with Brian James of the Damned and we we're screamin' at each other for about 3 hour 'cause he stands for enjoying himself and I stand for change and creativity.

Joe—I'd rather play to an audience and them not enjoy it, if we we're doin' what we thought was honest. Rather than us go up and sing - Get outta Denver, baby and do what we didn't think was honest.

Mick—If they enjoy us then they come with us. If you ask me what I think of groups like the Hot Rods, I think they're a load of bozos and they're not telling the audience to do anything other than stay as they are. They're playing old stuff and I don't think much of their orginals. The situation is where the Hot Rod's audience are bozos and it's easy to identify with a bozo. I mean, obviously they're goin' down ... like, people queing outside the Marquee, they've got a great thing goin' for themselves, but it's not to do with change, it's just keeping people as they are!

SW—What do you think the scene needs now?

Mick—Ten more honest bands!

Joe—More venues...

Mick—More events!

Joe— ... just more people who care, if we could get out hands on the money and get something together ... immediately. None of the promoters running any of the venues in London, care. Ron Watts, the 100 Club bloke, has done something but no one else really cares. They don't give a shit about the music, not one shit!

END.

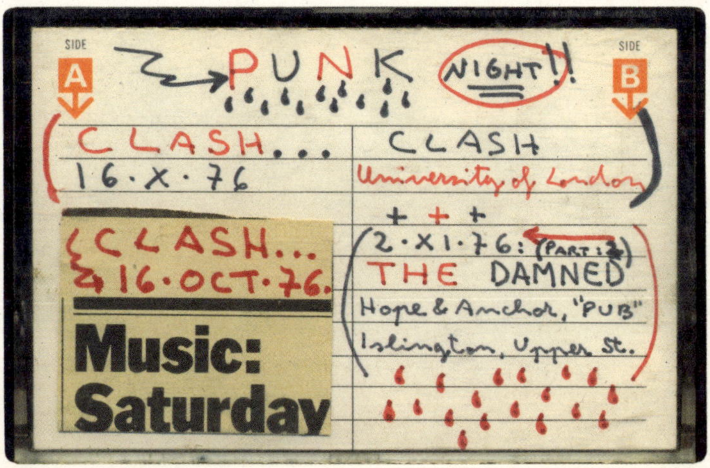

Portada d'*Sniffin' Glue*... 4, on surt publicada l'entrevista amb els Clash. | Coberta de K7 amb els concerts dels Clash a la University of London, 16.10.76, i dels Damned al Hope & Anchor Pub, 2.11.76.

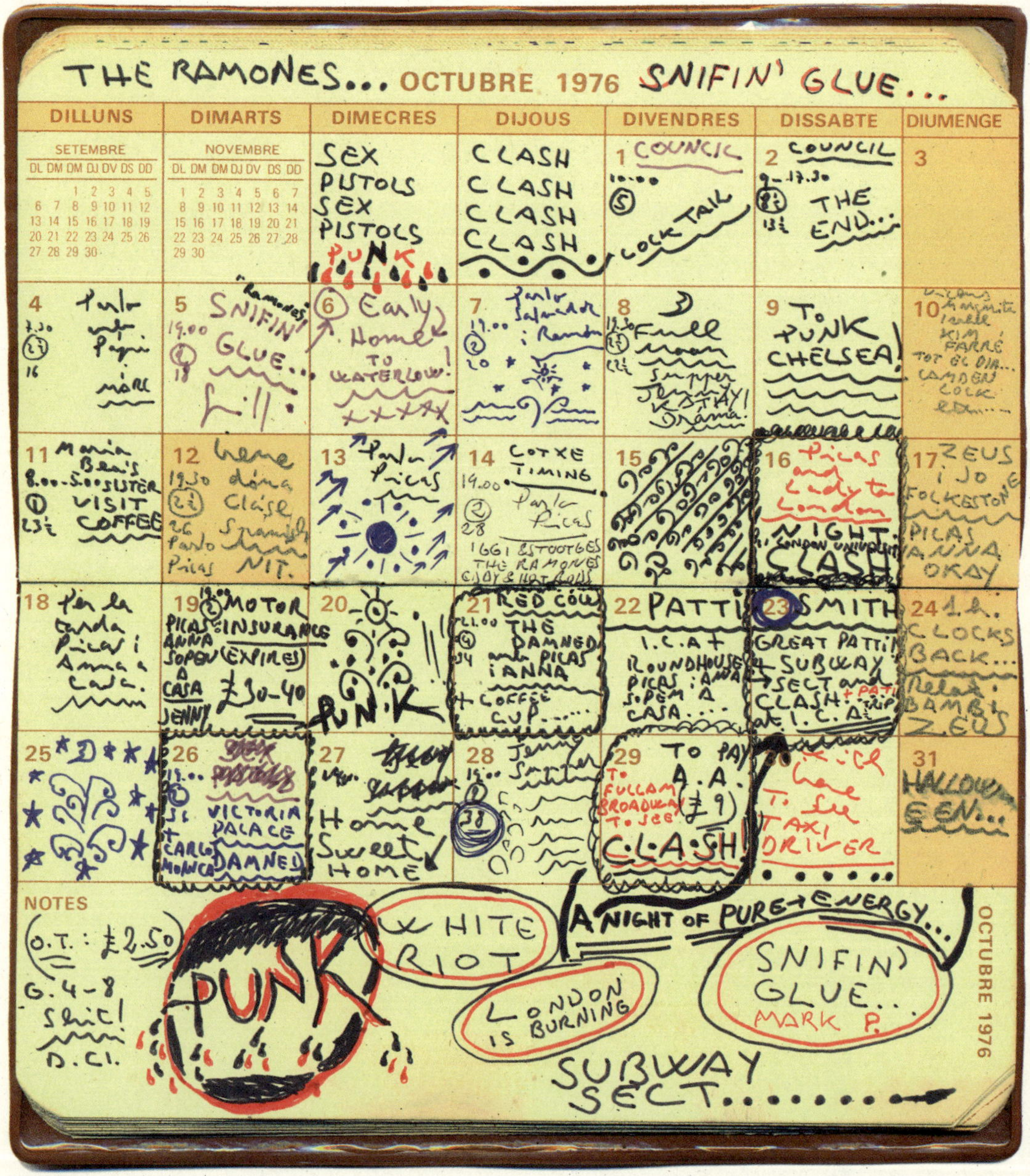

Pàgines de l'agenda de Jordi Valls, 1976. | Cares A i B de la cinta TDK amb els concerts dels Clash i els Damned a Fulham Old Town i Hope & Anchor Pub respectivament.

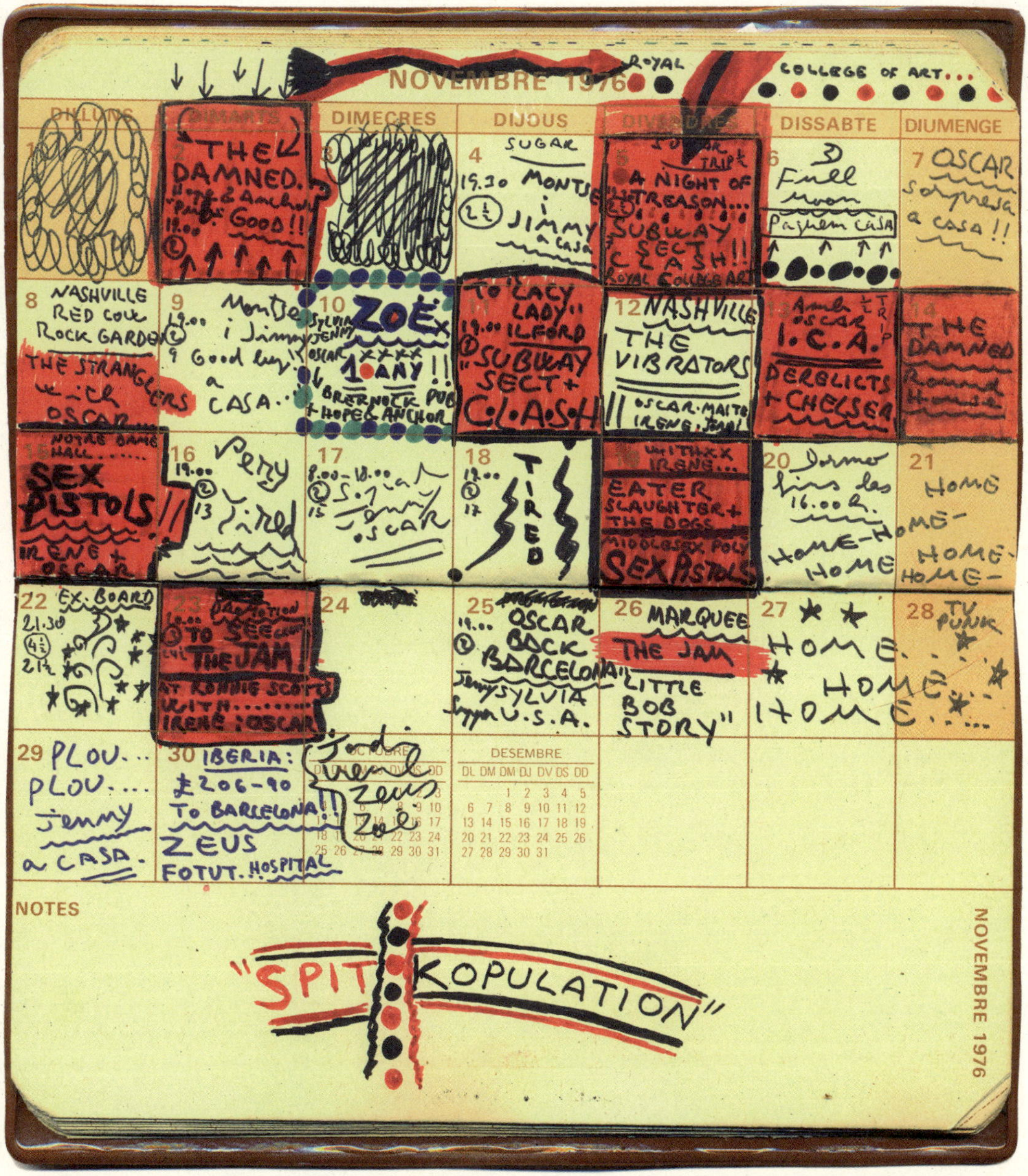

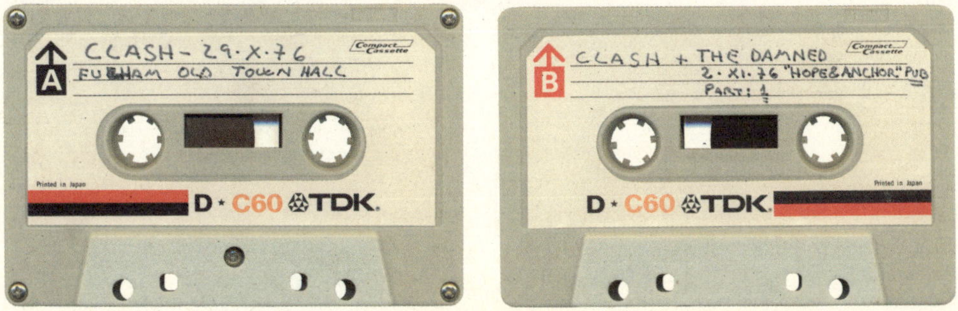
CLASH - 29·X·76
FULHAM OLD TOWN HALL
CLASH + THE DAMNED
2·XI·76 "HOPE & ANCHOR" PUB
D·C60 TDK

DAMNED. INTERVIEW.

Mark Perry (SG).
Sniffin' Glue... núm. 3, setembre 1976.

SG-You've not played many gigs, what's happening?

RAT-We'll play anywhere that'll have us except pubs.

SG-Except pubs?

RAT-You realy get a shitty reputation for one thing and it's very difficult to break out of the pub circuit. Most of the pub audiences like to sit, have a drink and chat about the weather ... we're too loud for pubs anyway.

SG-There isn't anywhere else really.

RAT-Places like the Nashville are alright. It would be nice to get a tour or somethin'.

SG-The songs you play .....

RAT-They're all our own songs except ... the only ones that ain't ours are 'Help', the Dolls one, 'It's Too Late' and the Stooges' number, '1970'.

SG-What sort of stuff do you listen to?

BRIAN-I listen to the Stooges and the Dolls.

ANDREW-All their influences are the same, that is why they came together.

RAT-No they're not ...

BRIAN-You like Dave Clark!

RAT-It's not that .... it's like, yea Dave Clark started me playing but I mean .... I was very young when Dave Clark came in.

SG-What about the stuff you see playing in pubs?

RAT-There ain't nothin'!

BRIAN-There's nothing going on so far in this country, you tell us what have you seen?

SG-To us there's no good or bad ...

RAT-To get the scene going ...

SG-It's no good putting bands down, it's great that there's bands trying.

RAT-The biggest thing around at the moment is the Rods. The Pistols are trying to make a dent but whether they will or not I don't know. About the only two bands ... I don't know about Sister Ray 'cause I ain't seen 'em yet.

SG-What you think of the Rods?

BRIAN-They're alright, they need to progress a bit though. They're going back on old stuff but they're good though.

DAVID- They do generate excitment don't they?

RAT-I really like Eddie and the Hot Rods and you, Barrie Masters .... we've all got differant influences, getting back to that. Ray used to listen to Marc Bolan until he discovered Iggy Pop.

DAVID-Until he got Iggy's t-shirt he means!

SG-He tried to swop me that ... Iggy's shirt for a Marc Bolan t-shirt!

RAT-You ...

RAY-I was talking about somethin' else.

RAT-That's what we got has a bass player ...

SG-He wears a nice line in shades.

RAY-I bought these for 5p would you believe?

RAT-No, basically... our music fires off so well'cause we hate each other ....

SG-Every band says that!

RAT-It's true ... we don't see each other at all socially.

SG-What have you done before the Damned?

RAT-I was on holiday like ... that's the last thing I was doing. We all had varied backgrounds.

RAT-Yea, I was a toilet cleaner ... yer, print that!

DAVID-I'm still working as a grave digger, a guy who digs graves, he don't dig'em he digs graves ....

RAT-Yea, we don't see each other at all socially, we hate the sight of each other and (pointing at David) I'd kick his head in if I got half the chance!

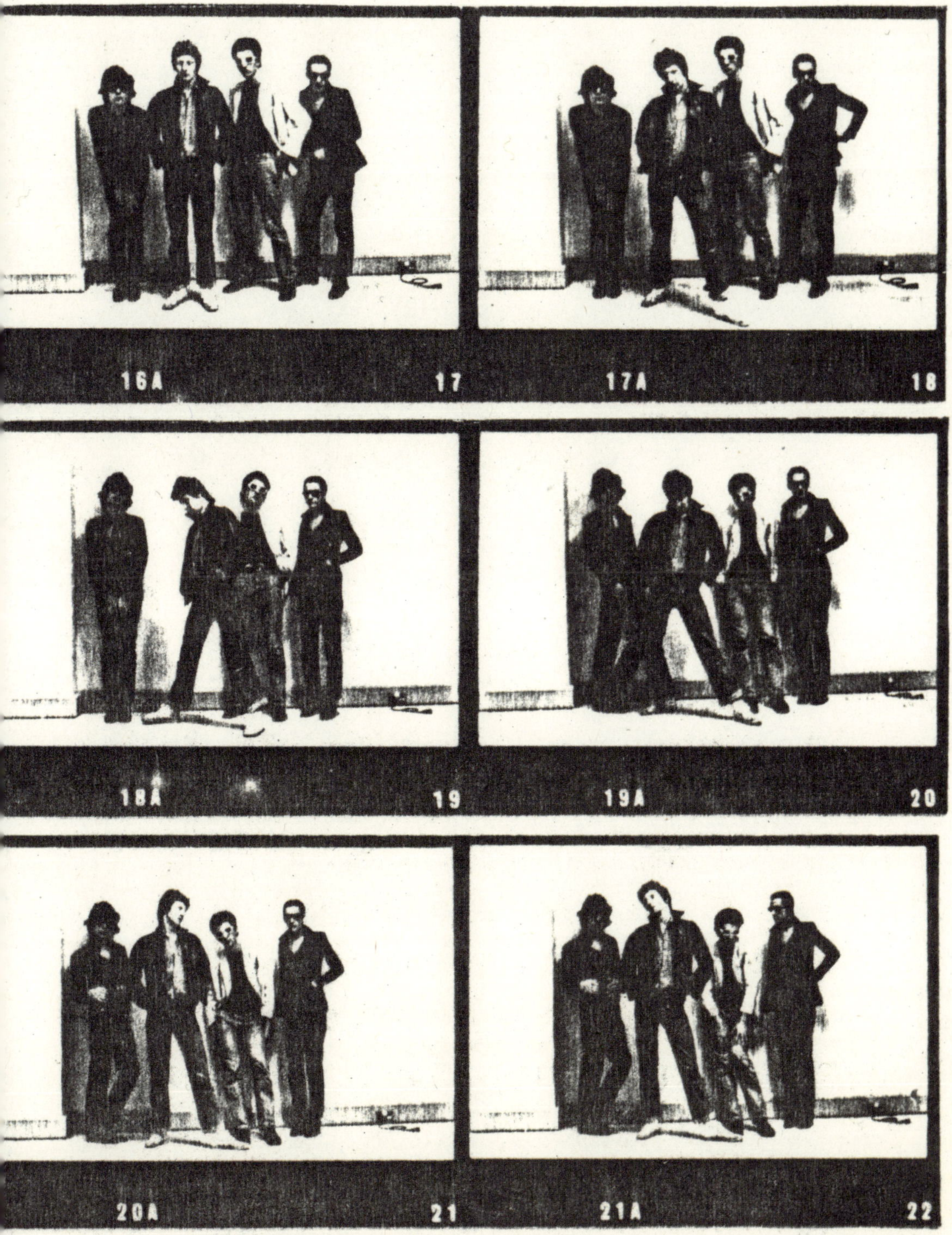

THE DAMNED. Brian James (21), Rat Scabies (19), Ray Burns / Captain Sensible (22) i David Vanian (20). Fotocòpies que il·lustren l'entrevista de Mark Perry.

PUNK ROCK?

RAT-You can call it punk-rock but I don't think I like that definition ... Punk!

BRIAN-It's the word people use ...

RAT-Yea, but it's like a tag, the thing is I hope it don't go to far ... I dunno, what's a punk?

SG-It's a ruffian, isn't it?

DAVID-The actual definition means worthless.

BRIAN-No one playing in a band's worthless!

RAT-You've got to have talent to sorne degree to get up on stage to do it!

BRIAN-If someone says you're a punk, it mean they think you're stupid ....

RAT-It's just a slag down, I can see how the tag came about but I don't see how it applys to me.

DAVID-Or anyone else in this group!

SG-How would you describe your music?

DAVID-There isn't a name at the moment.

RAT-It's not rock'n'roll but it's like ....

DAVID-It's music for NOW!

BRIAN-Power music ...

RAT-Get up of yer arse music! We'll drive you out to the other bar in the Nashville!

SG-They were sitting there stunned at the Nashville, when you were supporting S.A.L.T.

RAT-We've had that at a few gigs ... well two of 'em. Our second gig we just played and there was nuthin', except we were throwing bottles at some gays things like that. Afterwards they were calling for an encore. There was nothing after every song but by the end they went mad!

SG-What about the stunt at the Nashville, you know, kicking the drums?

RAT-It wern't a stunt, we were playing so badly, well, I was anyway, and that number just wern't goin' right. I couldn't take anymore, it had to stop and I knew that ounce I got rid of

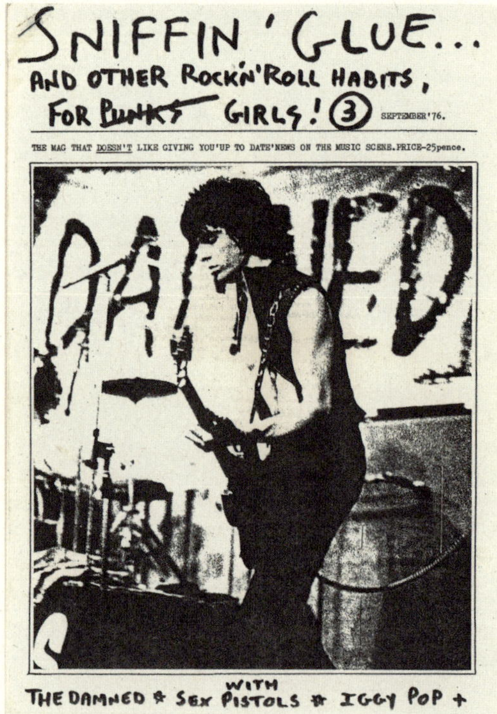

that initial outburst it could go a bit better, which it did. Except S.A.L.T. closing the curtains on us, we was into our last number when they done it as well. Then again, it looked good I suppose. It was a laugh afterwards, you expect hippys to be friendly people but ...

SG-S.A.L.T. really wanted to get you off ...

RAT- ... 'cause we was too much of a threat to them.

DAVID-We didn't even do our fifty minutes.

RAT-We was contracted to do an hour, but it was still great, the guy from Chiswick, Roger Armstrong came up and asked us to do somethin'.

SG-You gonna do it?

RAT-It'll be a one off deal.

SG-It's all rock'n'roll on Chiswick at the moment.

RAT-I think rock'n'roll ... you mean the 101'ers single?

SG- ... and the Count Bishops, great rockin' stuff!

THE LONDON SCENE.

RAT-Who wants to see and hear 45 year old rock stars?

BRIAN-45 year old people!

RAT-What about the sixteen year old kids on the streets who ain't had no life, they're the ones we're going for.

ANDREW-We wanna satisfy the young audience.

SG-We need a club in London where you've got it every night, like New York at the moment!

RAT-In New York there's loads of clubs ...

BRIAN-There's only about three or four ...

RAT- ... more than there is over here though ain't there?

BRIAN-There's a scene, there's not that sort of community feel here.

RAT-Joey Ramone was saying that they all know each other. There's competion but they are all good mates as well.

SG-That's the feeling we should get here.

BRIAN-That's what 'Sniffin'Glue ... 'is all about.

DAVID-That's what we wanna do, make people do somethin' rather than just sit and talk about it.

BRIAN-There's no fun around at the moment.

RAT-London's a real dead town anyway, like that Pistols thing we done, it was'uncool' to clap another band, you know?

BRIAN-But Johnny's alright.

RAT-Yea, I like Johnny Rotten ...

SG-Ask the Rods what they think of'em!

RAT-I don't think they're very fond of them somehow.

BRIAN-It's sad, the Stranglers as well.

DAVID-It's a hazme 'cause really all these young bands should be friendly, it should be a whole scene.

RAT-I think we're the only bands that talks to the others on a friendly level ... except S.A.L.T.! It works both ways, if you're good to a band they'll work with you. One good turn deserves another, it don't seem that way with a lot of 'em.

ANDREW-That's where the punk tag relates to the scene.

SG-Are you associated with Sister Ray?

BRIAN-I know the singer and the guitarist.

SG-They're really good ...

ANDREW-They're a bit dated though.

SG-They sound a lot like Mott the Hoople ...

ANDREW- ... and sixties R&B!

RAT-He's a good guitarist.

BRIAN-Yea, Kelvin, the singer's good too.

SG-Getting back to you, what song are you hoping to do for the single?

RAT-We're thinking of doing a slow twelve-bar actually, called 'My Baby Left Me and I Ain't Got a Shirt On My Back' and it goes de, do, de, dum, da, de, do. It goes from E up to A up to B-flat and back to E again!

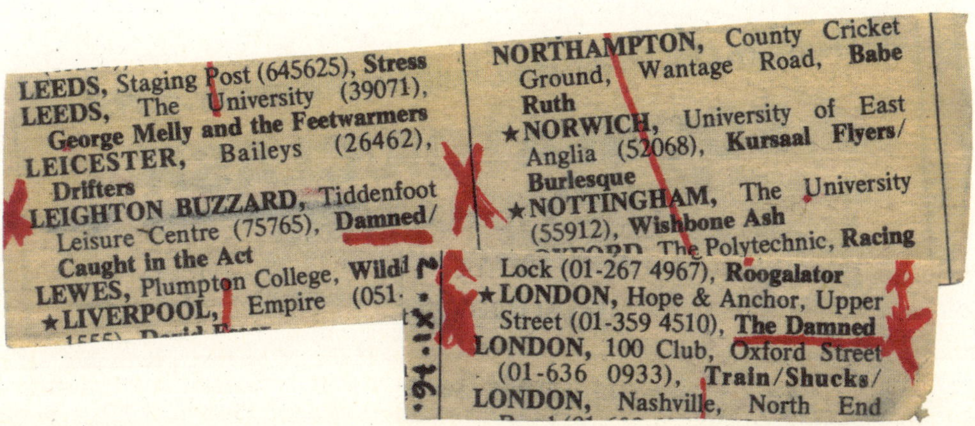
LEEDS, Staging Post (645625), **Stress**
LEEDS, The University (39071), **George Melly and the Feetwarmers**
LEICESTER, Baileys (26462), **Drifters**
LEIGHTON BUZZARD, Tiddenfoot Leisure Centre (75765), **Damned/Caught in the Act**
LEWES, Plumpton College, **Wild**
★LIVERPOOL, Empire (051-
NORTHAMPTON, County Cricket Ground, Wantage Road, **Babe Ruth**
★NORWICH, University of East Anglia (52068), **Kursaal Flyers/Burlesque**
★NOTTINGHAM, The University (55912), **Wishbone Ash**
The Polytechnic, **Racing**
Lock (01-267 4967), **Roogalator**
★LONDON, Hope & Anchor, Upper Street (01-359 4510), **The Damned**
LONDON, 100 Club, Oxford Street (01-636 0933), **Train/Shucks/**
LONDON, Nashville, North End

Portada d'*Sniffin' Glue*... 3, on surt publicada l'entrevista amb els Damned el setembre del 1976. | Retall de diari amb anuncis de concerts dels Damned, 1976.

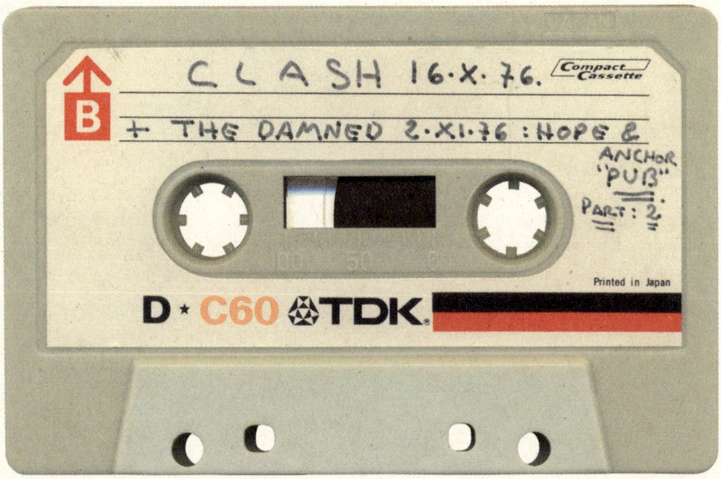

K7 amb el concert de The Damned al Hope & Anchor Pub, Londres, 2.11.76.

YEA?

RAT–It's like a vicious circle ... still hassling gigs ... you get on to an agent and ask "come down and see us 'cause we're looking for an agent". They say "OK maybe I will". Of curse they don't come so they ask for a tape and we take 'em one and they say "We can't really tell from that". They won't give you a fucking gig to start off, at one of their placeso ... it's such a vicious circle!

"YOUR PRETTY FACE IS GOING TO HELL".

RAT–Dave Vanian, what makes you tick?

DAVID–Tick, tick, tock: I havn't got an image on stage, whatever I do is just like .....

RAY–Chuck Berry smells! (He had to get that in).

DAVID– .... images, I don't like anything contrived. I think images should come naturally, just do what happens at the time–work off the audience. A panther? Thats mostly 'cause I hate the audience. No I don't really, we love all the punks!

RAT–Keep on booking us kids ....

RAY–Buy our records!

RAT–There's to much plasticness around ....

ANDREW–Yea, in the record business!

RAT–Funny man, no, there's too much posing.

DAVID–They're being far to serious about the image a not about the music. Like, we're here to have a bit of fun.

RAT–Just do what you wanna do, that's why my kit went over, it just happened!

RAT–I'm the only one with a dynamic personality in the group.

SG–Shut up! Where do you hope to be playing next year?

RAT–Stockwell, we wanna do a tour of Andy's house!

DAVID–We wanna do by dad's garage.

SG–You gonna cram an audience in?

DAVID–We don't play to audiences, only cockroaches.

SG–Audiences bore you?

RAT–Only when there's no response.

SG–What do you do then?

RAT–We don't responed back. If they throw bottles it's fair enough, you know?

BRIAN–Good or bad, it's a reaction .... but when you get absolutely nothin' ....

SG–It's like playing to a brick wall!

BRIAN–Yea, right!

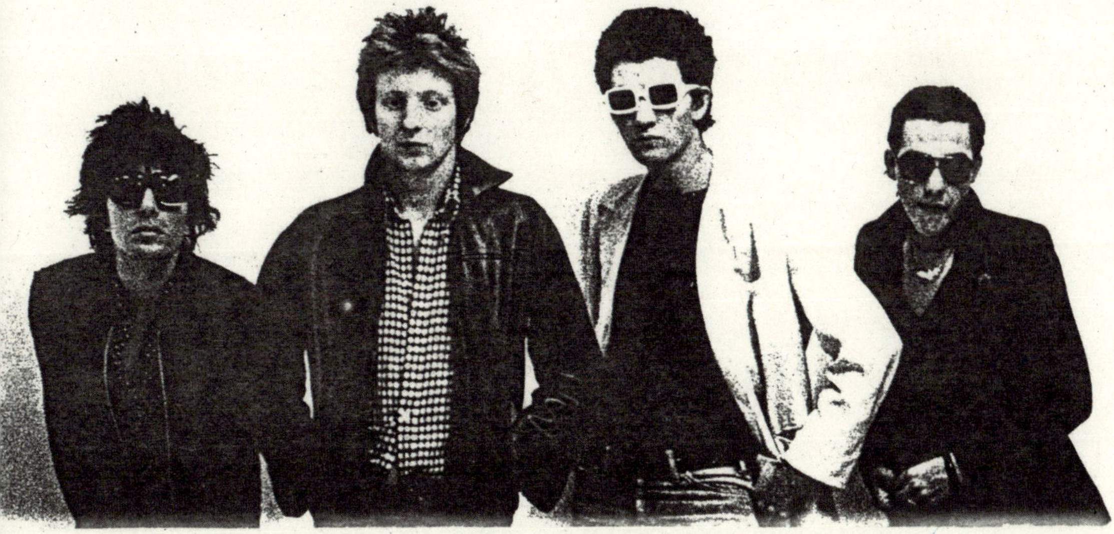

Brian James, Rat Scabies, Ray Burns/Captain Sensible, David Vanian.

DAVID—When we get nothing we usually try harder.

BRIAN—We don't usually get a non-reaction ...

RAT—Well, we did at St. Albans though, didn't we?

BRIAN—No, throwing beer and bottles .... very good that.

SG—What do you think audiences most like about the band?

BRIAN—The energy.

RAT—I think that's our main selling point.

SG—It's not just your dynamic stage personality then?

RAY—They like me as well ...

RAT—It's, my dynamic stage act!

RAY—They like me.

RAT—Why do they like you Ray?

RAY—They come to see what sunglasses I've got on.

SG—Do you wear a differant pair each night?

RAY—I keep on losing'em.

SG—Do you feel frustrated, not being able to reherse today? (Somebody had 'Borrowed' their gear)

RAY—No.

SG—You don't care?

RAY—I care but it doesn't get me down.

SG—How long have you been playing for?

RAY—A couple of years or so ...

SG—Would you say that you had any influences?

RAY—No, not really ....

SG—You just thought that you'd like to play.

RAY—I don't play like anyone else, you know?

SG—Does it irritate you ... not being able to buy a cheeseburger?

RAY—Yer, that irritates me!

SG—Do you practice much?

RAY—I never practice!

SG—What, do you just play when you're together?

RAY—Yea, I don't need practice.

SG—You reckon it was just born in you to play?

RAY—Not really ... I saw Bolan on 'Top Of the Pops'.

SG—He doesn't play bass though, does he?

RAY—No.

SG—What made you lot play?

RAT—Failed me 11+ and I thought I'd get me own back. No, I dunno ... I just like hitting things. To relieve that inner frustration!

THE END

SUBWAY SECT

Steve Mick (SM).
Sniffin' Glue... núm. 5, novembre del 1976.
Fotografies: Subway Sect.

SM–What's in the name, Subway Sect?

Paul–Ah?

SM–Err ... the name?

Paul–What's in it? Well, we used to go busking down Hammersmith subway and ...

Vic–Not busking!

SM–AH of ya?

Vic–Na, just three of us ... but it wasn't busking so much as we wanted to see what it was like to play to people. Even though they were just walking by ... So we weren't really down there to get any money'cause you've gotta join aunion to do that really, havn't you? We just played a couple of Velvet Underground numbers down there a couple of times and we evolved from there.

SM–So, who was the other musician?

Vic–No, there's just ... I was singing and the guitarist, Rob, was playing and he (Paul) was just standing there.

Paul–Yer, banging a can against the wall most of the time'cause I don't like standing there and doing nothing.

SM–You've been playing for about 4 months?

Vic–Well ... practising.

SM–Rob has, hasn't he?

Vic–Well, he's been playing guitar. Paul's been playing bass for about 4 months havn't ya?

Paul–Coming up to 4 months.

Vic–The drummer though, he's only been playing for about 2 months. He's done really well.

SM–How many gigs have you played now?

Vic–Two ...

SM–I thought you played a party or something –a wedding.

Vic–That was good that was. We did Sex Pistols'numbers, a couple of ... not the ones they've written, we did "Steppin' Stone" and a couple of ones lid written then which we donlt do now. We did a complete 'noise' first, at that party –that's what made everyone walk out– where everyone smashed their guitars around. I just chanted some poetry over it all.

Paul–At the time I wasn't very good on bass and I reckon I got about three notes right in the whole set. I had my back to the audience so they couldn't see what I was doing.

SM–Did they pay you for that?

Paul–No!

Vic–Joking!

Paul–They kicked us ...

SM–What did you think of yourselves at the punk fest?

Vic–I thought I wasn't going to like going on stage but when you get up there it's just like you're one of the audience. When we play I always take the attitude that we're just practiaing in front of a load of people. So it seems to me, we do exactly the same when we're practicing as when we play live. There's only

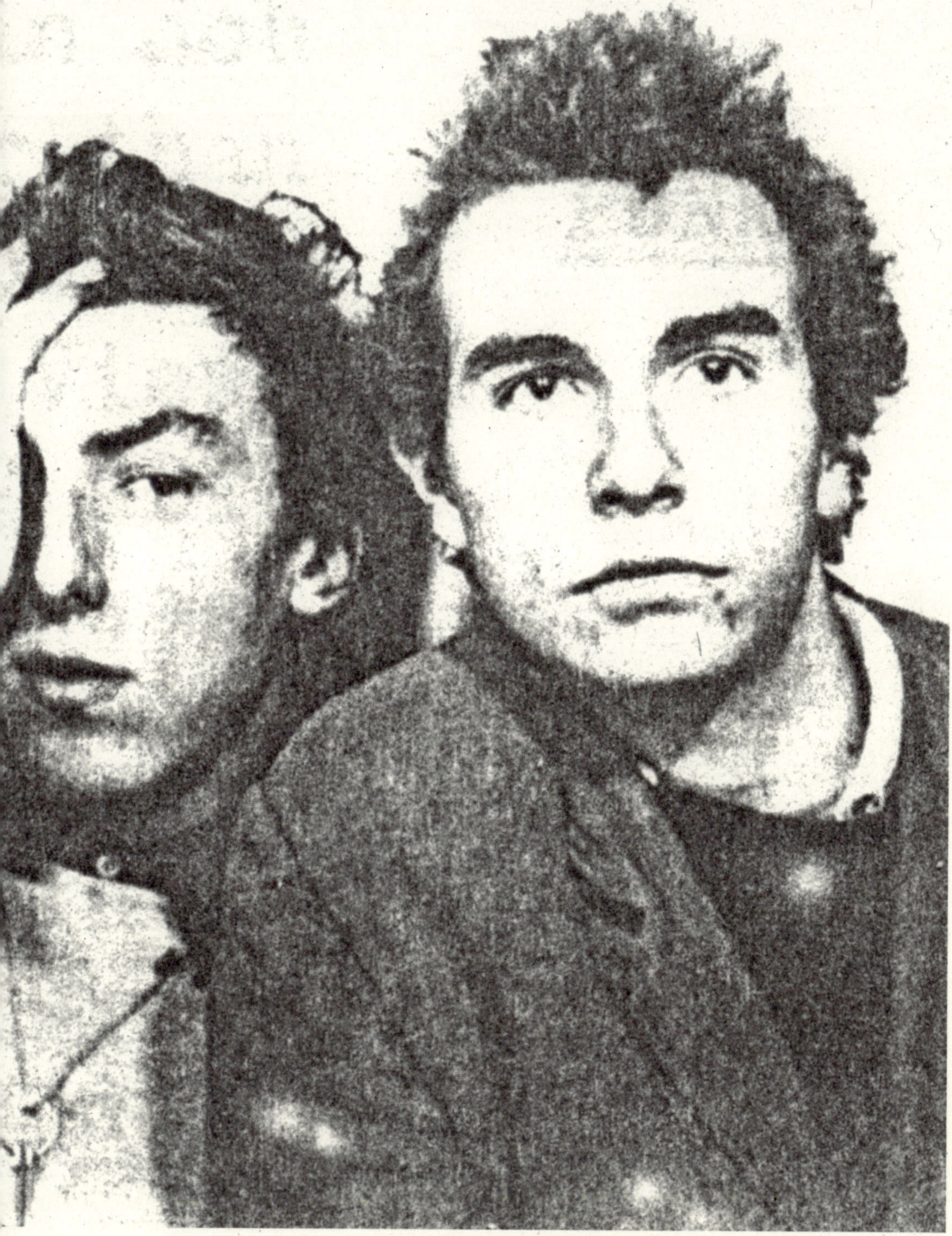

SUBWAY SECT. Vic Godard (19) i Paul Myers (19) fotocopiats a *Sniffin' Glue*...

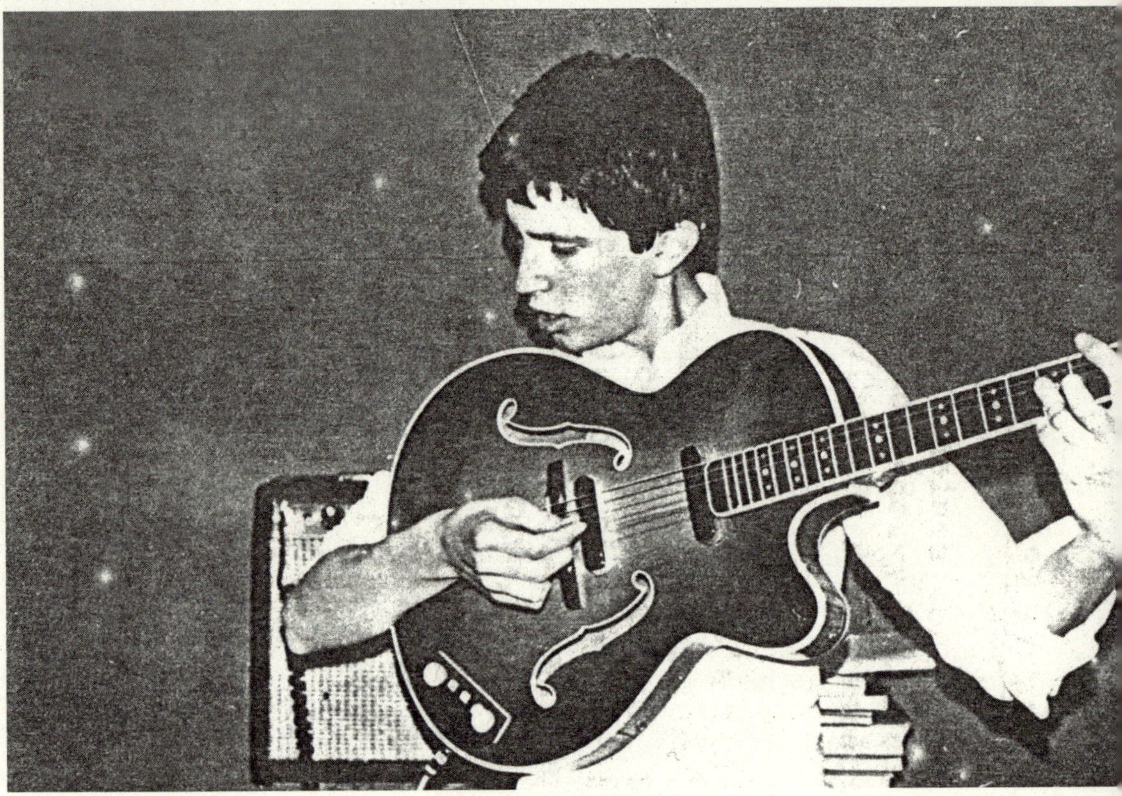

Robert Miller (19)

one difference - when we practice and we do something wrong we stop but when we play live and we do something wrong we just carry on.

SM-You look bored on stage, is that natural or is it all planned?

Vic-We're not trying to make it an image or anything.

Paul-The reason I don't move is ... if I moved I wouldn't be able to play the bass. I'd miss all the notes, so I just stand still. If it is an image I'm glad it's original anyway.

Vic-The reason we do it is that those two can't move 'cause they're not good at playing, so they just stand there and concentrate. It'd look a bit silly if that lot stood still and I jumped all over the place. So I stand still as well.

SM-What'do you care about (Getting serious-Ed)

Vic-I care about being involved in society.

SM-You think you're involved enough?

Vic-I'm not saying that my playing is being involved in society. I'm talkin' about being inolved in doing things that ... causes that you stand up for ... things like that.

SM-What sort of causes do you stand up for?

Vic-Well ... things like radicting oppression of workers and thinks like that, you know?

SM-Are you political through your music?

Vic-None of the rest of the group are political but my songs ... some of 'em have got political ideas in them. What I meant by "getting involved" was things like ... You know what I did the other day? I'll tell you what I did. Everyone else will take the piss out of this! There's some Californian grape farmers and, they're being opressed by the Mafia-big business and they're not unionised which means they really ... about 20 quid a week and they are really worked to the bone.

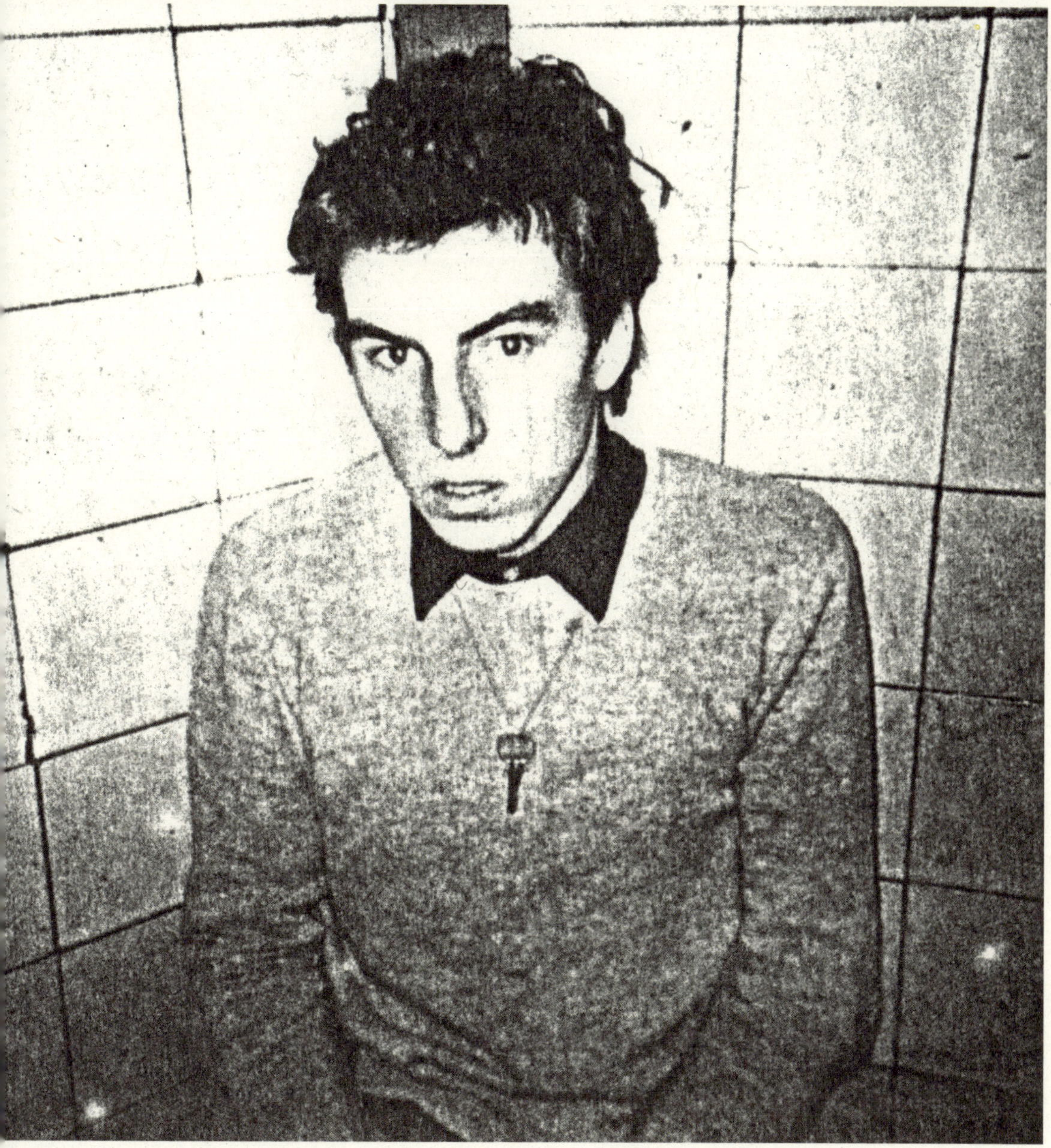

Vic Godard

All their grapes are coming over to England and ... I don't know if you've heard about it -United Farm Workers Cooperative, you heard of that? All these grapes are coming over to England. Now, they'll be here from October to March. All the red grapes you see in England, about 70% of those will be from California and what they were trying to do was boycott anyone from eating those red grapes. I've been round all the local greengrocers in my area asking them not to stock red grapes. I know it seems petty but there's a lot of ... what happened was, in 1971 these red grapes were brought over to England and all the dockers refused to take'em but now, with the advant of containers all the grapes are mixed up so it's gotta be done by the consumers if anything is to be done ...

SM–You say you're "political". What do you think of the "anarchy" and that?

Vic–Rather than go around with "ANARCHY" written all over ya self you should do something like what I did. It's sounds petty but you should get involved with things. If you're an anarchist, well ... I think all the people that go about with "anarchy" written over themselves I don't think they're anarchists. They don't go around blowing up things!

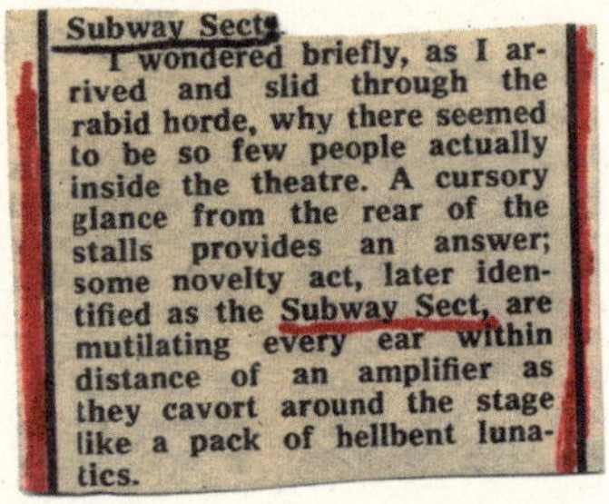
Subway Sect

I wondered briefly, as I arrived and slid through the rabid horde, why there seemed to be so few people actually inside the theatre. A cursory glance from the rear of the stalls provides an answer; some novelty act, later identified as the Subway Sect, are mutilating every ear within distance of an amplifier as they cavort around the stage like a pack of hellbent lunatics.

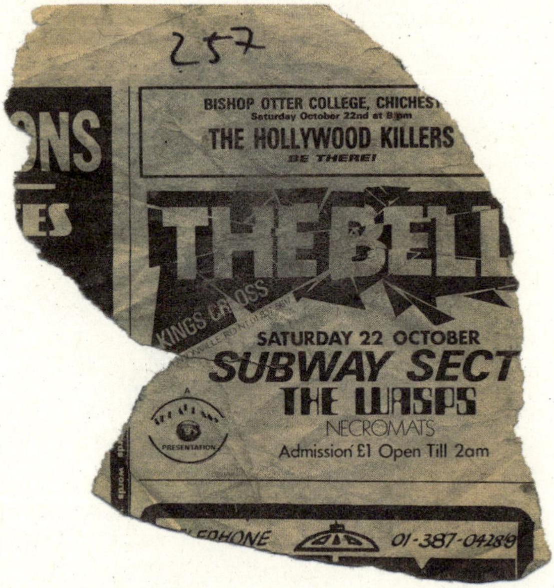

NEWSPAPER.

SM–What was that about,the newspaper at the ICA gig?

Vic–What newspaper?

SM–The newspaper you held in yer hand on stage?

Vic–What mine?

SM–Yeah, I'm sure it was.

Vic–Oh. That was the words of the songs. We were doing three songs and I hadn't long written them so I wasn't sure of the words of some of'em.

SM–'Cause I thought you was going to suddenly stop the show and read out some headline.

Vic– Oh no, it wasn't that.

Paul–He had to tell us when to change.

Vic–That's right, yeah. You mean when I kept putting it up? That was when they dhanged chords.

Paul–We kept looking at him when to change.

Vic–'Cause they were new numbers and they had to look at me when to change'cause they don't know the words all that well. When I put my hand up ... that means they change and we go into the chorus or something like that, you know?

Paul–Well, we couldn't hear what he was singing so it didn't matter anyway.

END.

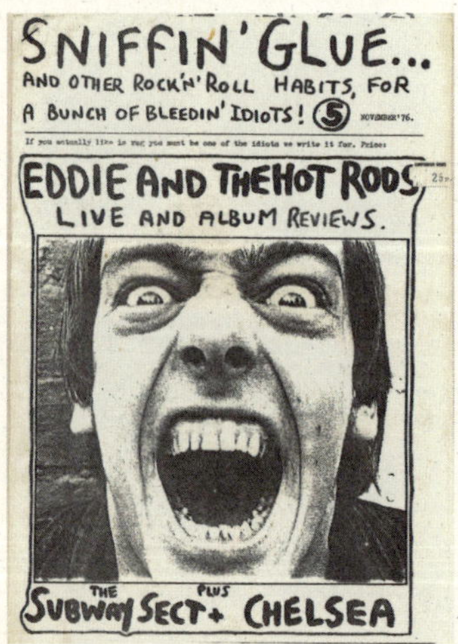

Retalls de diari. | Portada d'*Sniffin' Glue*... 5, on surt publicada l'entrevista amb els Subway Sect, novembre del 76. | Lletra de la cançó "Nobody's Scared" i K7 amb els concerts de Subway Sect i Clash al Royal College of Art, novembre del 76.

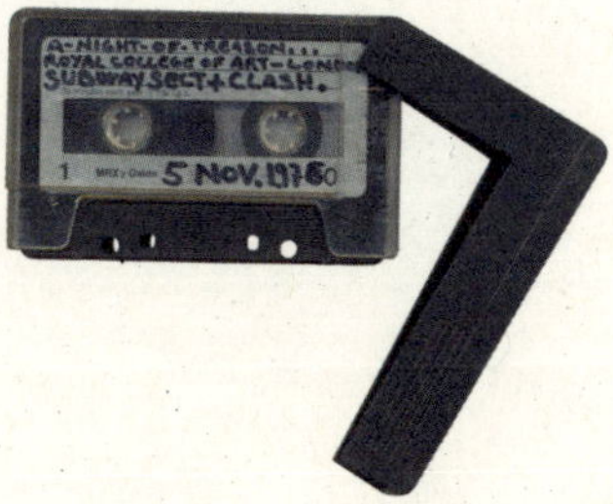

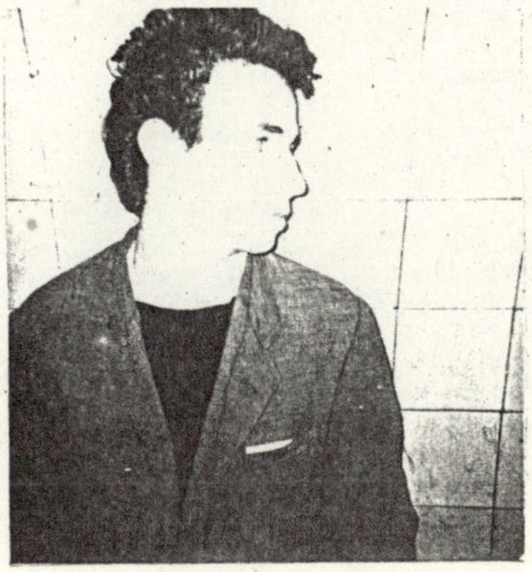

Paul Myers

<u>Nobody's Scared</u>

Nobody's scared
Everyone's a prostitute
Singing the song in prison
Moral standards the wallpaper
The wall is a bad religion

Media teach me what to speak
Take my decisions
It's how to find your inner self time
On the television

No one knows what they're for
No one even cares
We'll shout out publicity handouts
Nobody's scared

The language we use is what we want
Does it not project the force
The subject to object journeys mean
That a word loses course

So take me talking with cliches
Betray yourself for money
Having is more than being now
Nobody is sorry

No one knows what they're for
No one even cares
We'll shout out publicity handouts
Nobody's scared

(Vic Godard / Subway Sect)

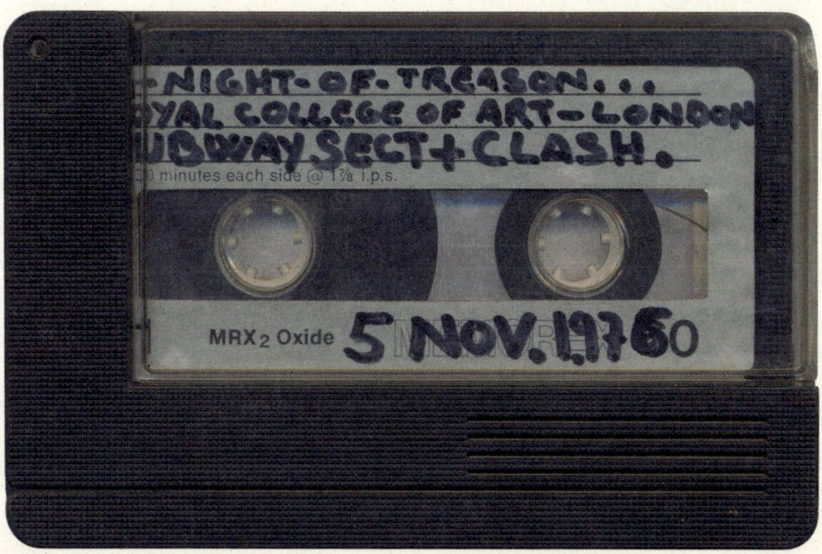

October 19th-26th 1976

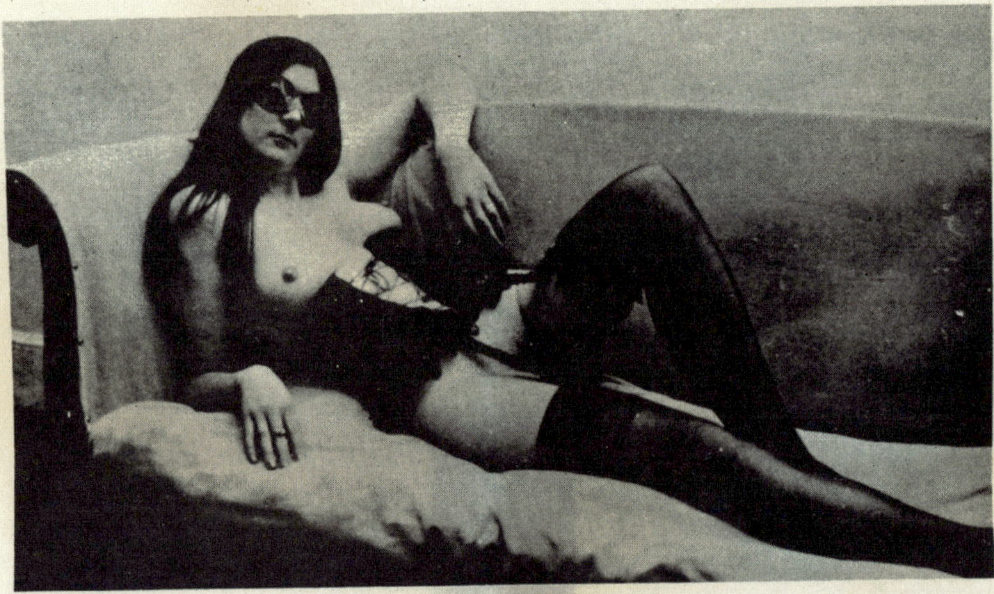

SEXUAL TRANSGRESSIONS NO. 5

PROSTITUTION

COUM Transmissions:- Founded 1969. Members (active) Oct 76 - P. Christopherson, Cosey Fanni Tutti,Genesis P-Orridge.Studio in London.Had a kind of manifesto in July/August Studio International 1976. Performed their works in Palais des Beaux Arts,Brussels; Musee d'Art Moderne, Paris; Galleria Borgogna, Milan; A.I.R. Gallery, London; and took part in Arte Inglese Oggi, Milan survey of British Art in 1976. November/December 1976 they perform in Los Angeles Institute of Contemporary Art;Deson Gallery,Chicago;N.A.M.E. Gallery,Chicago and in Canada. This exhibition was prompted as a comment on survival in Britain,and themselves.

2 years have passed since the above photo of Cosey in a magazine inspired this exhibition.Cosey has appeared in 40 magazines now as a deliberate policy.All of these framed form the core of this exhibition.Different ways of seeing and using Cosey with her consent,produced by people unaware of her reasons,as a woman and an artist, for participating.In that sense,pure views.In line with this all the photo documentation shown was taken,unbidden by COUM by people who decided on their own to photograph our actions.How other people saw and recorded us as information.Then there are xeroxes of our press cuttings,media write ups.COUM as raw material.All of them,who are they about and for? The only things here made by COUM are our objects. Things used in actions,intimate (previously private) assemblages made just for us. Everything in the show is for sale at a price,even the people. For us the party on the opening night is the key to our stance,the most important performance.We shall also do a few actions as counterpoint later in the week.

PERFORMANCES: Wed 20th 1pm - Fri 22nd 7pm
Sat 23rd 1pm - Sun 24th 7pm

INSTITUTE OF CONTEMPORARY ARTS LIMITED

NASH HOUSE THE MALL LONDON S.W.I. BOX OFFICE Telephone 01-930-6393

21.9.76 Top Rank, Cardiff, Wales
22.9.76 Stowaway Newport, Wales
23.9.76 Bubbles, Swansea, Wales
24.9.76 76 Club, Burton On Trent
27.9.76 Outlook Club, Doncaster
28.9.76 The Place, Guildford
29.9.76 Strikes Club, Stoke
30.9.76 Cleopatras, Derby
1.10.76 Didsbury College, Manchester
2.10.76 Priory Ballroom, Scunthorpe - CANCELLED
12.10.76 Technical College, Dundee, Scotland, UK
13.10.76 Lafayette Club, Wolverhampton
14.10.76 Mr Digby's, Birkenhead
15.10.76 Eric's, Liverpool
20.10.76 Bogarts, Birmingham
21.10.76 Queensway Hall, Dunstable
15.11.76 Notre Dame Hall, Leicester Place, London
19.11.76 Hendon Polytechnic, London
29.11.76 Lancaster Polytechnic, Coventry

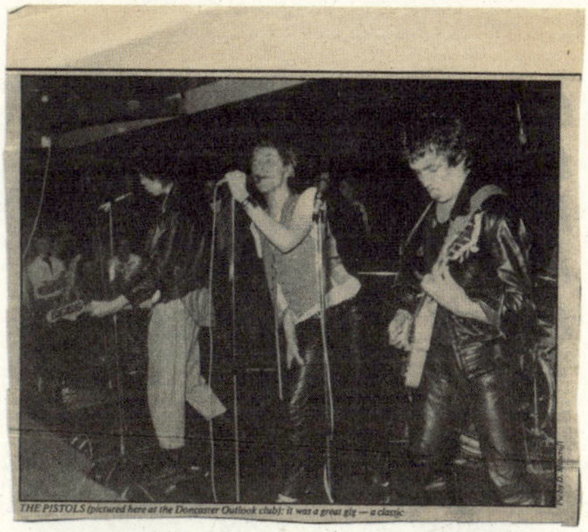

I WANNA BE ME

CANNIBALISM AT CLASH GIG

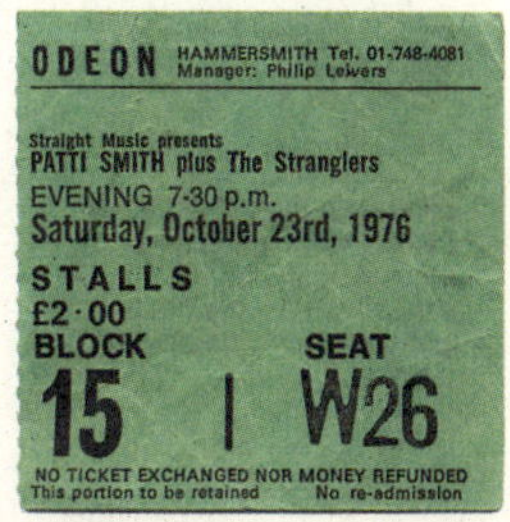

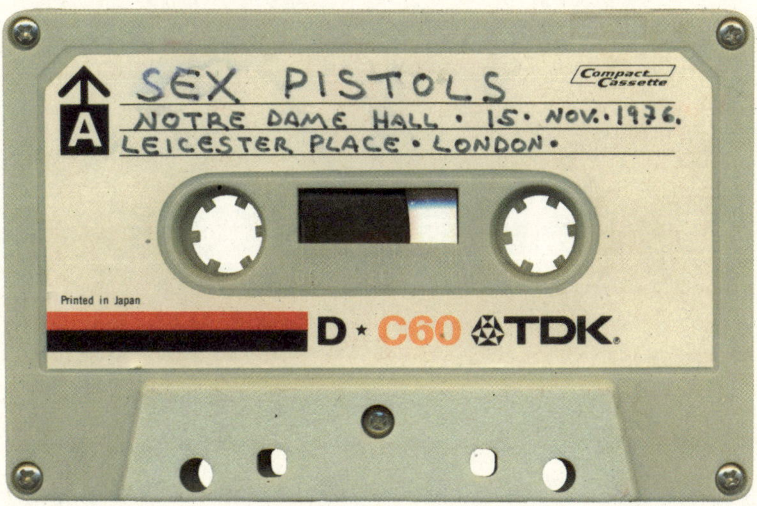

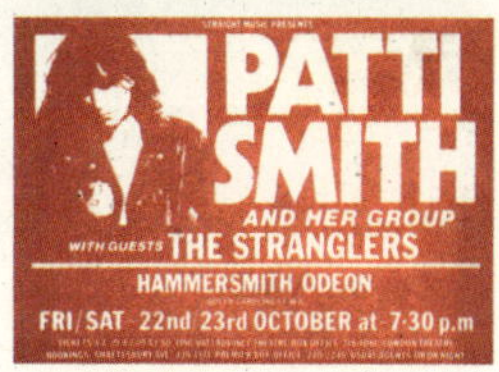

Full volant anunciant l'exposició "Prostitution" de COUM Transmissions, la qual va fer exclamar al parlamentari conservador britànic Nicholas Fairbairn: "Aquesta gent són els enderrocadors de la civilització". Els membres de COUM Transmissions integren el grup Throbbing Gristle des del seu debut el 6 de juliol del 76 a l'Air Gallery de Londres i comencen l'era de la música industrial. | Concerts dels Sex Pistols de setembre, octubre i novembre del 76. | Retall de diari amb els Sex Pistols fotografiats per D. Muscroft a l'Outlook Club de Doncaster, 27.9.76. | Titular sensacionalista de la revista *New Musical Express*, 6.11.76. | Títol d'una de les cançons dels Sex Pistols. | Entrada i full volant dels concerts de Patti Smith i The Stranglers al Hammersmith's Odeon, 23.10.76. | K7 amb el concert de Sex Pistols al Notre Dame Hall, a Leicester Place, Londres, 15.11.76.

Aquest quadrat negre sobre fons blanc és la funda que conté el primer disc dels Sex Pistols. Cara A: "Anarchy in the UK". Cara B: "I Wanna Be Me". Cook/Jones/Matlock/Rotten. EMI Records, 26.11.76. Prohibit a la ràdio i amb moltes crítiques negatives a la premsa, "Anarchy in the UK" sonava com mai res s'havia escoltat abans. | Cara A del disc i lletra de la cançó "Anarchy in the UK".

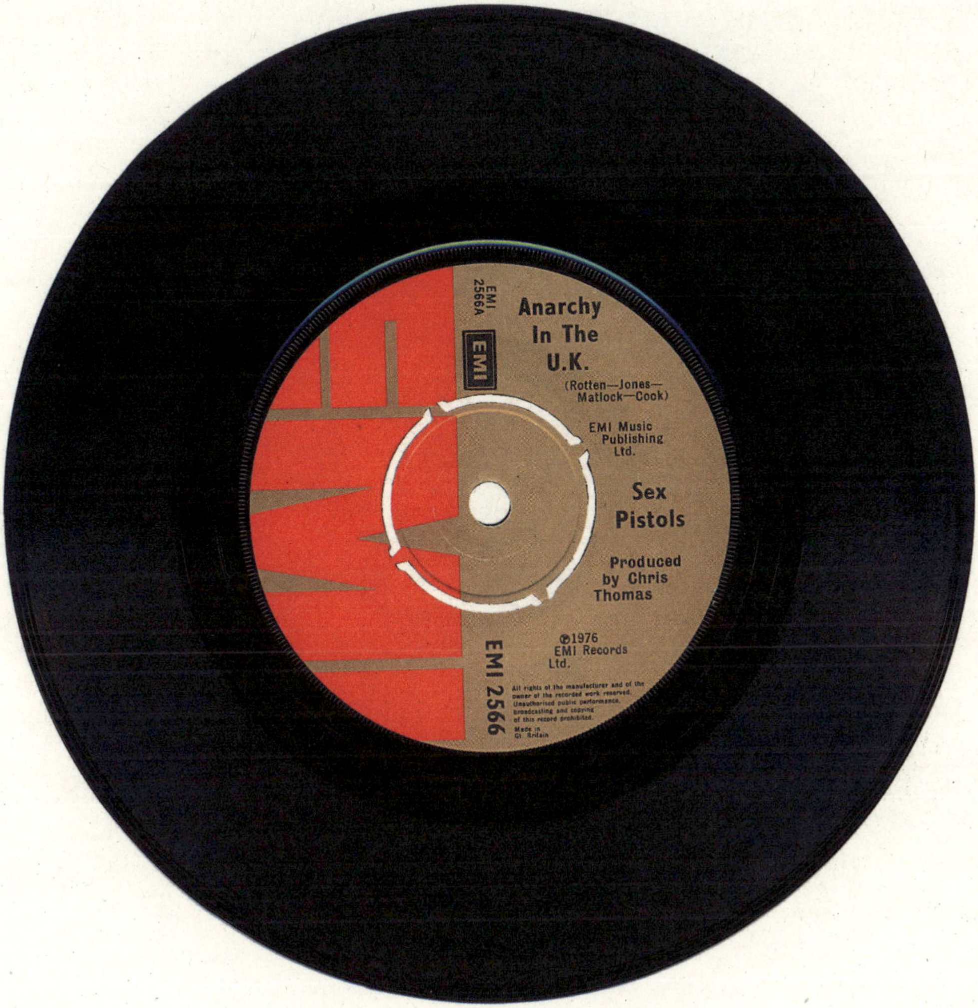

Anarchy in the UK / Right / Now / Ha, ha, ha / I am an antichrist / I am an anarchist / Don't know what I want / But I know how to get it / I wanna destroy passer by / Cause I / Wanna be / Anarchy / No dogs body / Anarchy for the UK / It's coming sometime and maybe / I give a wrong time stop at traffic line / Your future dream is a shopping scheme / Cause I / I wanna be / Anarchy / In the city / How many ways to get what you want / I use the best / I use the rest / I use the enemy / I use anarchy / Cause I / Wanna be / Anarchy / It's the only way to be / Is this the MPLA / Or is this the UDA / Or is this the IRA / I thought it was the UK / Or just / Another / Country / Another council tenancy / I wanna be / Anarchy / And I wanna be / Anarchy / Know what I mean / And I wanna be / Anarchist / Get pissed / Destroy / (Cook/Jones/Matlock/Rotten)

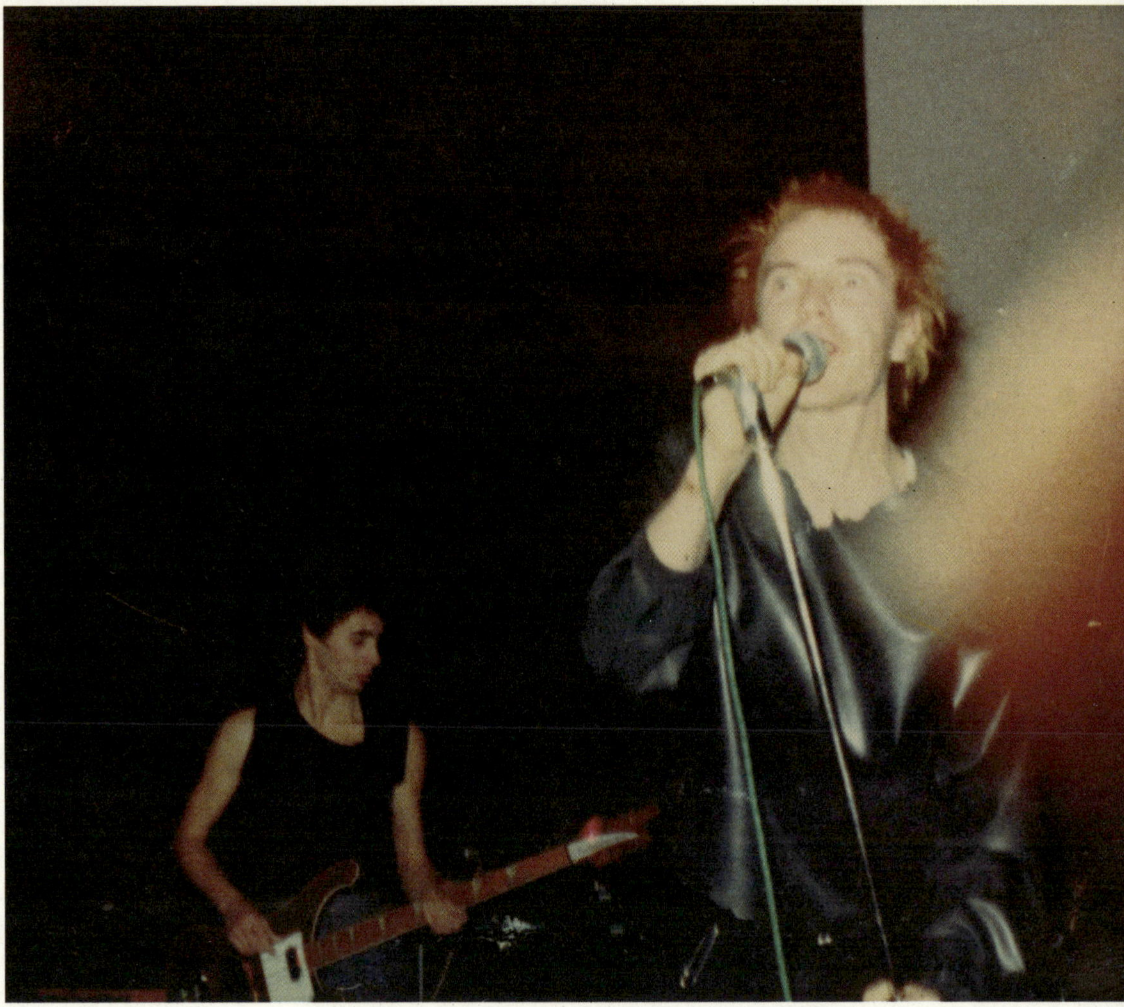

PHOTOGRAPHS BY BEN BROWTON

NEVER MIND THE DOG'S BOLLOCKS

"I had been taking photos since the age of nine, when I had a Kodak Brownie. I still have a lot of the prints; my family on top of a mountain in the Lake District, Hadrian's Wall, the monument at Waterloo and so on. I continued taking stuff through my teen years, and it was probably no surprise that I happened to have an Instamatic camera on my person on the evening of November 29th 1976, when a friend and I trekked to Lanchester Polytechnic in Coventry to see The Clash and The Sex Pistols playing. I guess it's a bit like buried treasure; these images have never been seen before." / Ben Browton (for trakMARX, 2005)

"I had copped my first whiff of a revolution in October 1976 when I saw The Vibrators and The Stranglers live in Oxford. I met up with a couple of punks on the train from Leamington and started to realise something was brewing amongst my generation. A month later, something was unleashed before me, which gave me hard proof. I went with a friend and

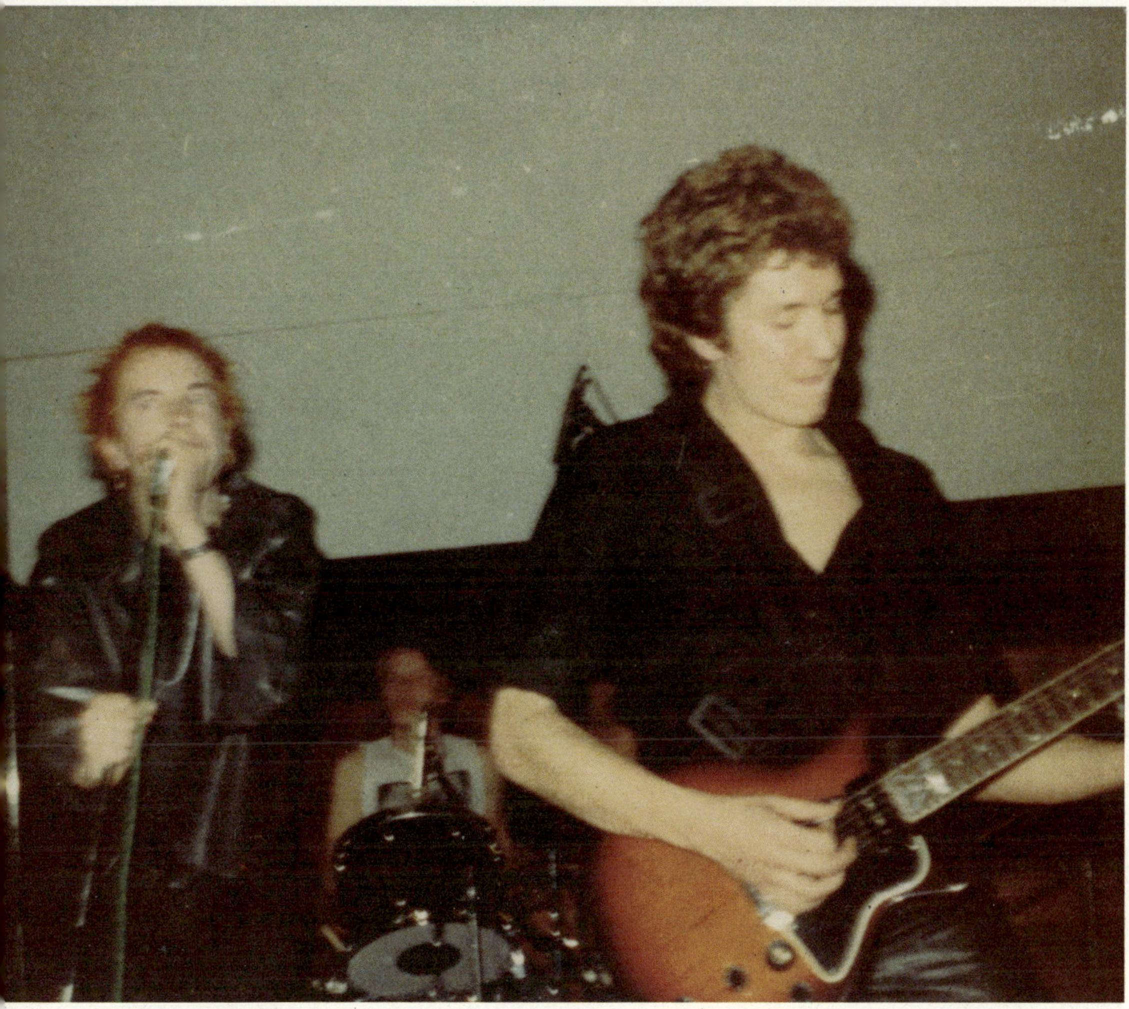

my camera to nearby Coventry and spent an intoxicating evening with those musicians who were spearheading the nascent punk movement. First on stage were The Clash, who performed their set at breakneck speed with hardly a pause between songs - they were a jangling, urgent, colourful, electric blur of anger, with Joe Strummer spitting out his shards of venomous diatribe over a wall of cacophonic metal. With scarcely a pause for breath, the Sex Pistols then shambled laconically on stage, led by Rotten in a magnificent rubber top, spiked orange hair and with cigarette burns on his arms. The Pistols set was less urgent than The Clash, and they regularly took long ironic breaks between songs, tuning up/tuning down their instruments, during which time a bug-eyed confrontational Rotten would harangue the audience with taunts like "We know you love it!". I was entranced and spellbound by this man, and in retrospect, he changed my life for ever. To cap it all, my friend and I were invited backstage afterwards, where we saw both bands consuming a vast rider of beer. We chatted with them for a while and then departed. We were so stunned when we left the venue, we walked the twelve dark miles home in a daze of brimful excited energy, knowing we had witnessed a new dawn awash with the spirit of anarchic disobedience..." / Ben Browton

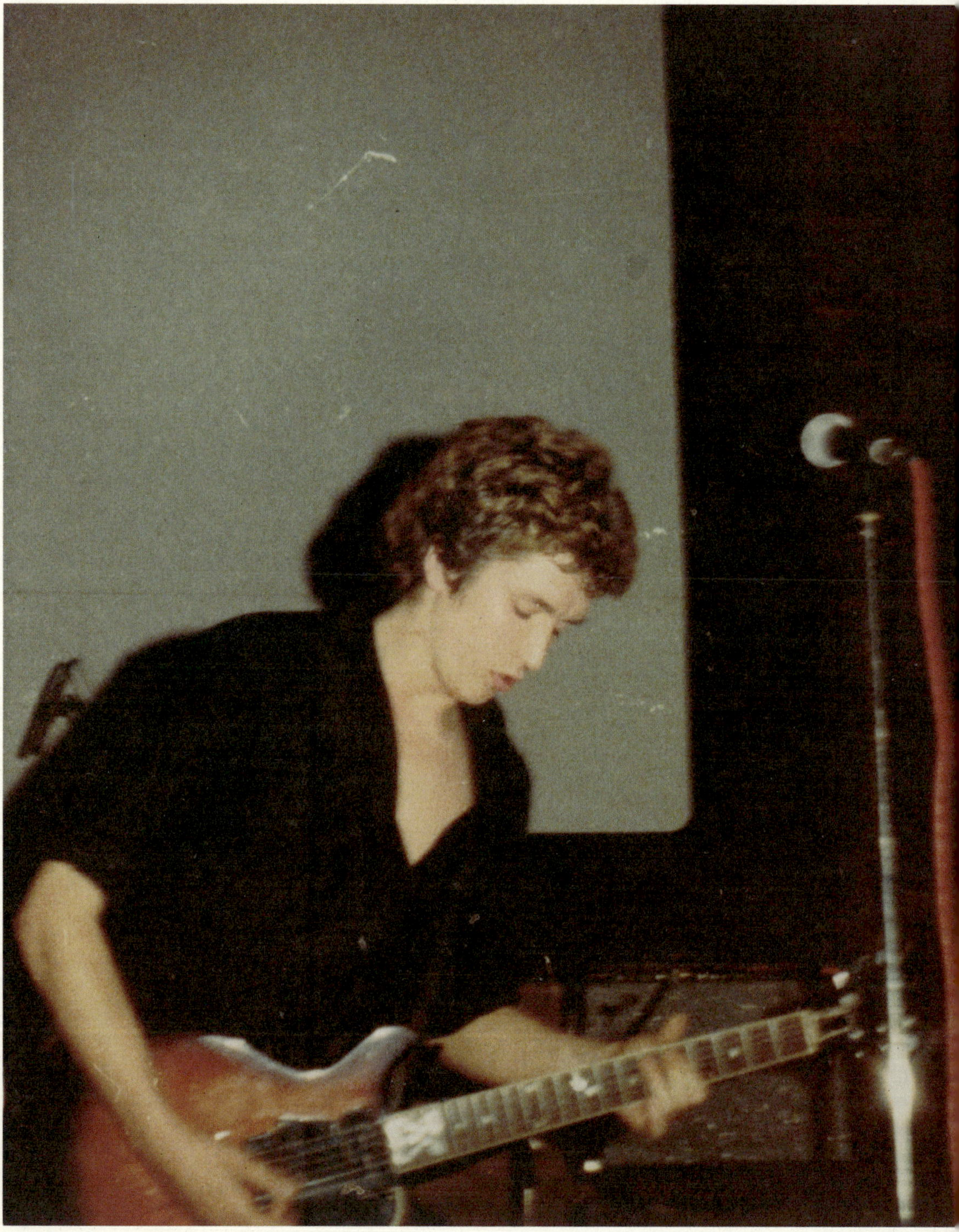

Steve Jones al Lanchester Polytechnic, Coventry. | Pàgines anteriors: SEX PISTOLS. Glen Matlock (20), Johnny Rotten (20), Paul Cook (20) i Steve Jones (21) fotografiats per Ben Browton al Lanchester Polytechnic, Coventry, 29.11.76.

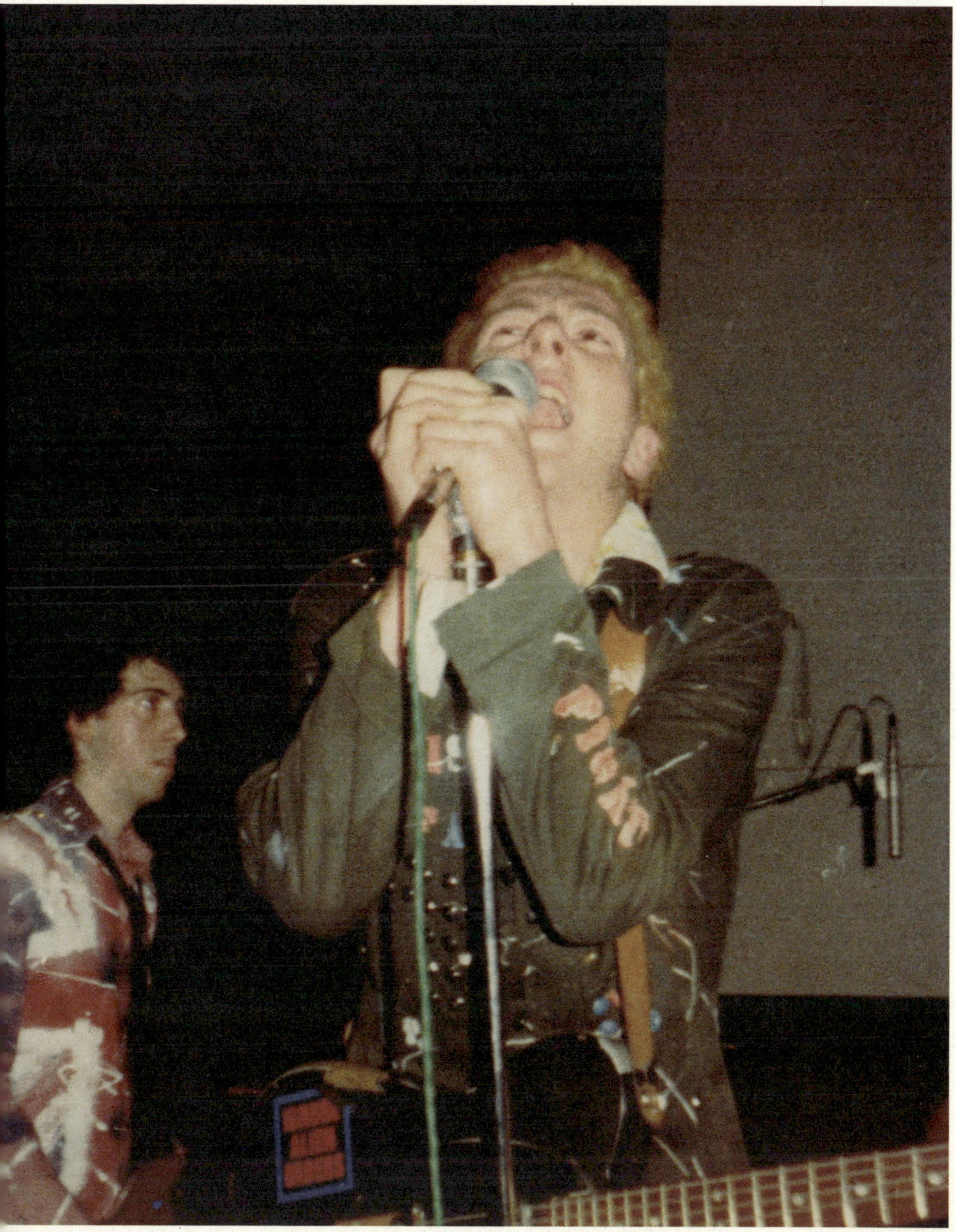

THE CLASH. Mick Jones (21) i Joe Strummer (25). | A les pàgines següents: Joe Strummer, Terry Chimes (20) i Paul Simonon (20) al Lanchester Polytechnic, Coventry, 29.11.76.

Photographs by Ben Browton

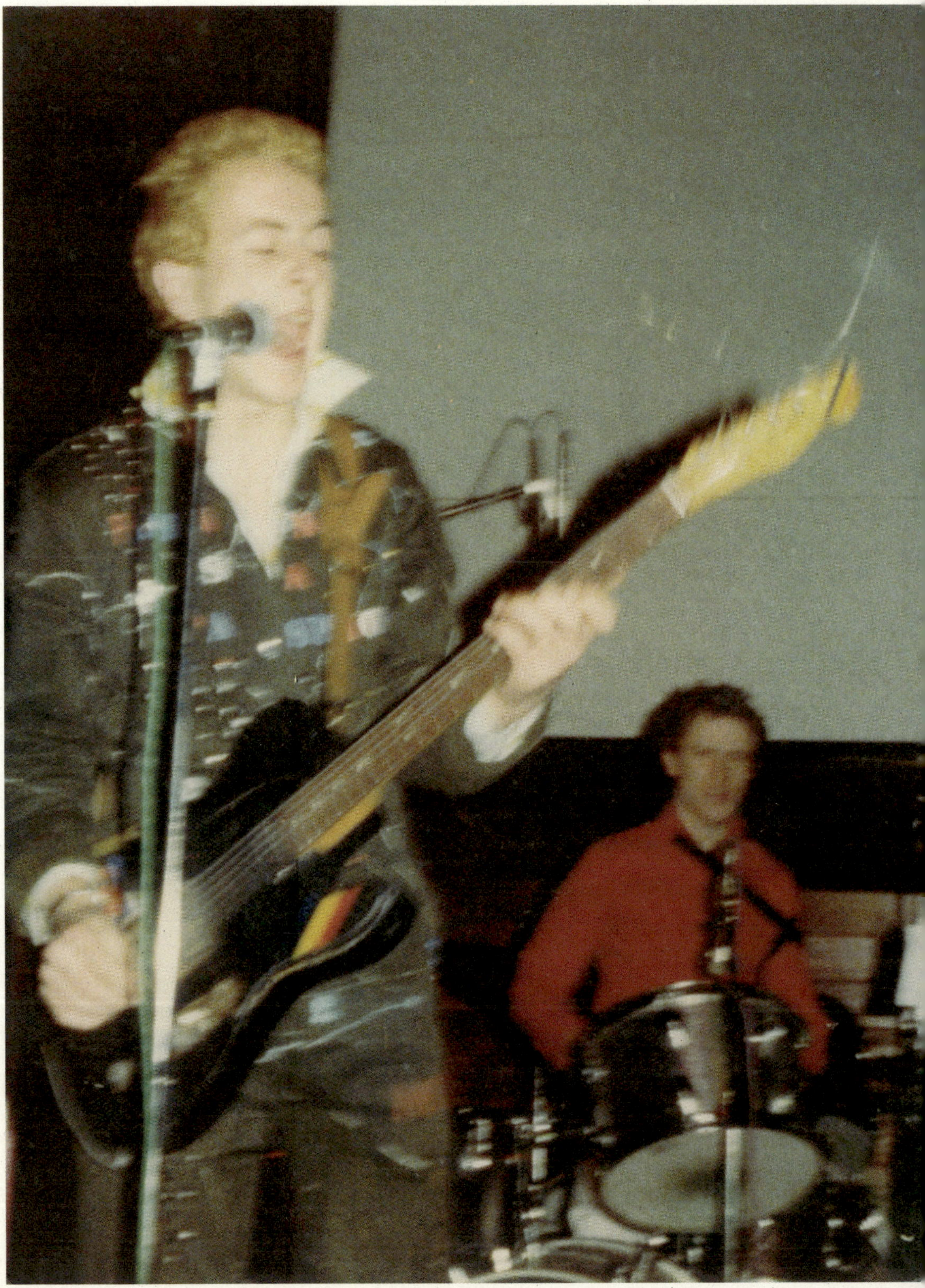

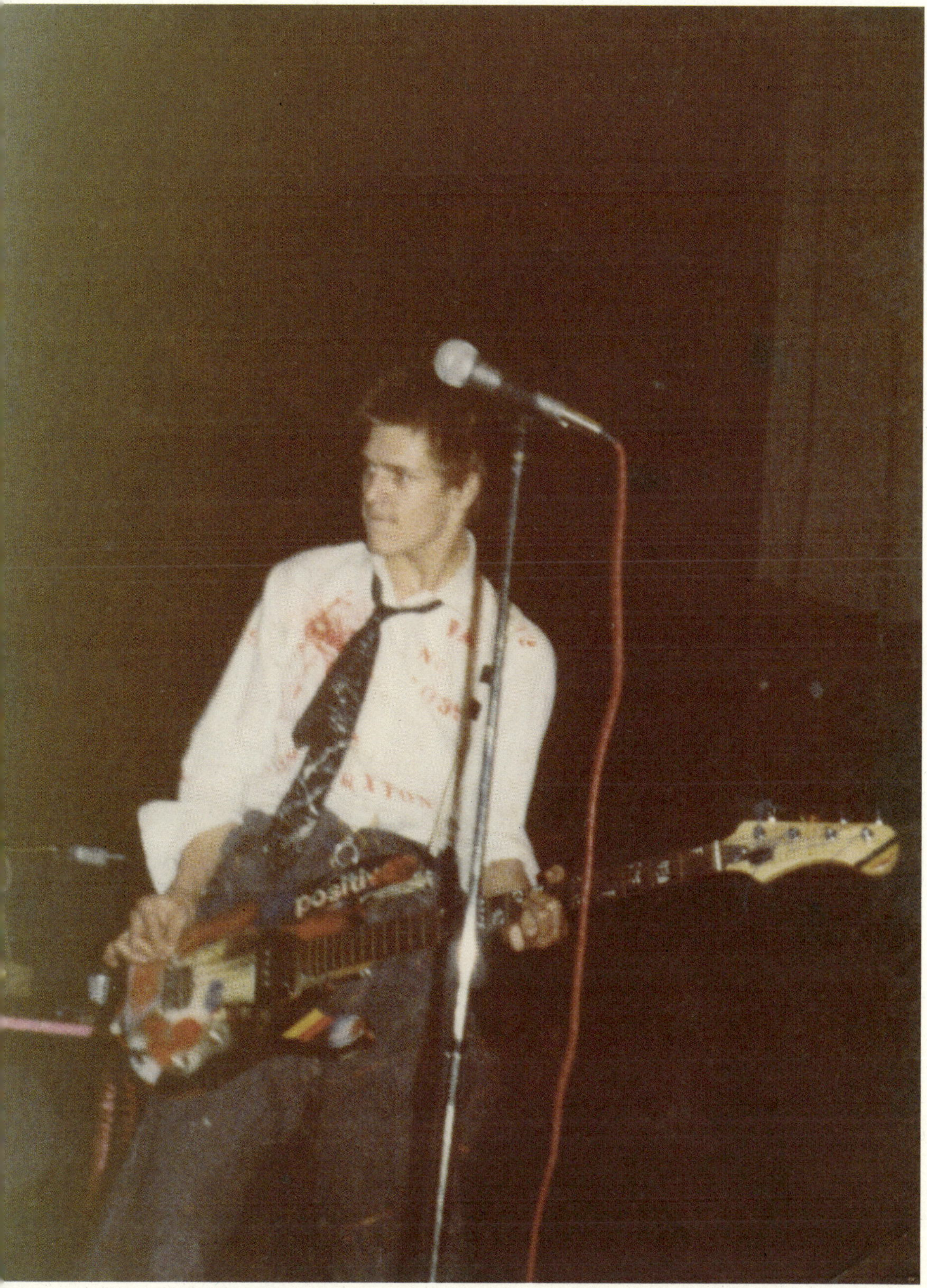

You dirty sod.

You dirty bastard!

You dirty fucker!

What a fucking rotter.

IT'S 1976 OK AN YOU STILL CAN'T SAY FUCK ON TV

YOU'VE SEEN ALL THE CRAP IN THE PAPERS AND TV PROBABLY ABOUT THE SEX PISTOLS AND HOW THEY OFFEND PUBLIC DECENCY AND ALL THAT SHIT AND NOW THERE'S THIS BIG ROW ABOUT THEM CALLING BILL GRUNDY NAUGHTY NAMES ON TV. The people who Run the Roxy have cancelled the Boxing Day gig and the Chairman of EMI told them they've got a week to become nice well-behaved rockstars or he might consider cancelling their contract because "public duty" comes before financial considerations. How boring. What a load of shit. Since when did EMI or any of those old cunts put "public duty" before their precious money or the security it gives them. What it really is is they feel that security is threatened just by what the Pistols represent. And how could anything that appears on ITV offend public decency. There isn't any public decency – people only know what's decent by being told by ITV and the rest of the media and EMI too.

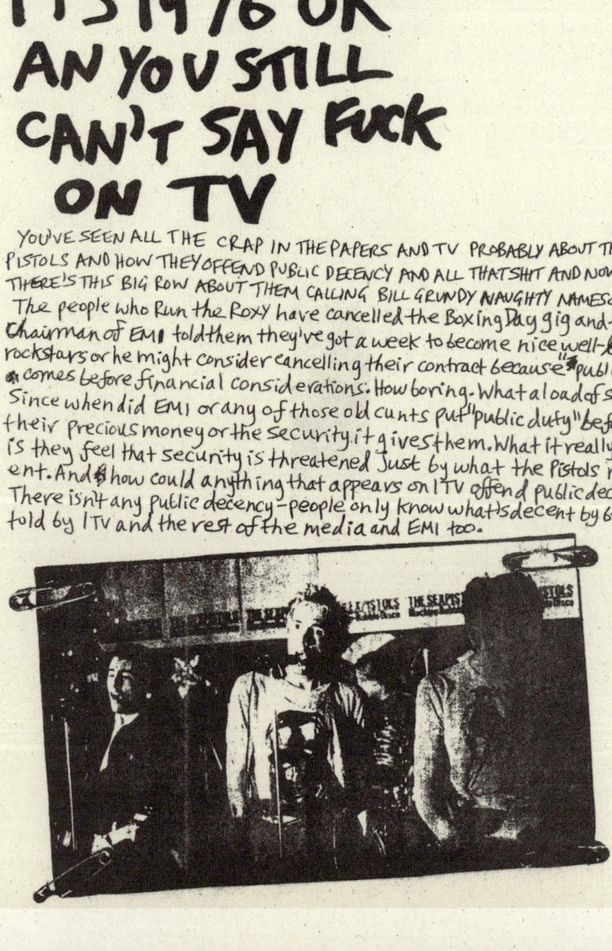

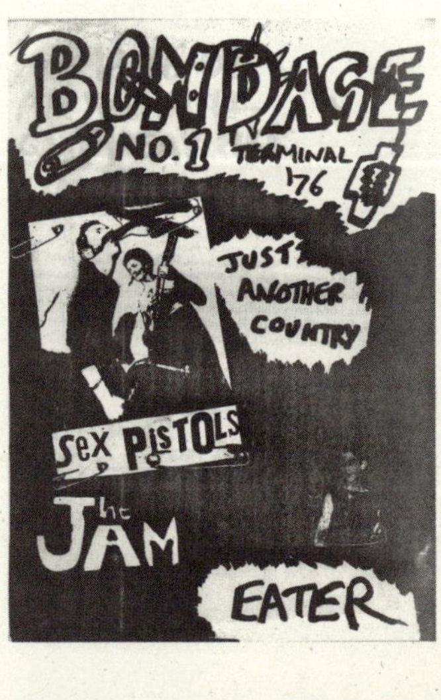

You dirty old man!

William "Bill" Grundy
(18.5.1923 – 9.2.1993)

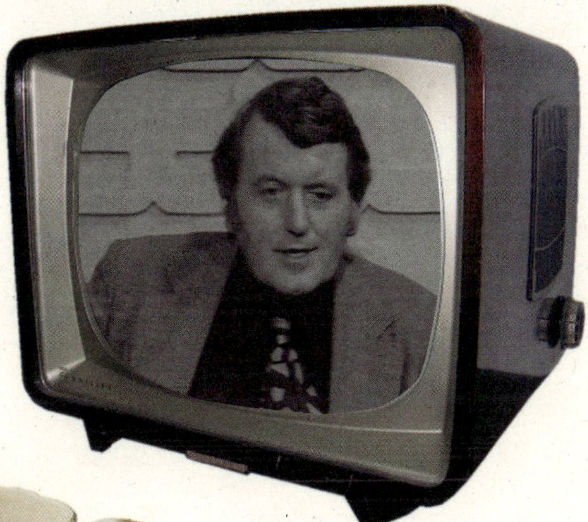

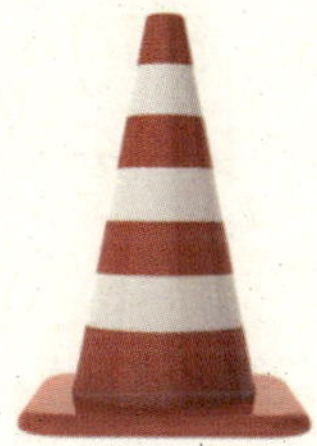

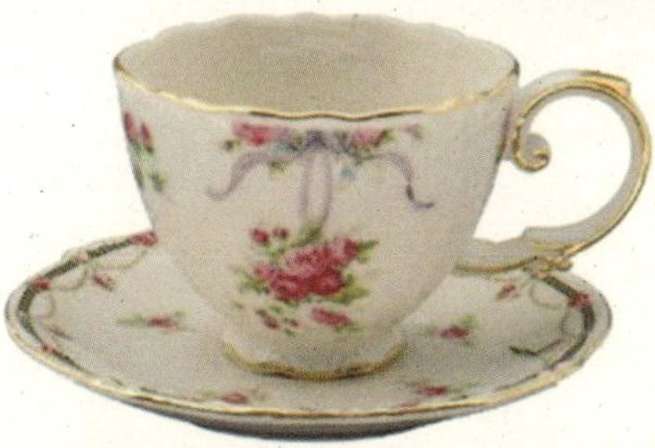

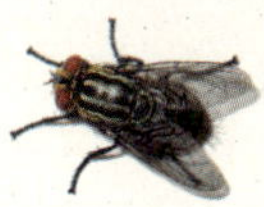

Grundy: (To camera) They are punk rockers. The new craze, they tell me. Their heroes? Not the nice, clean Rolling Stones ... you see they are as drunk as I am ... they are clean by comparison. They're a group called the Sex Pistols, and I am surrounded by all of them ...

OBNOXIOUS!
OUTRAGEOUS!

SEE PAGE 21

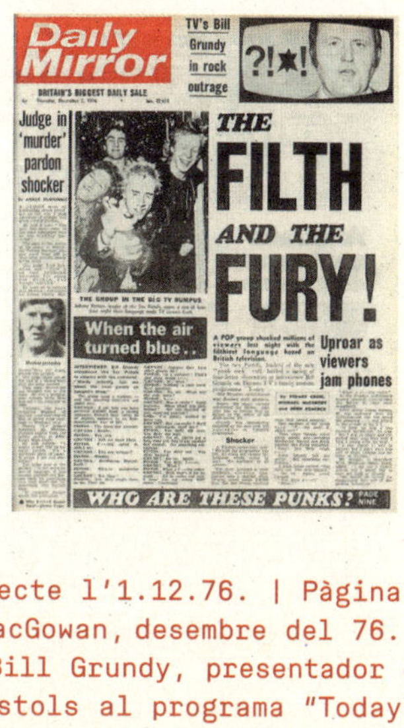
Daily Mirror
BRITAIN'S BIGGEST DAILY SALE
TV's Bill Grundy in rock outrage
?!*!
Judge in 'murder' pardon shocker
THE FILTH AND THE FURY!
When the air turned blue...
Uproar as viewers jam phones
WHO ARE THESE PUNKS?

Insults d'Steve Jones a Bill Grundy televisats en directe l'1.12.76. | Pàgina i portada del fanzine *Bondage* 1, fotocopiat per Shane MacGowan, desembre del 76. | Sang. | Televisor dels anys setanta amb la imatge de Bill Grundy, presentador de Thames Television, durant l'entrevista amb els Sex Pistols al programa "Today", 1976. | Tassa de te victoriana. | Mosca universal. | Paraules de Bill Grundy. | Reaccions de la premsa anglesa, desembre del 76.

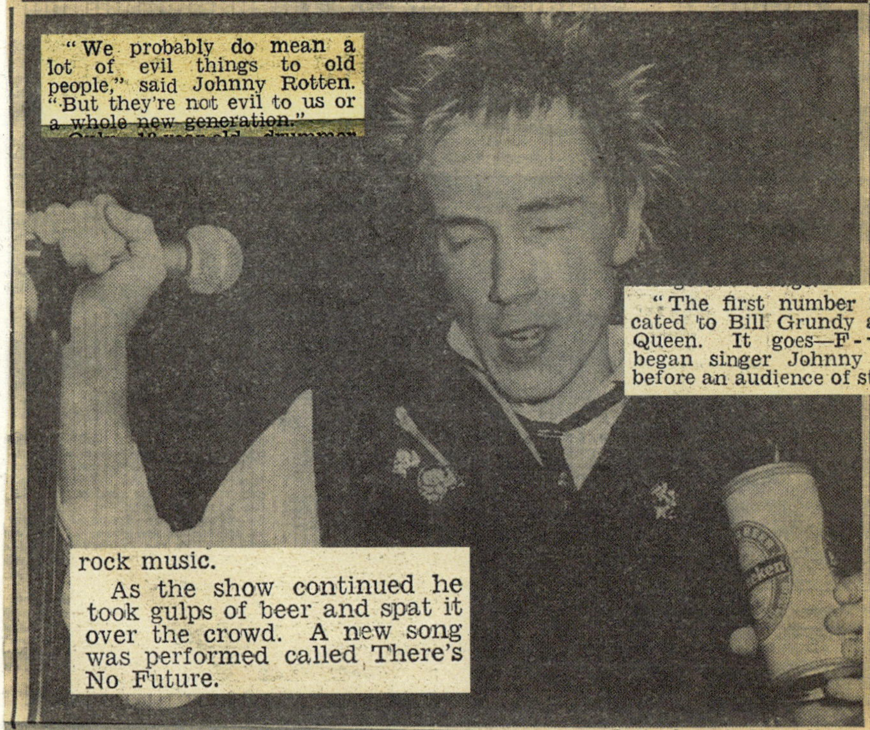

Evening Standard : Richard Young

MIKE in one hand, can of beer in the other—Sex Pistols singer Johnny Rotten in action last night.

Sex Pistols insult Queen

By James Johnson
LEEDS, Tuesday.

THE PROMISE to cut out drinking and swearing quickly disintegrated when Britain's m o s t notorious group, the Sex Pistols, were allowed to play on-stage last night for the first time since their controversial four-letter-word appearance on television.

It was too much for some of the students at the Leeds Polytechnic gig. They walked out claiming the music was "rubbish" and "too crude".

Before the show started local students' union leader Ian Steele was told by the tour manager that the group had cleaned up their act.

But as soon as the Sex Pistols hit the stage it was obvious they were determined to live up to their crude and belligerent image.

"The first number is dedicated to Bill Grundy and the Queen. It goes—F - - Ya," began singer Johnny Rotten before an audience of students,

Cont. Back Page, Col. 2

Retall de diari amb notícia sobre el concert al Leeds Polytechnic, el primer i un dels pocs concerts de l'Anarchy Tour que es van poder realitzar. Convertits en enemics públics per l'aparició televisiva al programa de Bill Grundy, els Sex Pistols són criticats al Parlament i a tota la premsa. El temor i la censura dels responsables de les sales va fer que es cancel·lessin la majoria de concerts programats a la gira.

Anarchy Tour / December '76

Sex Pistols / Johnny Thunders' Heartbrakers / The Damned / The Clash /

3.12.76 Norwich University, Norwich - CANCELLED
4.12.76 Kings Hall, Derby - CANCELLED
5.12.76 City Hall, Newcastle - CANCELLED
6.12.76 Leeds Polytechnic, Leeds - PLAYED!
7.12.76 Village Bowl, Bournemouth - CANCELLED
9.12.76 Electric Circus, Manchester - PLAYED!*
10.12.76 Lancaster University, Lancaster - CANCELLED
11.12.76 Stadium, Liverpool - CANCELLED
13.12.76 Colston Hall, Bristol - CANCELLED
14.12.76 Top Rank, Cardiff, Wales - CANCELLED
14.12.76 Castle Cinema, Caerphilly, Wales - PLAYED!**
15.12.76 Apollo, Glasgow, Scotland, UK - CANCELLED
16.12.76 Caird Hall, Dundee, Scotland - CANCELLED
17.12.76 City Hall, Sheffield - CANCELLED
18.12.76 Kursaal, Southend - CANCELLED
19.12.76 Civic Hall, Guildford - CANCELLED
19.12.76 Electric Circus, Manchester - PLAYED!**
20.12.76 Town Hall, Birmingham - CANCELLED
20.12.76 Winter Gardens, Cleethorpes - PLAYED!**
21.12.76 Woods Centre, Plymouth - PLAYED!
22.12.76 400 Ballroom, Torquay - CANCELLED
22.12.76 Woods Centre, Plymouth - PLAYED!**
23.12.76 Paignton, Penelope's Ballroom - CANCELLED
26.12.76 The Roxy, London - CANCELLED

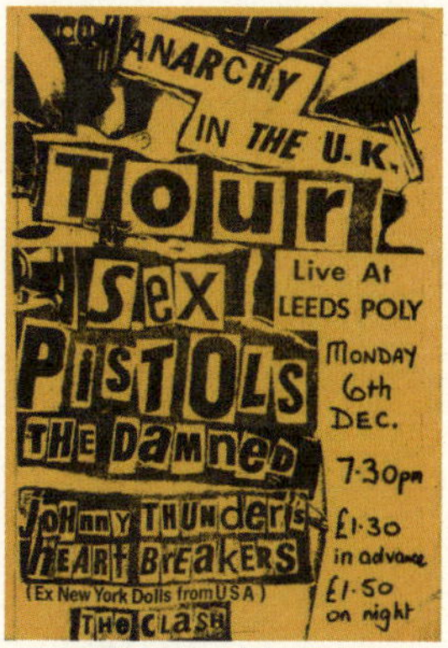

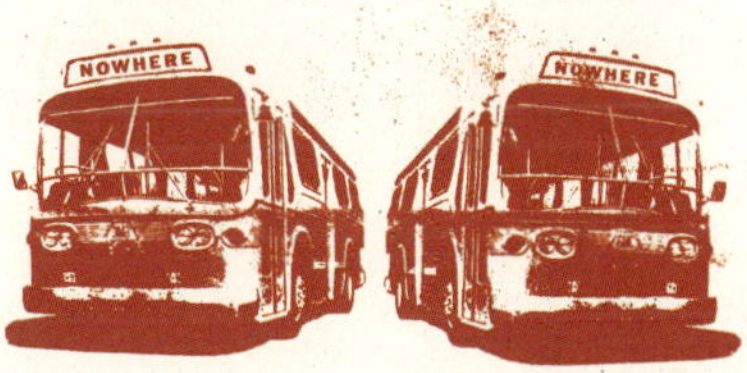

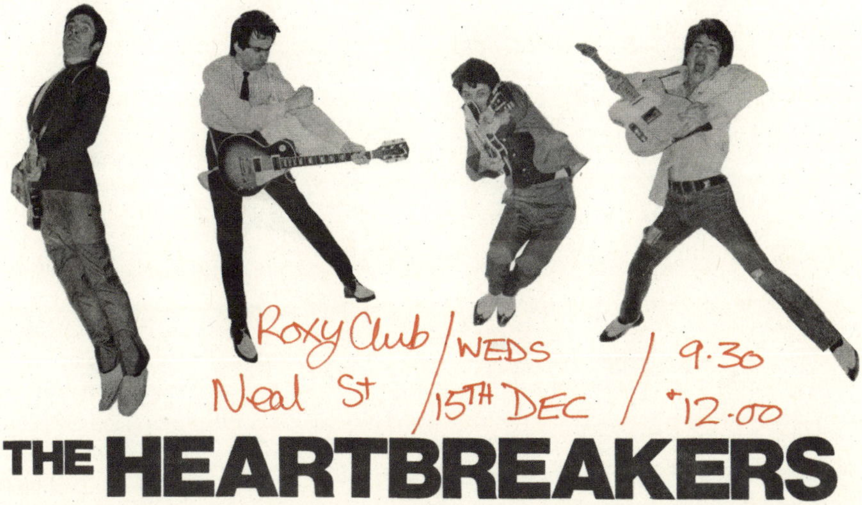

Concerts i cartell de l'Anarchy Tour. * Els Buzzcocks passen a integrar l'Anarchy Tour en substitució dels Damned. ** Concerts tornats a contractar a causa de la cancel·lació de la data original. | Autobusos de Jamie Reid publicats al fanzine dels Sex Pistols *Anarchy in the U.K.*, 1976. | Cartell del primer concert dels Heartbreakers al Roxy Club: Billy Rath, Walter Lure, Johnny Thunders i Jerry Nolan, 15.12.76.

Generation X

Rich Defame (RD). 48 thrills núm. 2, inicis del 1977.

RD: Why are you called generation X?

Billy: Well, it's that we're speaking for our generation. For people like us.

Tony: The idea is that its meant to be Generation Positive rather than Generation Blank which is the American idea.

Billy: We've got something to say.

Tony: They're sort ot saying 'We're the blank generation, we're so bored' but we're saying that we want to be positive. Politically we're not Left or Right, just speaking for our generation.

RD: Is that what the song 'Your Generation' is about ?

John: In that we are talking about the older people, who have ruled the roost for too long. Everything's been modelled on whats gone before. Not enough people think about NOW - They dont think about todays kids and their problems.

Tony: 'Your Generation' is stating our standpoint - We're trying to get rid of that generation, using any way we can. It's hard to shake off previous influences. Like you don't want to be influenced by the old bands. You've got to forget all that and start something new right now!

John: Go forward and not think about any of that.

Billy: They've led us to a vacuum - a dead end in thinking.

Tony: Whenever you get change, there's always violence - as a reaction to change becaue people don't like it. We know that if we say to people, 'You're too old', or 'You're Boring', then another generation is gonna come up under us and say that we're old and boring! That's why we've got to get as much done while we can.

RD: How do you feel about making records ?

Tony: I think every group that's serious has to make records eventually.

Billy: It's a way of communication.

John: At the moment though we're gonna do as many gigs as we fuckin' can.

RD: What would you do if you made a lot of money and got big and famous ?

Tony: If that happened we'd have to make sure we're tough enougth not to loose our identity and get sucked into the establishment. It would be pointless for us to get money and save it, or get a big car and become part of the establishment like Pete Townshend. That's part of what we want to change!

John: The best thing we could do if we found ourselves with loads of money would be to open a club like the Roxy where kids could get up and do what they want to do!

RD: Your songs are a lot 'cleaner' and tuneful than some of the bands on the scene - aren't they ?

Tony: The important thing, apart from the message, is that you have a good melody and rhythm, so that people can hum the tune and hear the words going thru their head. If you don't have rhythm and melody, then people forget a song after they hear it, no matter how good the ideas are.

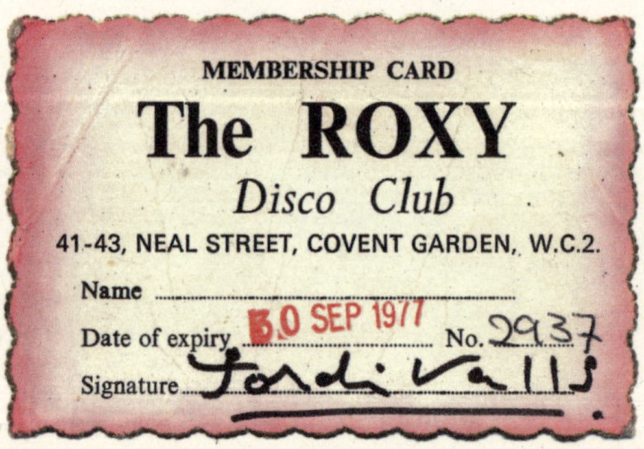
MEMBERSHIP CARD
The ROXY
Disco Club
41-43, NEAL STREET, COVENT GARDEN, W.C.2.
Name
Date of expiry 30 SEP 1977 No. 2937
Signature

Carnet del Roxy Club. Durant tot l'any 1977 i fins al seu tancament —l'abril de 1978—, el Roxy va oferir una programació frenètica de concerts; Don Letts n'era el discjòquei i va jugar un paper decisiu en la difusió de la música reggae.

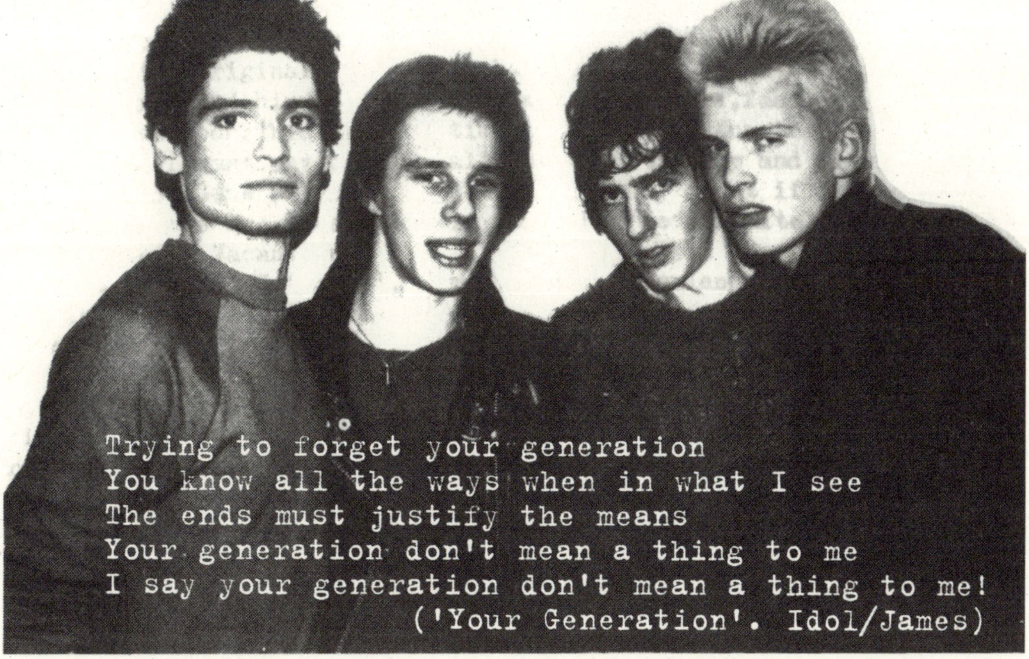

JOHN TOWE · BOB ANDREWS · TONY JAMES · BILLY IDOL

Otherwise if you ain't got good songs you should'nt be in a rock 'n roll band - you should be writing books or something. I think a lot of people critiscise us saying 'You're too musical' or 'You're too Poppy in your songs', but it's important to me that we got good songs.

Billy: The fact is that we are speaking the truth in our songs and that's important.

Tony: It ain't no good singing 'I got a brand new Cadillac' and stuff like that, because we haven't! It's OK as long as we're honest.

RD: How do you go about writing the songs ?

Tony: What happens with a lot of the songs is that I write the lyrics, Billy writes the melody and the music, and then the whole band get it together.

John: they come along with the framework and we all suggest our ideas.

Tony: It's important that everyone understands what a song's about before we play it. I write the words first so that the music interprets them.

HD: Is that song 'Ready Steady Go' about the Sixties and that ?

Tony: It's a bit dopey that one. It was one of the first ones we wrote when we were in CHELSEA with Jean October.

John: But even that song is about kicking out all the nostalgic stuff too.

Tony: We were managed by Acme Attractions when we wrote that and we were slightly into a Sixties type of thing. But the lyrics of that one were misquoted in Sounds a few weeks ago. They really go like this.... "I'm not in love with the King's Road ! / I'm not in love with Cathy McGowan ! / I'm NOT in love with Ready Steady Go !"

RD: What about 'Youth Youth Youth' - Is that one any closer to how you feel now ?

Tony: Yeah. That's one of the most recent ones written. The key line is: "Youth Youth Youth - Don't wanna ever be an adult". It means that I never want te have a house with ducks in the wall, or sign a mortgage and things

Generation X, fotocòpia d'una fotografia de Harry T. Murlowsky publicada a *Sniffin' Glue*... 6, gener 1977.

like that. To me 'adult' is like when your parents say you can't go out and you can't do this. I don't want to ever be like that- I allways want to be like a kid and do what I want to do.

RD: Do you do all your own songs now ?

Tony: Yeah. We only did stuff like 'Baby Come Back' because we didn't have enough of our own songs- when we started out in Chelsea.

John: The important thing then was that we started playing as quickly as possible. We didn't want to stagnate ! We only had seven songs so we had to do other people's.

Tony: Now we're writing songs quicker than before and learning them quicker too because everyone immediately relates to the material.

RD: Tell us how you got Bob as the lead Gultarrist ?

John: Well that's an amazing story. It's like a fairytale ! It's a gospel truth but it seems incredible!

Tony: We'd been trying for weeks with auditions and adverts and we'd given up hope, and this was like a week before our first gig as Generation X (at The Central Art School) so we were going to go out as a three-piece cos we didn't want to cancel the gig. Then on the saturday before the gig Billy went this party and there was Bob playing in this dopey little group and Billy thought... He's the Man ! So he rushed over and asked him what he was doing wasting his time in that group. Anyway we rehearsed with him on that Sunday and then on the Monday he phoned us and said that he wanted to join!

RD: So that was just four days before the gig !?

Tony: Yeah, we just had two rehearsals before the gig, and he's fitted in so well it's amazing. He'd never even seen a punk group before he joined us, just the Bill Grundy thing on TV. In the five gigs we've done with him so far he hasn't even played a wrong note - he's almost too good ! The last one we played was down in Brighton and he started moving about on the stage too, which he hadn't done in the London gigs!

Billy: Basically what we want to see is a more honest approach. Really it's only these new bands that are honest !

THE END

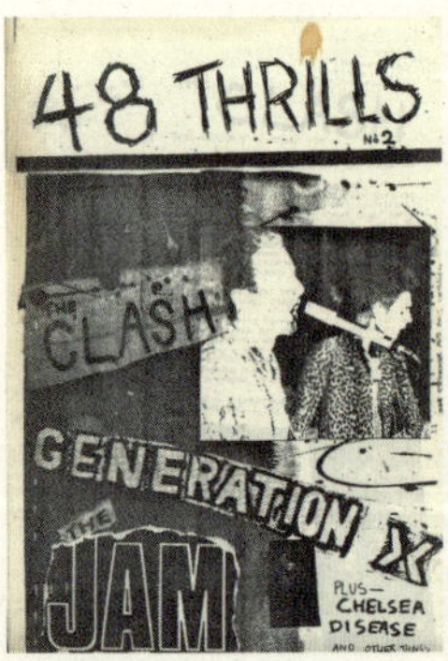

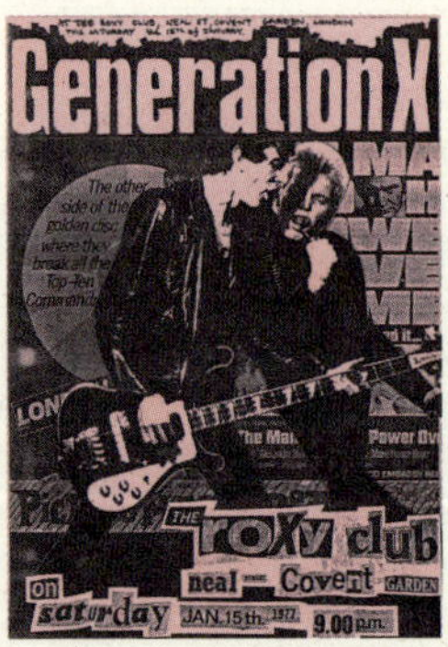

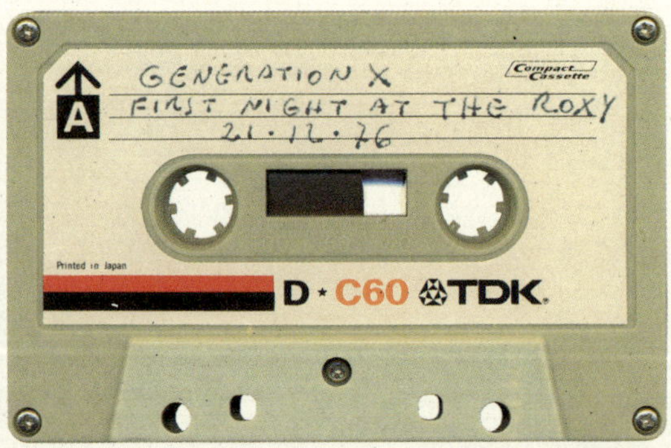

Portada del fanzine *48 Thrills*, 2, on surt publicada l'entrevista a Generation X. | Full volant anunciant una actuació de Generation X al Roxy Club, 15.1.77. | K7 amb la gravació del primer concert de Generation X al Roxy Club. | Billy Idol fotografiat per Ben Browton al Lanchester Polytechnic de Coventry el 1978. Diu Browton [a: trakMARX, 2005]: "M'agradava la música que feien en aquell moment: 'Ready Steady Go' i tot el seu rotllo. El Billy Idol era molt maco, anava de rocker amb cabell oxigenat de ros, amb la ganyota als llavis, i Generation X eren boníssims a l'escenari".

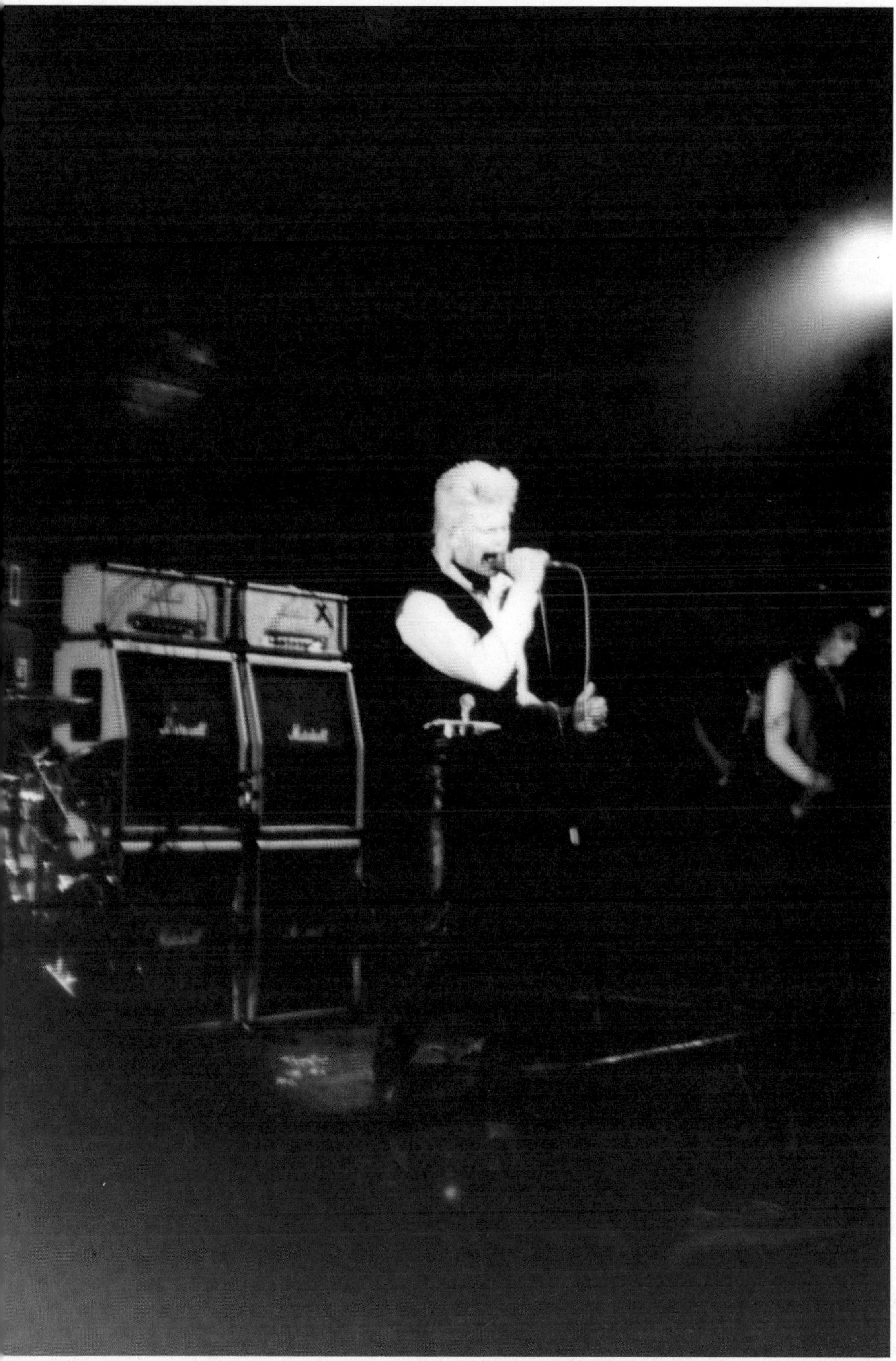

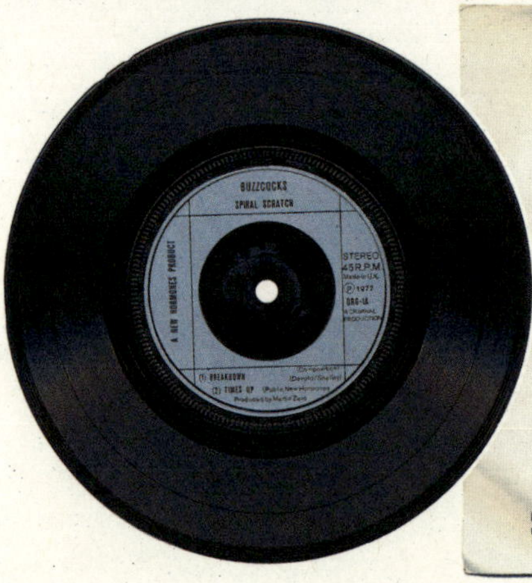

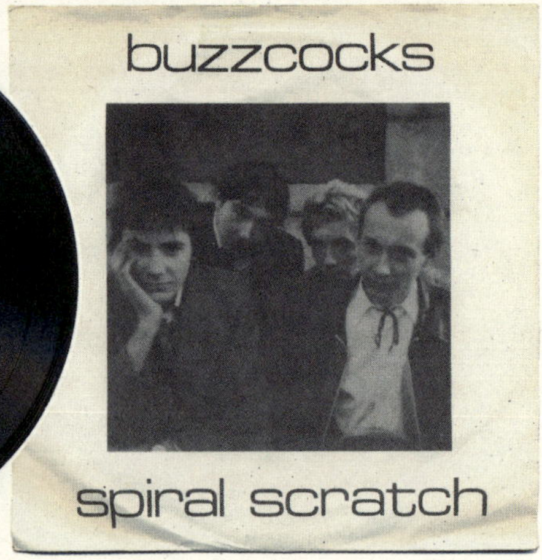

Side One	Side Two
BREAKDOWN (1.54)	BOREDOM (2.52)
3rd take No dubs	1st take Guitar dub
TIME'S UP (3.02)	FRIENDS OF MINE (2.13)
1st take Guitar dub	1st take Guitar dub

Photo left to right	All recorded 'live'
JOHN MAHER	Indigo Sound Studio Manchester
drums	28.12.76
STEVE DIGGLE	16 track
bass	Compositions Devoto/Shelley
PETE SHELLEY	New Hormones ©
starway guitar	Production Martin Zero
HOWARD DEVOTO	Polaroid Richard Boon
vocals	Heart beats up love

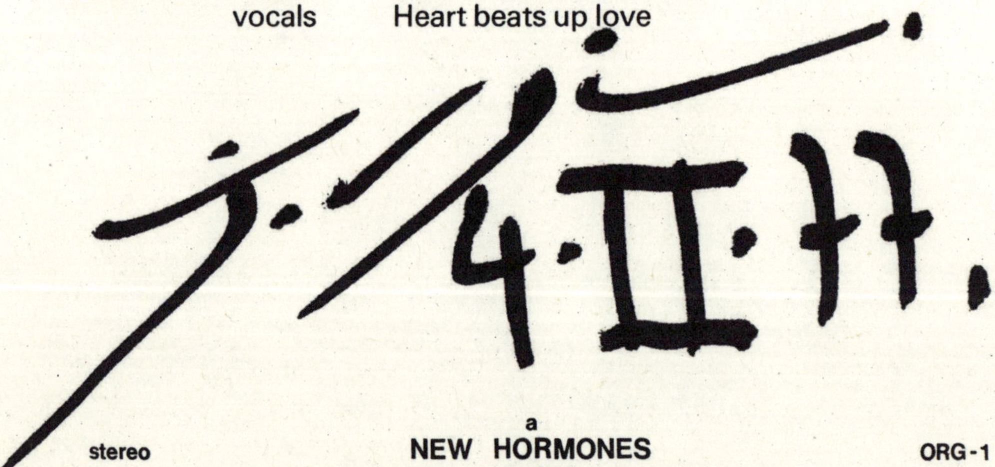

stereo

a NEW HORMONES product

182 Oxford Road, Manchester M13 9GP.

ORG-1

Disc, funda i crèdits del single *Spiral Scratch*, disc autoeditat pels Buzzcocks des del seu segell independent New Hormones. | Fragment de la cançó "Boredom". | Pete Shelley i Howard Devoto en una foto magnífica. | Coberta de la cinta amb el concert dels Buzzcocks al Coliseum de Harlesden, Londres, 11.3.77.

"Now there's nothing behind me,
And I'm already a has-been,
My future ain't what it was,
I think I know the words that I mean,

You know me-I'm acting dumb,
You know the scene-very humdrum,
Boredom-boredom-boredom".
('Boredom').

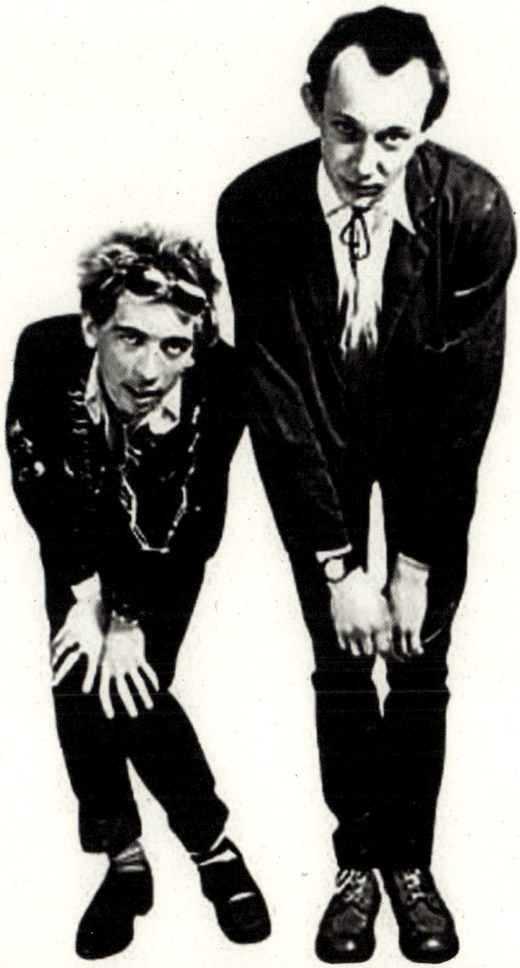

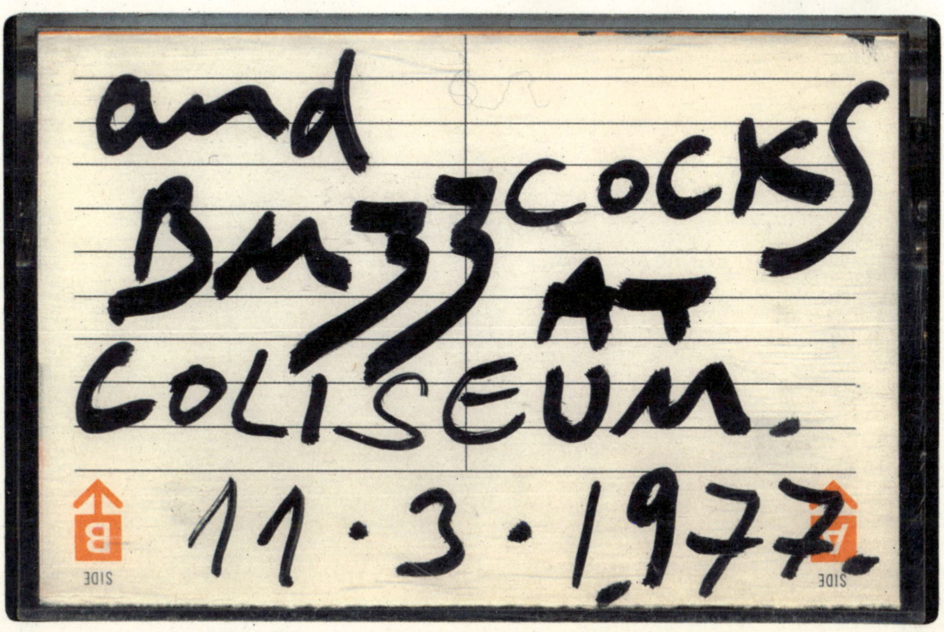

05.01.77 Paradiso Club, Amsterdam, Holland
06.01.77 Art Centre, Rotterdam, Holland
07.01.77 Paradiso Club, Amsterdam, Holland
21.03.77 Notre Dame Hall, Leicester Place, London
03.04.77 Screen On The Green Cinema, Islington, London *

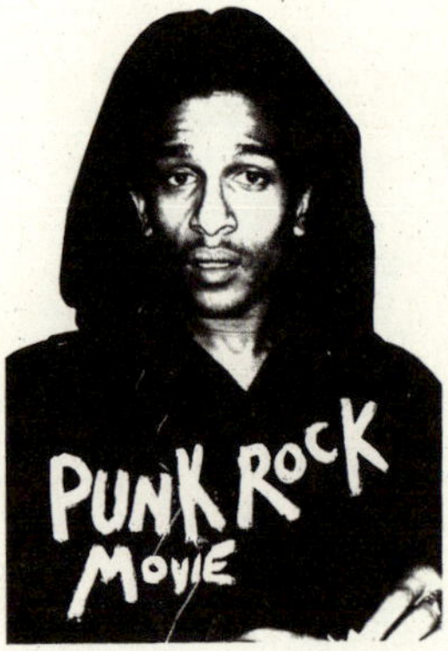

<u>DON LETTS:</u> Like,to me,the reggae thing and the punk thing...it's the same fuckin'thing.Just the black version and the white version.The kids are singing about change,they wanna do away with the establishment.Same thing the niggers are talkin'about,"Chant down Babylon",it's the same thing.Our Babylon is your establishment,same fuckin'thing.If we beat it,then you beat it and vise versa.

'Cause like,Johnny Rotten was telling me the other day.He's walkin'down the street now and the cops are hittin'on him. Takin'him in the van,tryin'to bust him for this and that.'Cause of the way he looks... it's the same shit we go through.Like,with me hair and the red,gold and green.Copper stopped me in me car and tell me I should walk,cops actually told me I should walk! 'Cause like he said,"People with red,gold and green nats shouldn't have enough money to drive flash cars"and all this crap,you know?

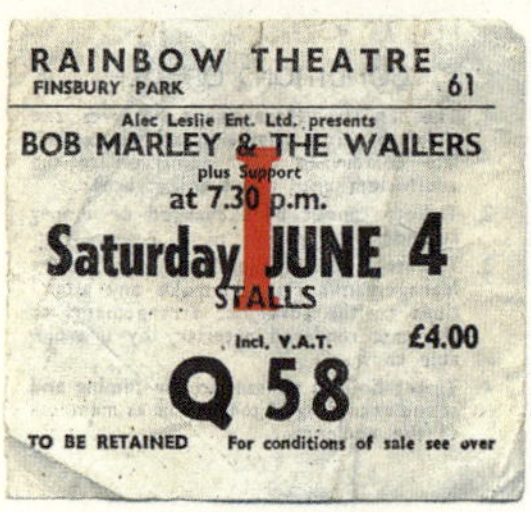

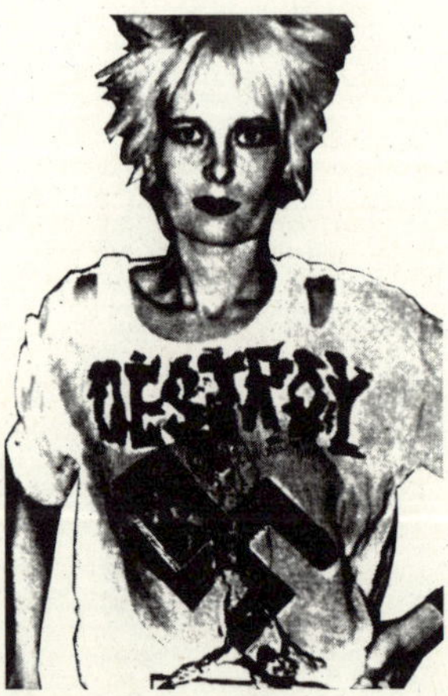

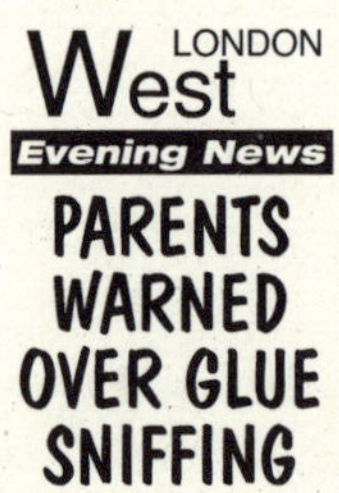

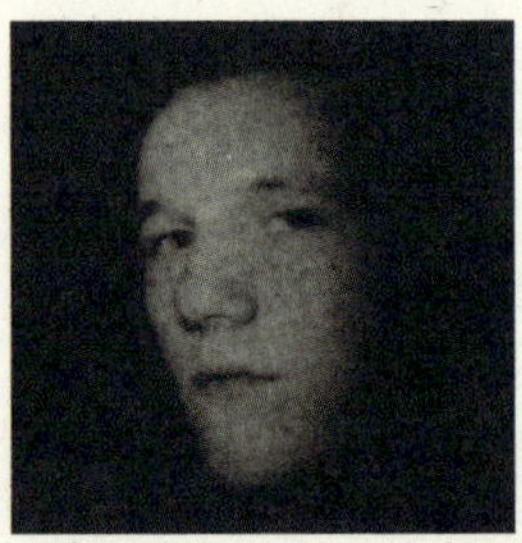

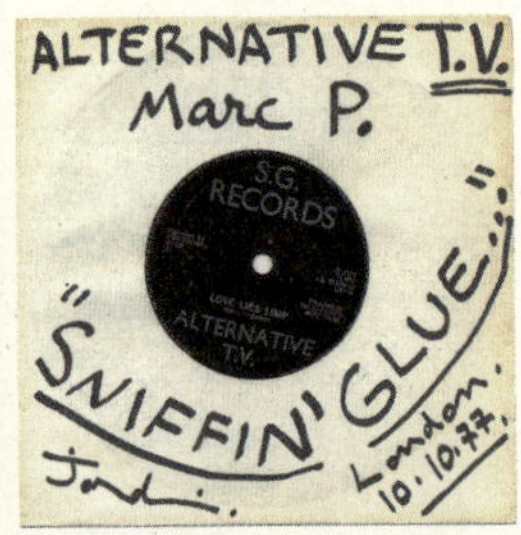

All you kids out there who read'SG',don't be satisfied with what <u>we</u> write.Go out and start your own fanzines or send reviews to the established papers.Let's really get on their nerves,flood the market with punk-writing!

Mark P.

Concerts dels Sex Pistols durant els primers mesos del 77. * Primer concert de Sid Vicious com a baixista dels Sex Pistols. | Fotografia i paraules de Don Letts publicades a *Sniffin' Glue...* 7. | Entrada pel concert de Bob Marley & The Wailers al Rainbow Theatre, 4.6.77. | Vivienne Westwood amb la samarreta "Destroy", que combina imatges d'un crucifix invertit, una esvàstica i una petita foto de la reina d'Anglaterra. Mal interpretat per molta gent, el grafisme és un atac al govern, la religió i el feixisme. | Notícia del diari *Evening News*, 1977. | Mark Perry fotografiat per Erica Echenberg, 1977. | Disc de vinil flexible regalat als lectors d'*Sniffin' Glue...* | Escrit de Mark Perry al cinquè número del seu fanzine.

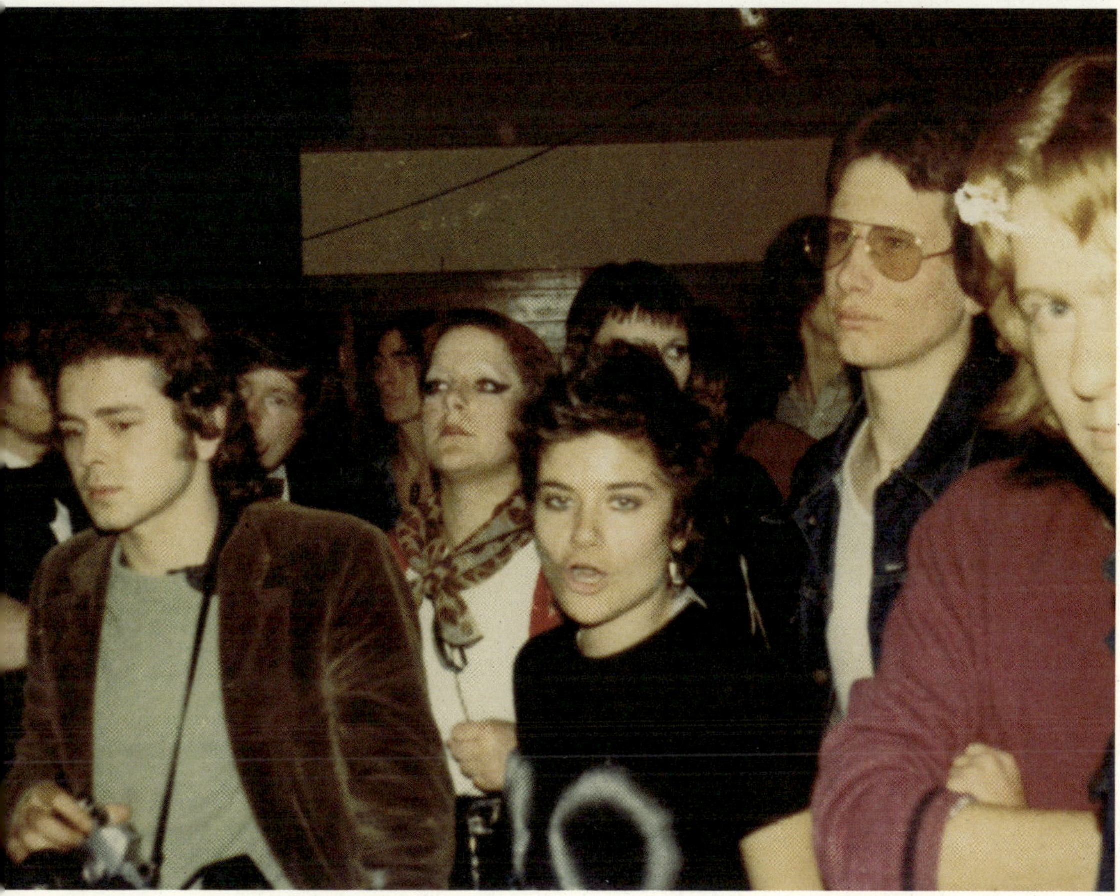

NUMBER ONE ENEMY
If you like white I'll be black
if you like black I'll be yellow
if you like the rational I'll be the impossible
if you like the reasonable I'll be the insane
if you like peace and flowers I'll carry knives & chains
I'm gonna be your number 1 enemy
all for the hell of it ..... (The Slits.)

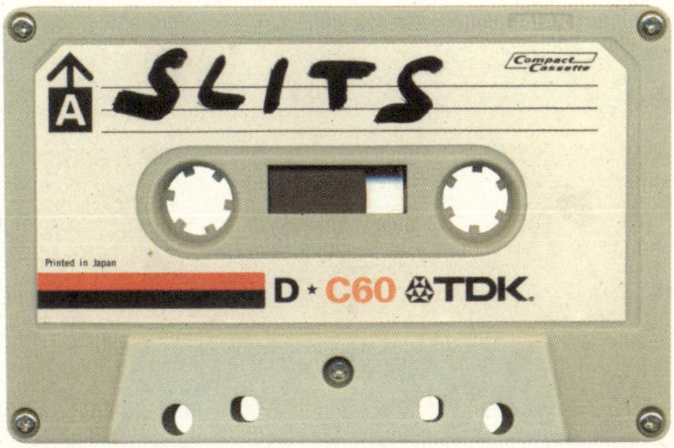

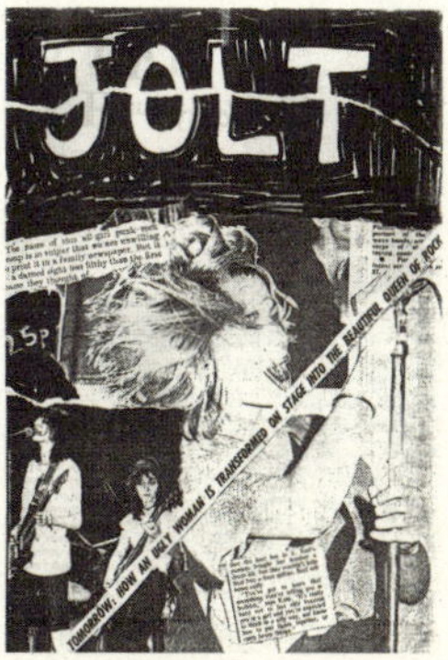

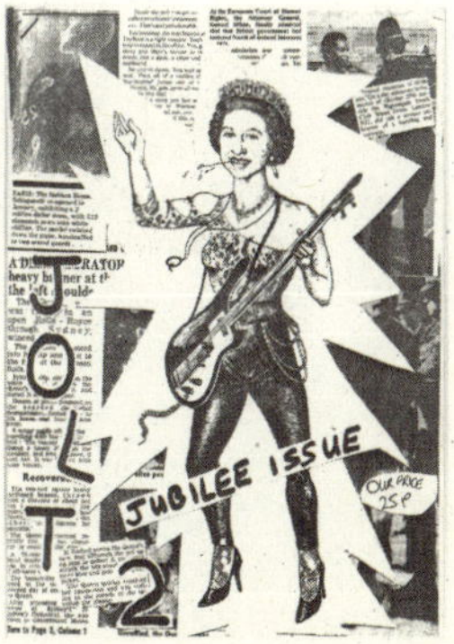

Palmolive, bateria de les Slits, fotografiada per Ben Browton al Lanchester Polytechnic, Coventry, 29.11.76. | Lletra d'una de les cançons de les Slits.| Cinta TDK amb el primer concert de les Slits al Harlesden Coliseum, 11.3.77. | Portades del fanzine *Jolt*, fotocopiat per Lucy Toothpaste a començaments del 77.

THE SLITS.

Lucy Toothpaste.
Jolt 2, març del 1977.

A few weeks ago my mum called me downstairs and told me there were some 'peculiar girls' to see me.

It was the SLITS, come to ask if I knew any girl bassists. Anyway we did a so-called interview, only I didn't have a tape and I didn't start writing anything down till halfway through so it's a bit jumbled up: I can't remember who said what.

Lucy: Were you very angry about the News of the World interview ?

Slits: Yes. The woman who came to interview us was so stupid, so stiff and posh. She wanted drugs, sex & violence, so that's what we gave her. We were just taking the piss out of her.

Ari: They said we had holes in our socks. We had shoes on!

Palmolive: They've got holes in their brains. They didn't even give us any money for doing the interview! We realised afterwards we should have asked for some. We don't care that much about what they wrote about us, because no-one with any brains would believe it anyway. But our advice to anyone else is, Don't agree to do an interview like that!

Lucy: If you couldn't find a girl bassist, would you accept a bloke ?

Slits: No, we're the Slits! It wouldn't matter so much if we'd already been going some time, but we want to start off as an all-woman band. We put an advert in for a bass guitar heroine, and three men applied! A woman applied, but when she found out it was a new wave band, she put the phone down!

Lucy: Have you tried Spare Rib etc. to find out if they know of anyone ?

Slits: Yes, but the women we spoke to didn't approve of our kind of music, they said it was cock rock.

Lucy: (I didn't say this exactly at the time, but this is what I think.)

I think it's a mistake for women to think they shouldn't play rock, should only play nice gentle folk songs and all that crap. New wave music is crisis music, and we're all in the crisis. Angry women should make an angry noise. Love and peace I didn't work. Rock is one of the ways in which women have been oppressed, I agree, but let's grab our chance to change that now.

Lucy: What is the most important thing to you ?

Ari: Getting our band together. Making things change.

Lucy: What about women ?

Palmolive: We are feminists in a way we don't want to tell anyone how to act, we just want to show them what we're doing, what girls can do.

Ari: Most girls don't push themselves enough. The world is changing, it'll leave us all behind if we don't change with it. One way to change things is for us to get on the stage.

Lucy: What do you think about love songs and songs about relationships ?

Slits: We're not anti love, but we're anti the idea of 'true love', anti the idea of a man buying you with money and presents. What most people call love is just status and security: just a facade. But we believe in friendship.

Lucy: What are your songs about?

Kate: We write songs about what happens to us, like, at the moment, shop-lifting. Lots of people do it, no-one's written about it yet. And lots of people don't do it! We're not saying they should, just letting them know it's there!

END

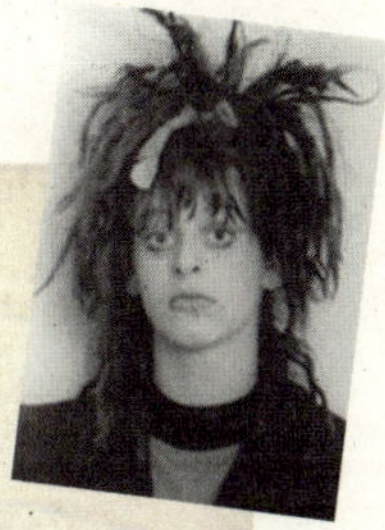

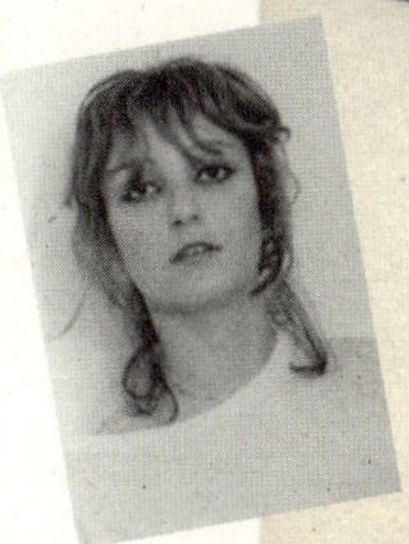

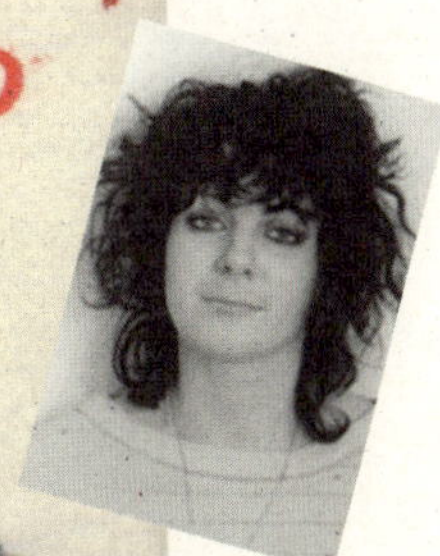

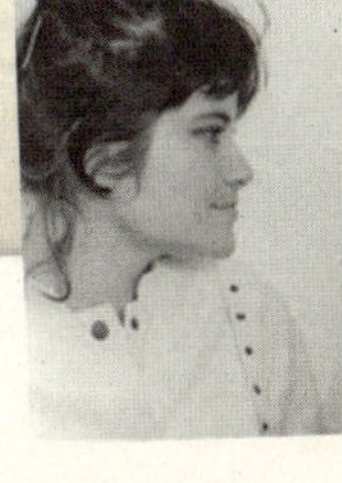

THE SLITS. Ari Up (14), Viv Albertine (22), Tessa (18), i Palmolive (22).

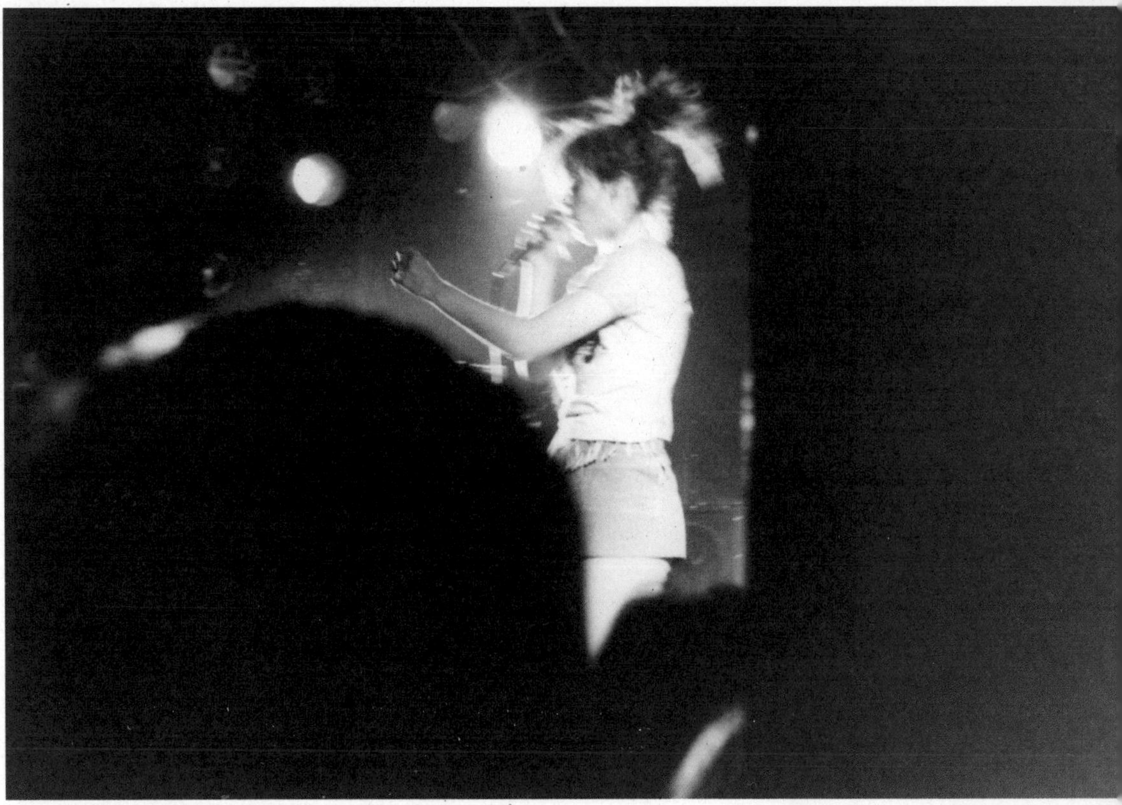

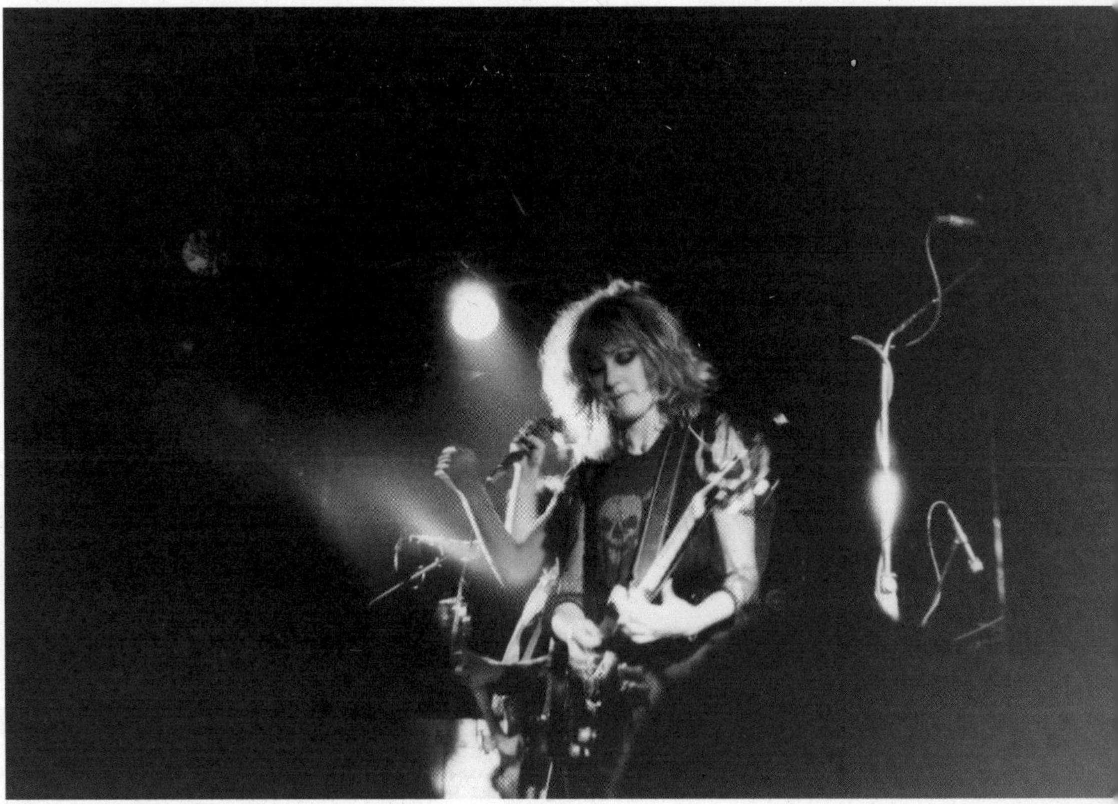

 The Slits fotografiades per Ben Browton al Tiffany's, Coventry, 1977.

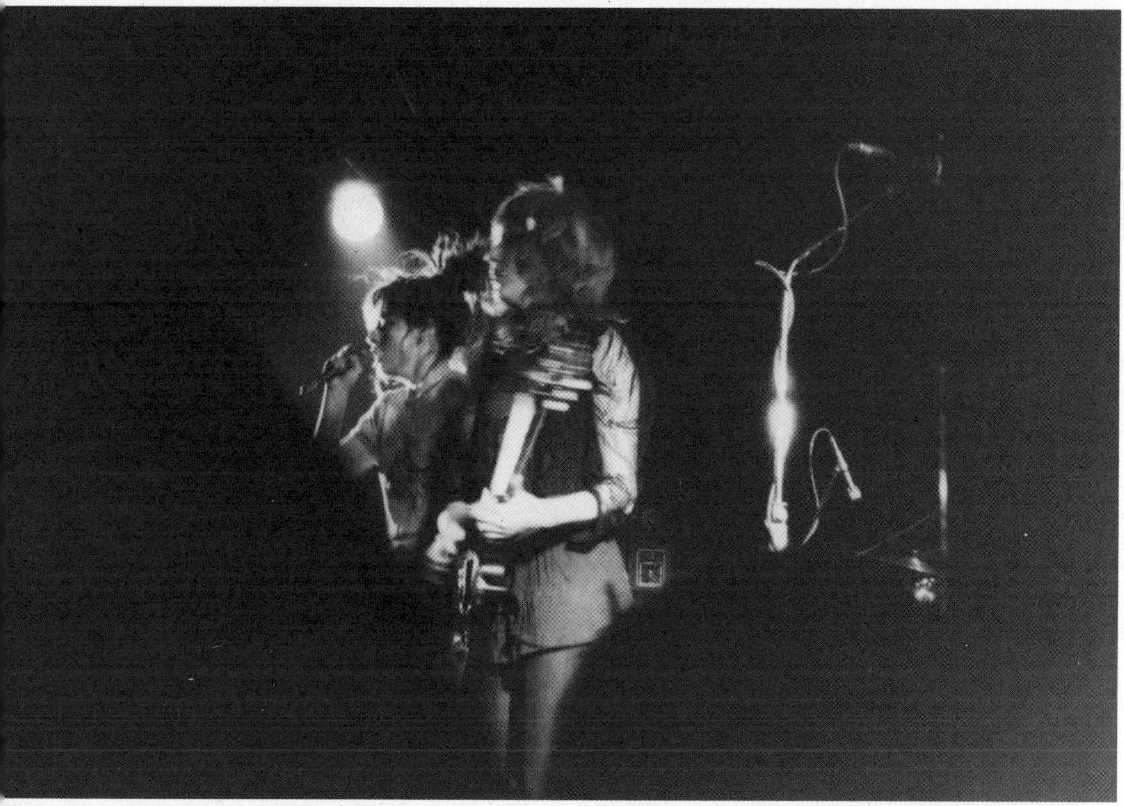

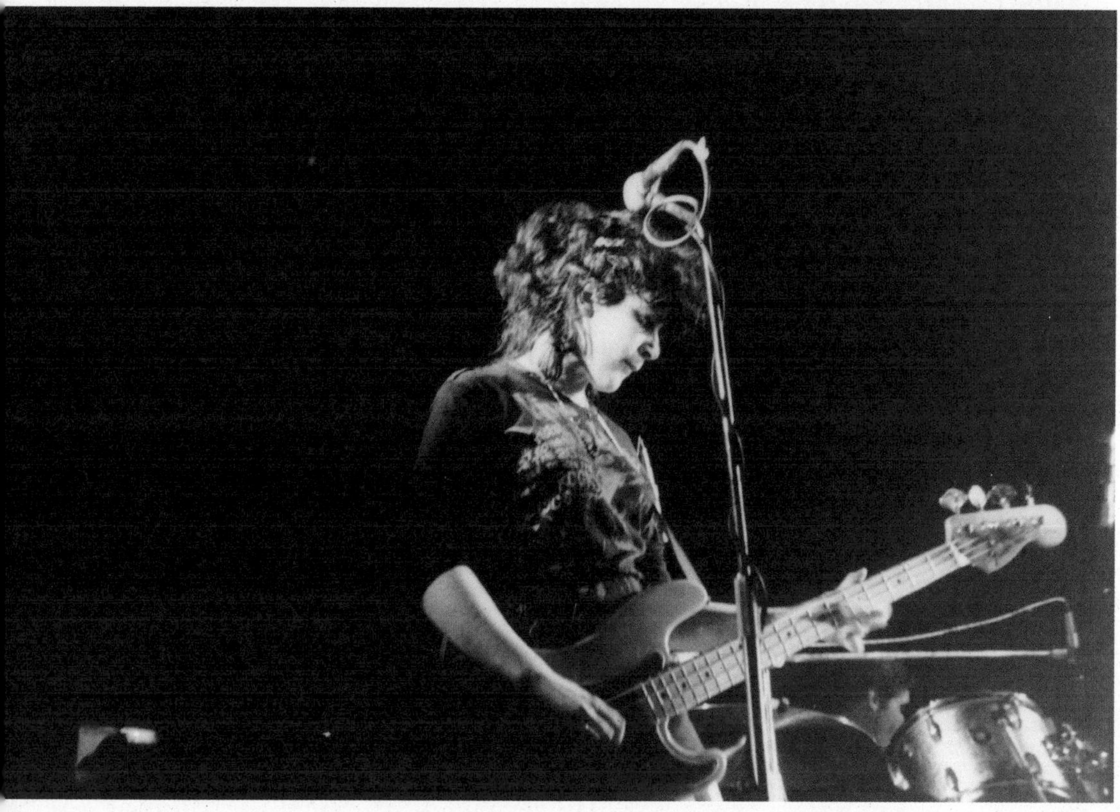

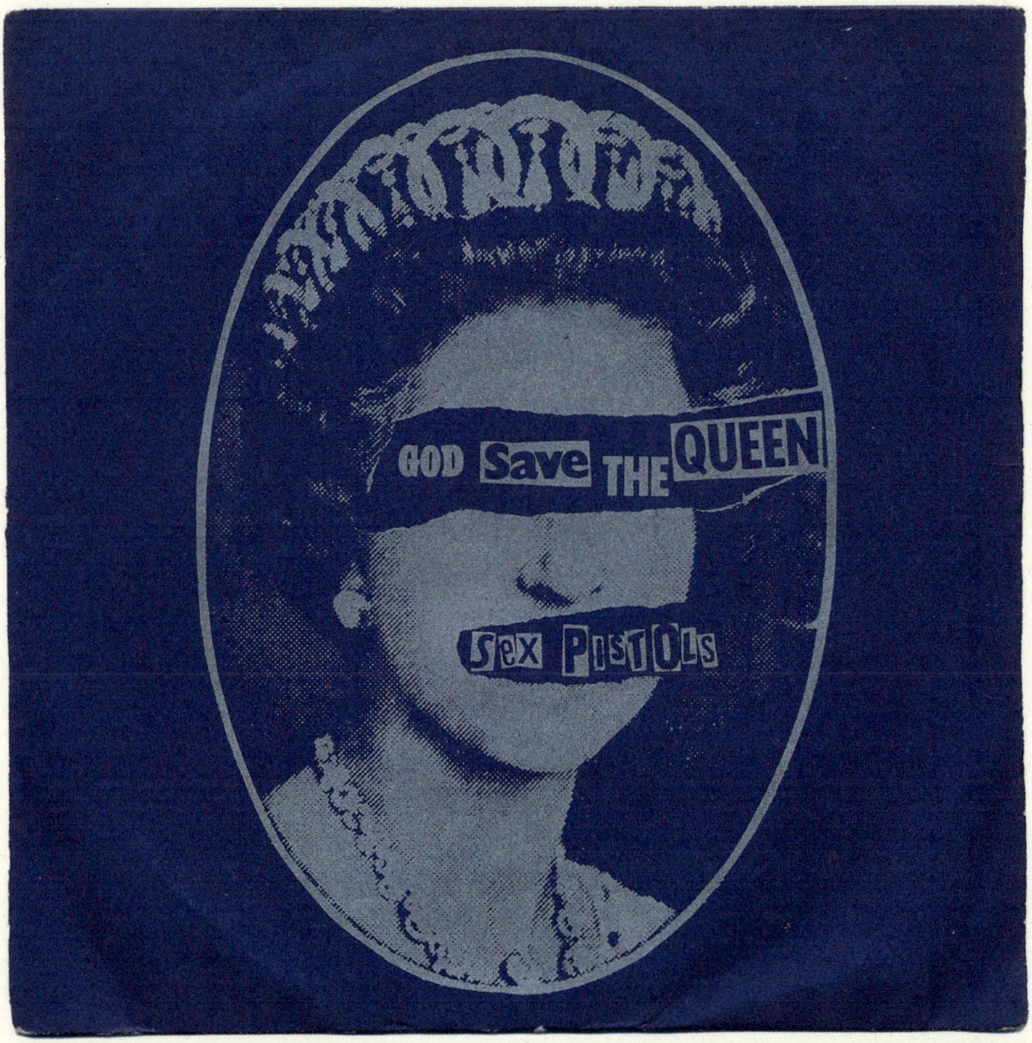

God Save The Queen, el segon disc dels Sex Pistols, va sortir just a temps per coincidir amb el *Queen's Silver Jubilee*, els actes de celebració del vint-i-cinquè aniversari de la coronació de la reina Isabel II d'Anglaterra. Fins aleshores ningú s'havia atrevit a qüestionar la monarquia tan públicament, i la cosa no va deixar de tenir les seves repercussions: els membres de la banda van ser atacats als carrers; fins i tot alguns membres del Parlament van demanar que els Pistols fossin penjats a la forca de la Traitor's Gate, la sinistra Porta dels Traïdors de Londres. Prohibit a les ràdios, a la televisió i a moltes botigues de música, aquest single va ser un èxit de vendes —se'n van vendre 150.000 en poc més d'una setmana— i va arribar al segon lloc de les llistes d'èxits [tot i que per volum de vendes li corresponia el primer lloc] sense que es mencionés, però, el nom de la banda. Cara A: "God Save The Queen". Cara B: "Did You No Wrong". Cook/Jones/Matlock/Rotten. Virgin Records, 27.5.77. Grafisme de Jamie Reid.

7.6.77 Queen Elizabeth River Boat, River Thames, London

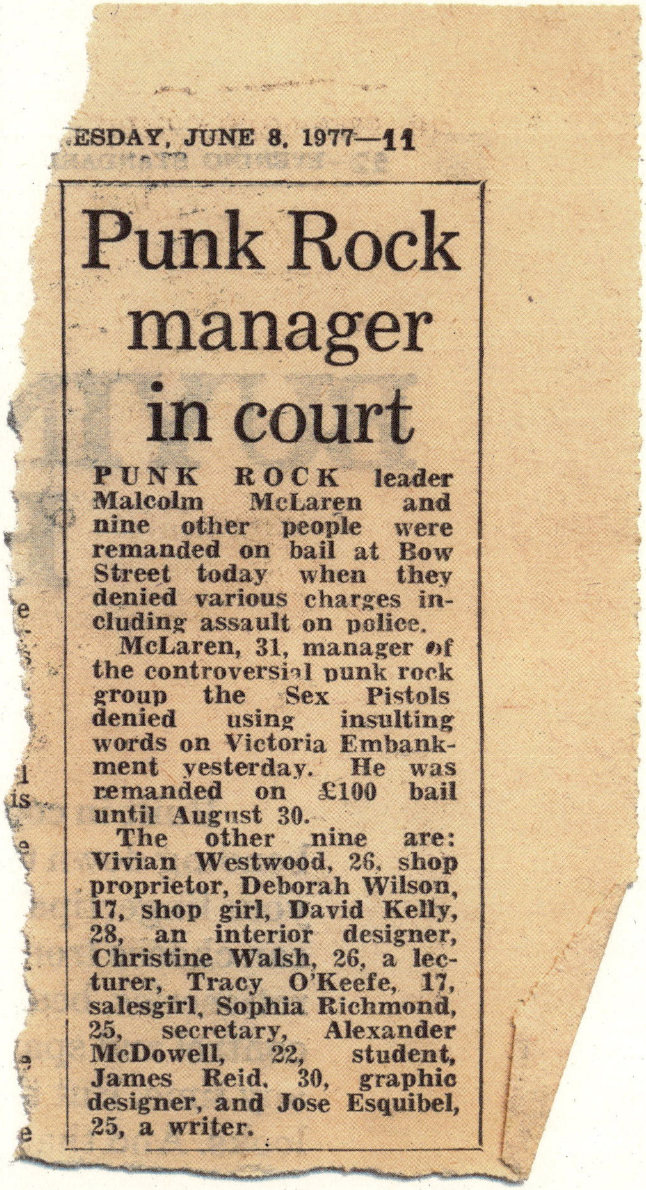
.ESDAY, JUNE 8, 1977—11

Punk Rock manager in court

PUNK ROCK leader Malcolm McLaren and nine other people were remanded on bail at Bow Street today when they denied various charges including assault on police.

McLaren, 31, manager of the controversial punk rock group the Sex Pistols denied using insulting words on Victoria Embankment yesterday. He was remanded on £100 bail until August 30.

The other nine are: Vivian Westwood, 26, shop proprietor, Deborah Wilson, 17, shop girl, David Kelly, 28, an interior designer, Christine Walsh, 26, a lecturer, Tracy O'Keefe, 17, salesgirl, Sophia Richmond, 25, secretary, Alexander McDowell, 22, student, James Reid, 30, graphic designer, and Jose Esquibel, 25, a writer.

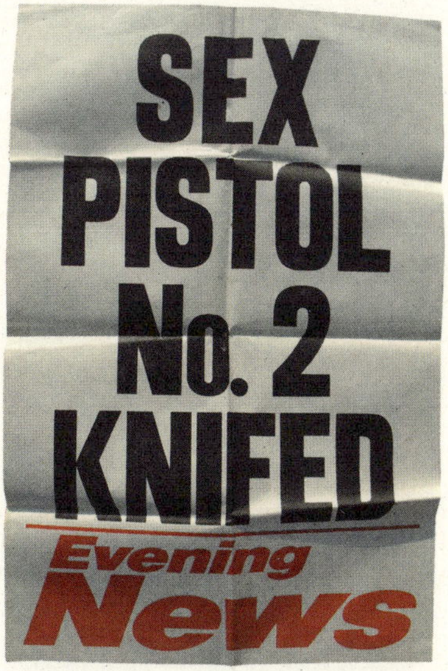

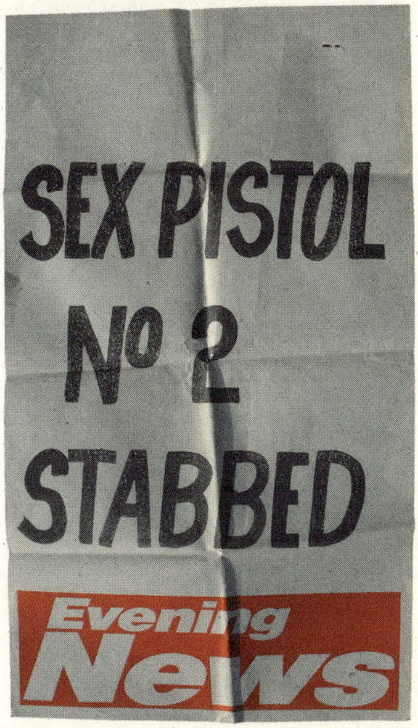

Retall de diari del 8 de juny del 77 informant de la llibertat sota fiança imposada a Malcolm McLaren i nou persones més pels fets del dia anterior. El 7 de juny —en plena celebració nacional del *Queen's Silver Jubilee*— els Sex Pistols desafien la prohibició de tocar en terra britànic i fan un concert des d'una barcassa navegant pel riu Tàmesi a l'alçada de l'edifici del Parlament a Londres. La policia aborda el vaixell creant un gran caos i passa a detenir diverses persones, entre les quals es troben Malcolm McLaren, Vivienne Westwood i Jamie Reid. | Cartells del diari *Evening News* amb la notícia "Sex Pistol apunyalat", referint-se a l'atac amb arma blanca que va ferir Johnny Rotten al braç el 18 de juny del 77. Paul Cook i Jamie Reid també van ser atacats amb barres de ferro.

Scandinavia Tour
13.7.77 Daddy's Dance Hall, Copenhagen, Denmark
14.7.77 Daddy's Dance Hall, Copenhagen, Denmark
15.7.77 Beach Disco, Diskotek Ostra Stranden, Halmstad, Sweden
16.7.77 Mogambo Disco, Helsingborg, Sweden
17.7.77 Discotheque 42, Jonkoping, Sweden
19.7.77 Club Zebra, Kristinehamn, Sweden
20.7.77 Pinvinen Restaurant, Oslo, Norway
21.7.77 Studenter Samfundet, Trodheim, Norway
23.7.77 Barbarellas Disco, Vaxjo, Sweden
24.7.77 Barbarellas Disco, Vaxjo, Sweden
27.7.77 Happy House, Student Kåren, Stockholm, Sweden
28.7.77 Happy House, Student Kåren, Stockholm, Sweden

PETER TOSH

S.P.O.T.S Tour
19.8.77 Lafayette Club, Wolverhampton - "S.P.O.T.S" (Sex Pistols On Tour Secretly)
24.8.77 Outlook Club, Doncaster - "Tax Exiles"
25.8.77 Penthouse, Scarborough - "Special Guest"
26.8.77 Rock Garden, Middlesborough - "Acne Rabble"
31.8.77 Woods Centre, Plymouth - "The Hamsters"
1.9.77 Winter Gardens, Penzance - "A Mystery Band of International Repute"

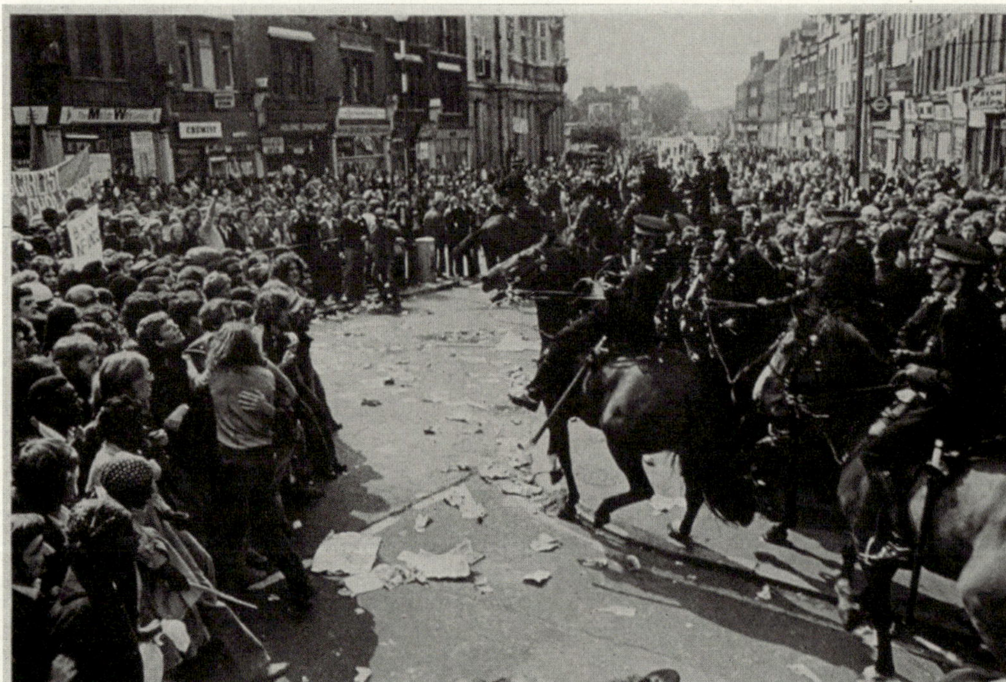

New Cross Rd. Anti-racists block route of National Front. Paul Trevor

LEWISHAM AUGUST 13, 1977

Gires dels Sex Pistols durant els mesos de juliol i agost del 77; a Anglaterra actuen amb diferents noms per esquivar la prohibició. | Nom. | Una gran concentració antiracista barra el pas als manifestants del National Front —custodiats per la policia— a Lewisham, barri del sud-est de Londres on viuen molts immigrants, 13.8.77. Fotografia de Paul Trevor publicada a la revista *Camerawork*, 8.

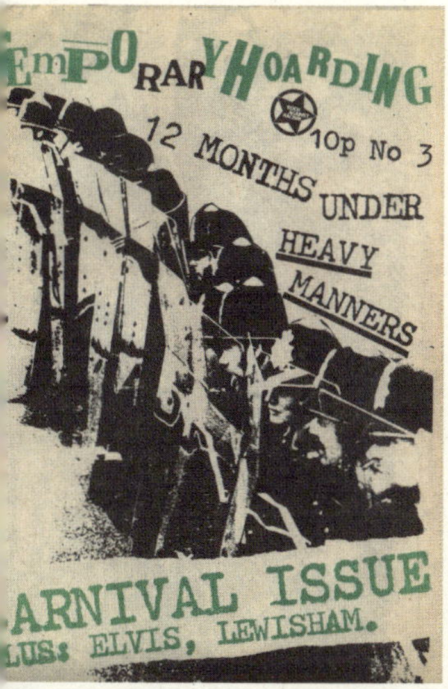

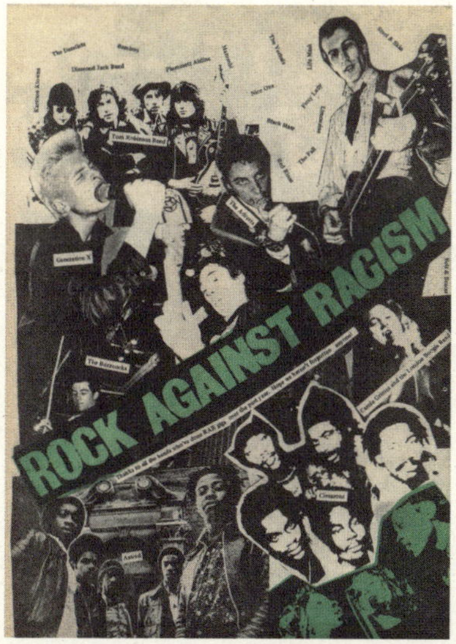

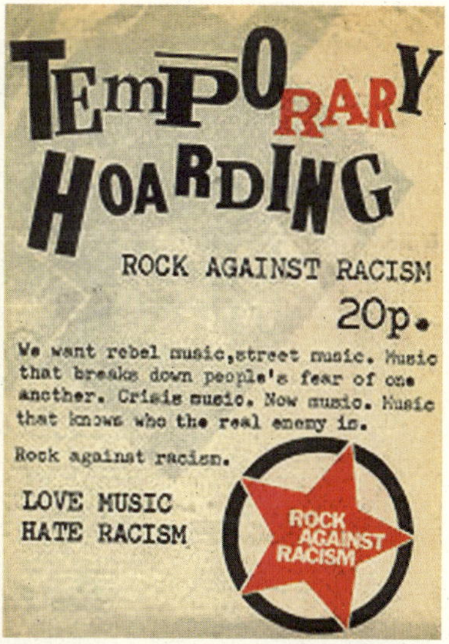

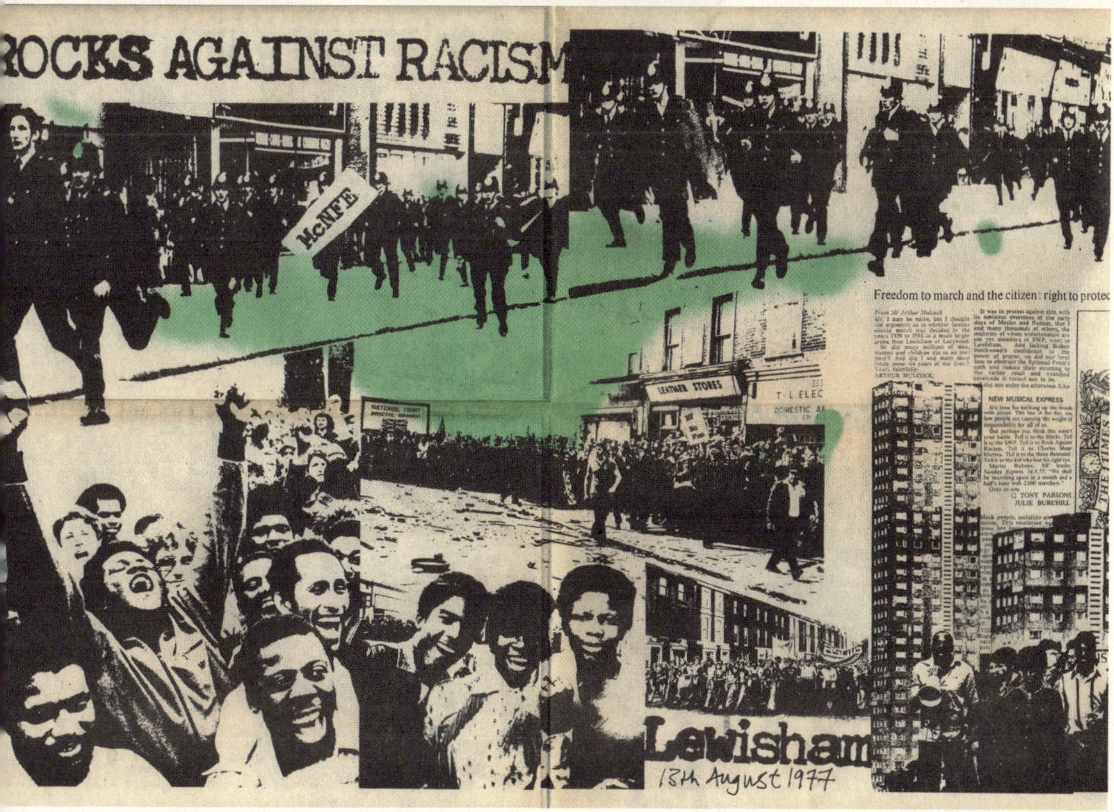

Pàgines del fanzine desplegable *Temporary Hoarding* publicat per Rock Against Racism i produït per Red Wedge Graphics i Lucy Toothpaste el 1977 i 1978. Durant els anys setanta, a Anglaterra, la crisi i l'atur van contribuir a enfortir el partit d'ultradreta National Front. El seu discurs racista i les accions violentes contra els immigrants anaven augmentant. Un dels moviments més combatius contra aquest ascens del feixisme a Anglaterra va ser Rock Against Racism, que va rebre el suport dels músics punk i reggae amb concerts de The Clash, X-Ray Spex, Buzzcocks, Tom Robinson Band, Steel Pulse, The Ruts, Sham 69, Generation X...

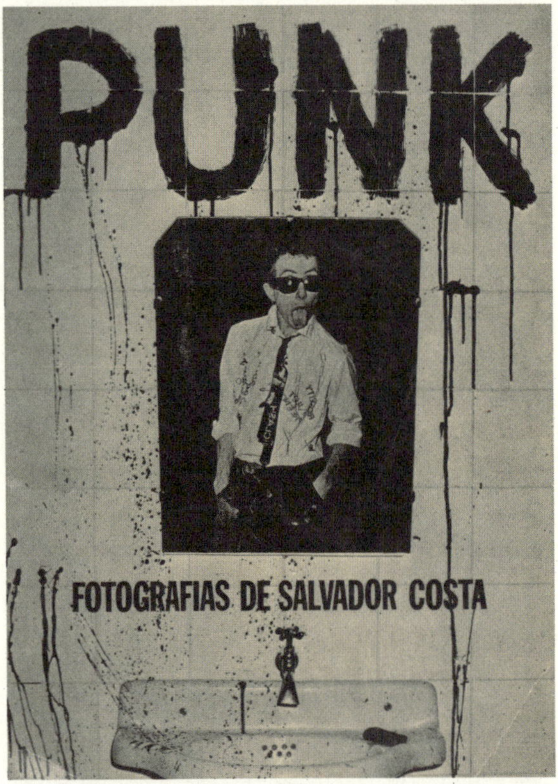

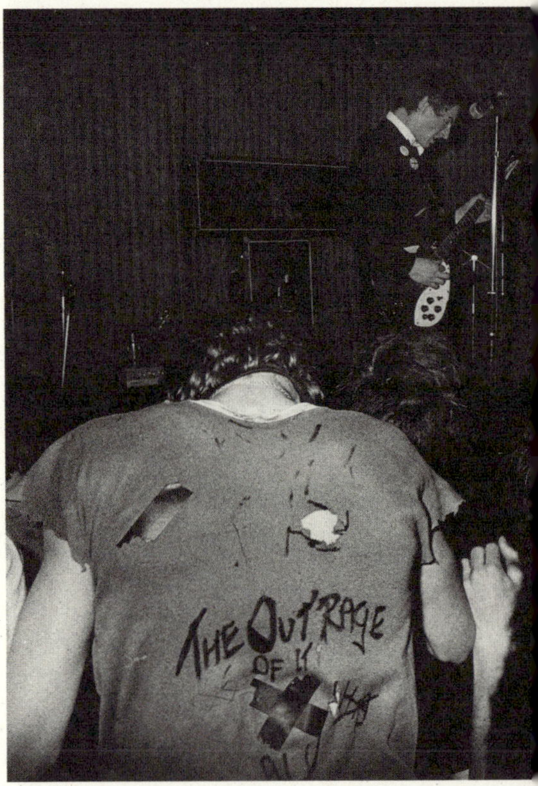

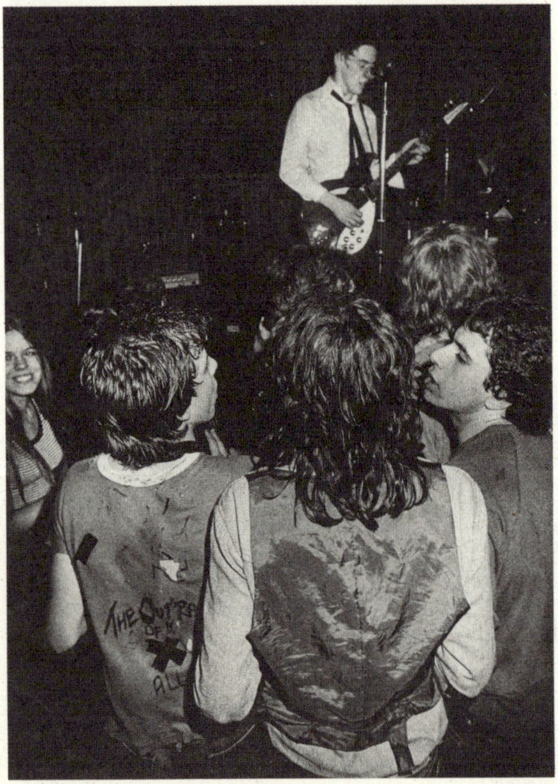

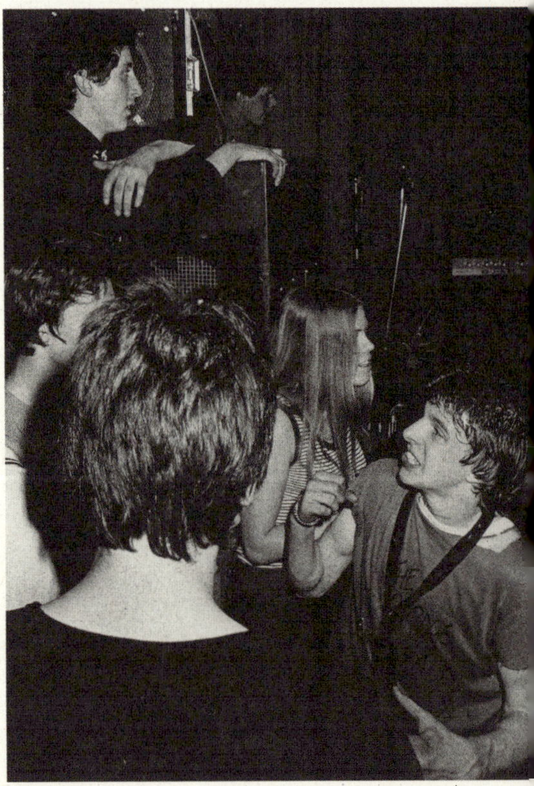

El 1977 Salvador Costa s'està una setmana a Londres i fotografia l'escena que hi troba. Aquell mateix any publica les seves fotografies al llibre *PUNK*, editat per Star Books a Barcelona, un dels primers testimonis publicats arreu.

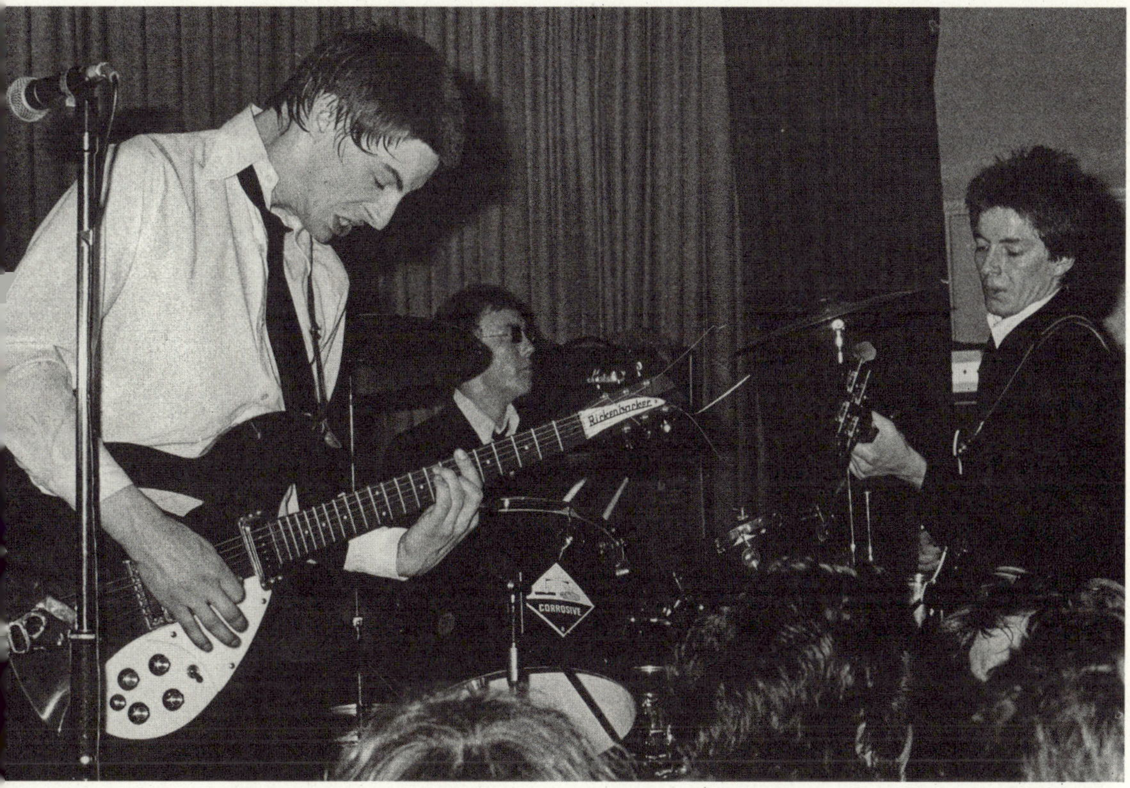

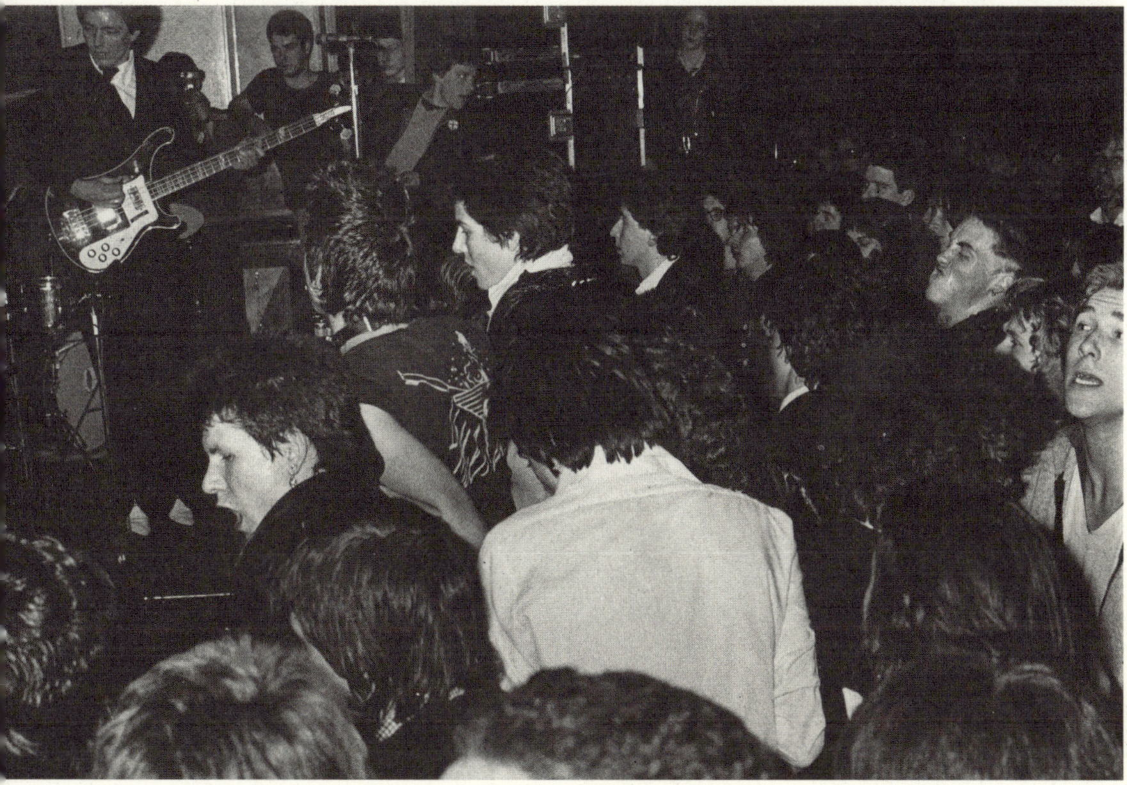

En aquestes pàgines: portada del llibre —amb grafisme i fotomuntatge del mateix Salvador Costa— i fotografies corresponents a un concert de The Jam, on es capta tota l'energia i la proximitat entre els músics i el públic.

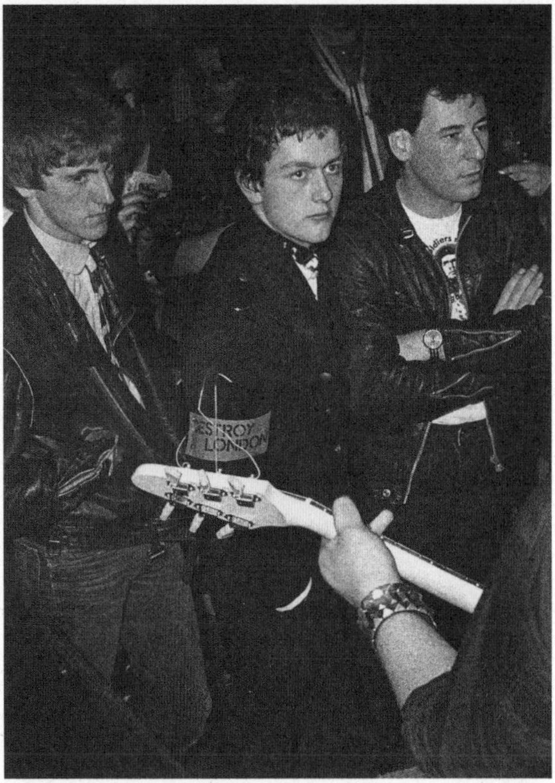

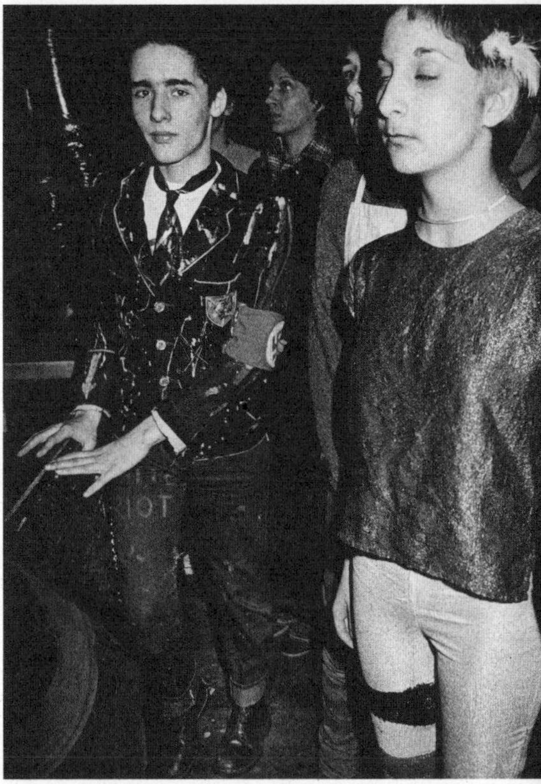

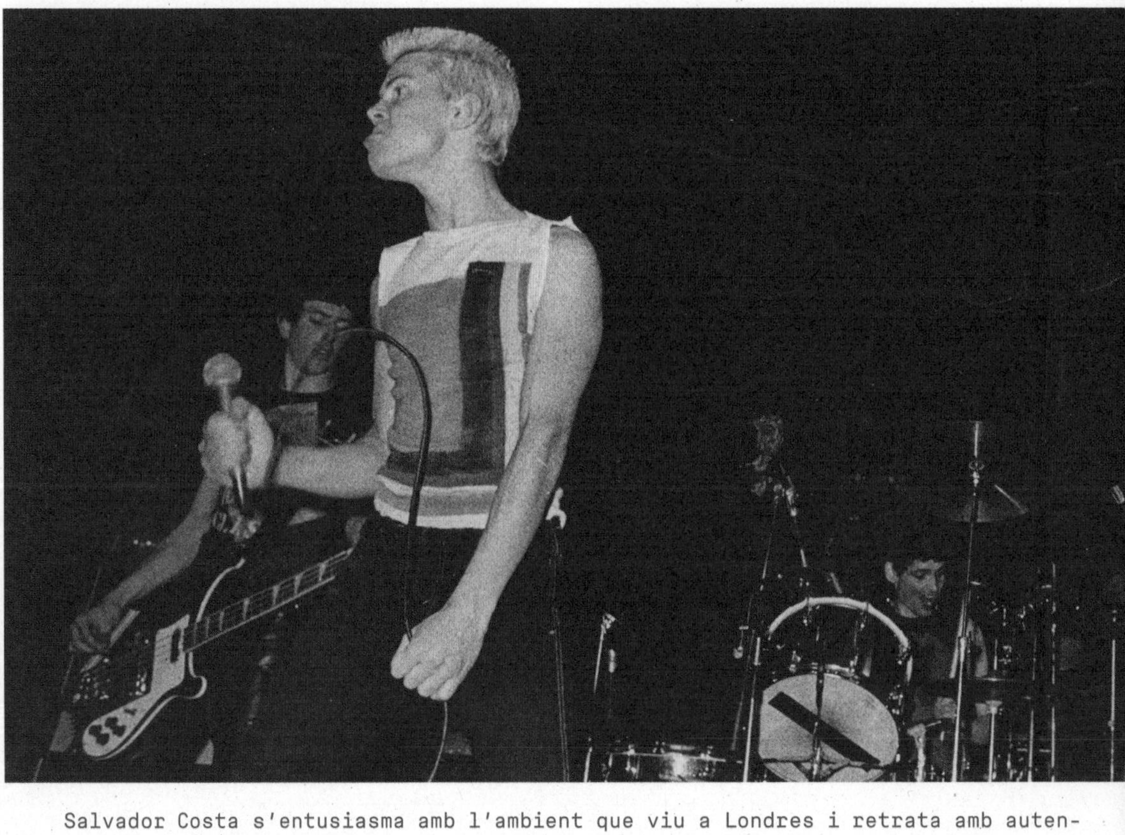

Salvador Costa s'entusiasma amb l'ambient que viu a Londres i retrata amb autenticitat l'actitud dels joves que assisteixen als concerts i dels conjunts en acció. La seva mirada atenta es fixa en els detalls i fotografia els concerts

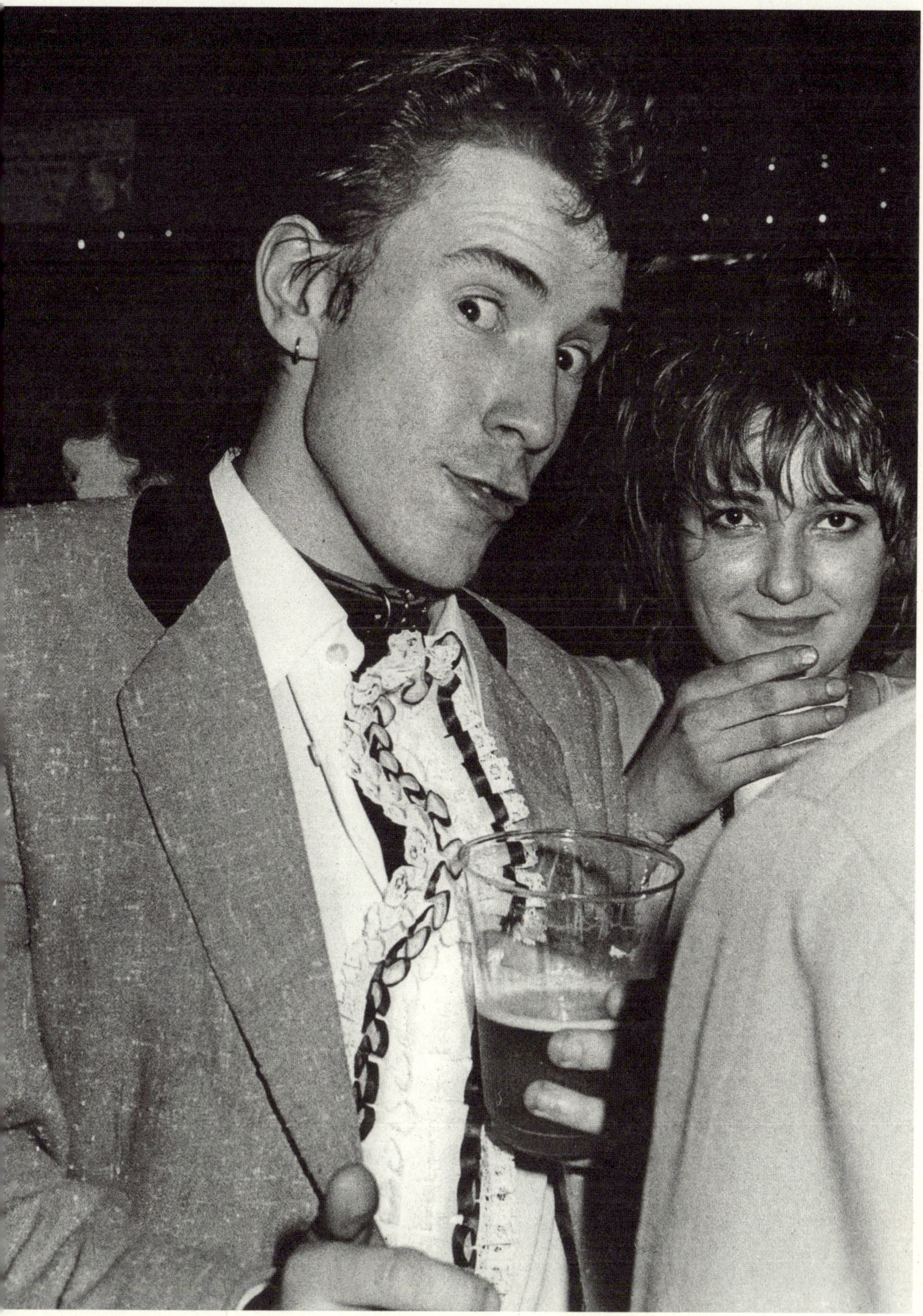

de The Model's, The Cortinas, Cherry Vanilla, The Police, The Jam, The Lurkers, XTC, The Stranglers, Johnny Moped i, com es pot veure en aquestes pàgines, Generation X i Johnny Rotten.

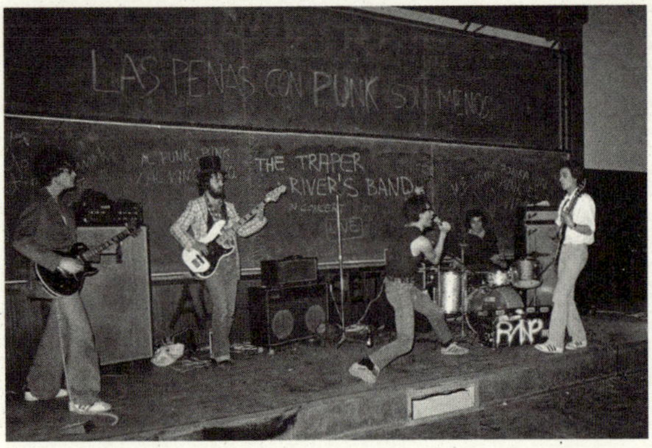

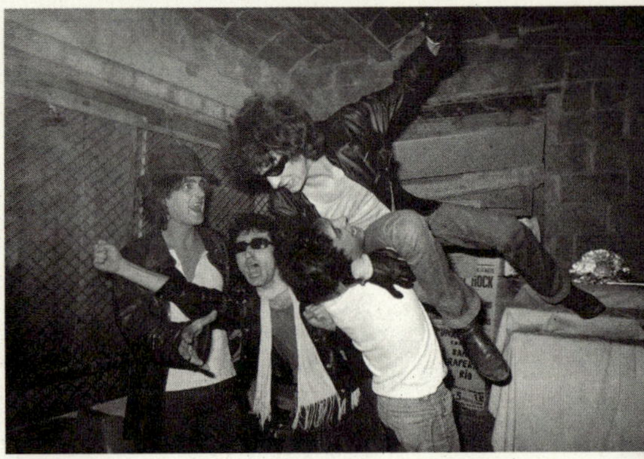

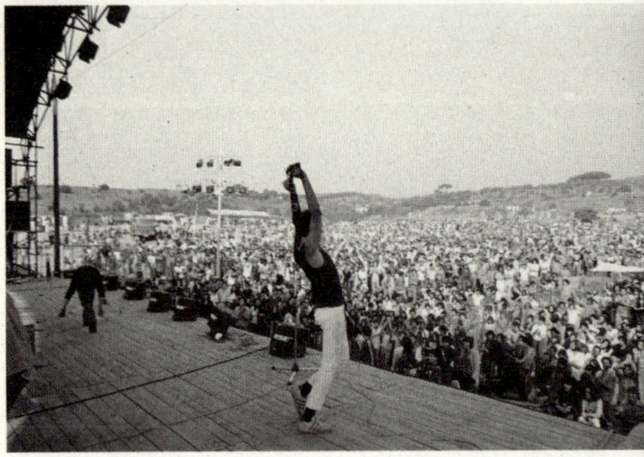

QUE PASA CON LA BANDA TRAPERA DEL RÍO

Antes del 13 de noviembre de 1976, Cornellá, la Satélite de San Ildefonso, era una cloaca sin marcha.
Cada noche, cuando el Morfi, el Chiri, el tio Modes, Raf Pulido, el Llobregat, después del curro querían divertirse un poco, un algo, un mucho, según el cuerpo, sólo tenían las ratas y los monos, los monos o las ratas, el olor a aceite barato, un paisaje desclasado y una cervecería con muchas puertas por abrir.
La falta de rollo y el gusto por el rock and roll provocó el nacimiento de la Banda Trapera del Río. Y desde el 13 de noviembre de 1976 Cornellá, la Satélite, es otra cosa. Hay todo un rollo, hay marcha, hay vida. Las ratas tienen compañía. Los monos se mantienen al margen.
La Banda trapera del Río comenzó tocando rock and roll tradicional. Todo el repertorio de los 60. Sin embargo la Banda Trapera del Río tenía un no sé qué que provocaba la marginación, el rechazo, la discriminación por parte de los núcleos mafiosos que controlan el business de la música joven.
Como es su costumbre, se limitaron a marginar y a rechazar y a etiquetar. "Antisociales" era el menos duro de los calificativos que le colgaron a la Banda Trapera del Río. Y esa rabia acumulada sirvió para que dejase de cantar rocks de los 60 y comenzara a sacar sus propios temas, como "La regla", como "Ciutat podrida", como "Venid a las cloacas", temas que nada tenían que ver con el rock Punk de los ingleses jodidos, pero que evidentemente tentaban al parentesco y al compadreo con Sex Pistols, Iggy Pop, Ramones y lo que usted guste mandar.
La verdad es que la Banda Trapera del Río estaba hasta los cojones de que se le pagara peor que a nadie, se le prestaran los peores equipos de sonido y se le hiciera actuar en los momentos más inoportunos. Por ejemplo, el Festival Punk de la Alianza del Pueblo Nuevo fué todo un poema. Mientras se anunciaba a Peligro, a Marxa, a Ramoncin y sus W.C.?, a Mortimer, La Banda Trapera del Río salió al escenario en primer lugar y sin previo aviso.

A Barcelona, Salvador Costa connecta amb La Banda Trapera del Río i passa a ser el fotògraf del grup i l'autor de les cobertes dels seus discos. Les seves fotografies són un tresor documental i es troben publicades al llibre de Jaime Gonzalo *La Banda Trapera del Río. Escupidos de la boca de Dios*, editat per

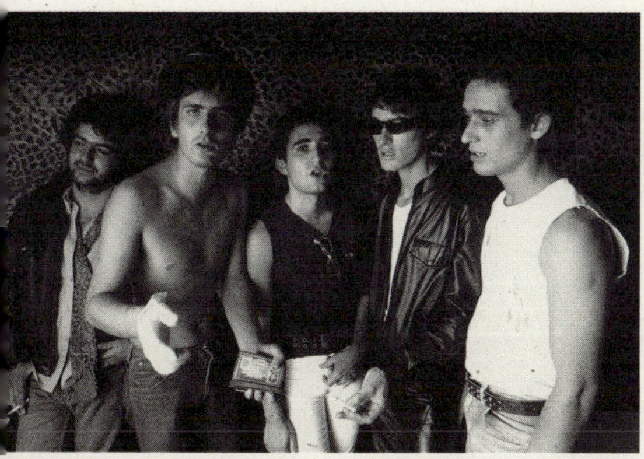

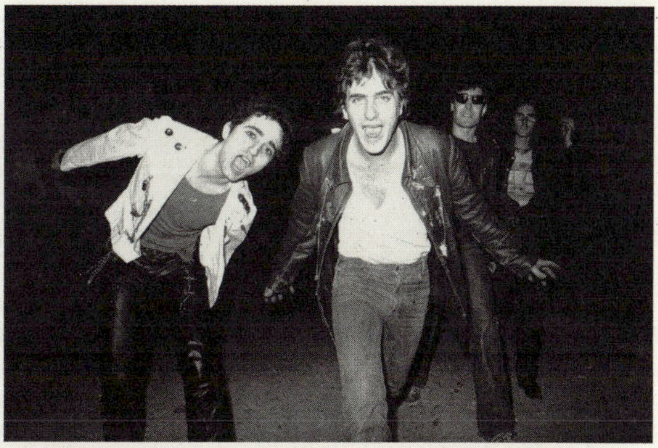

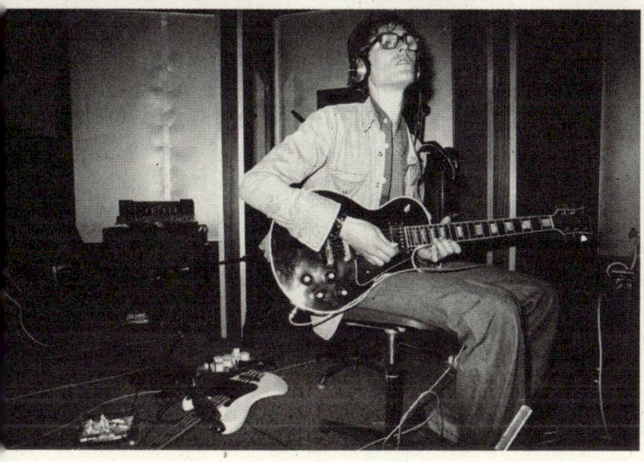

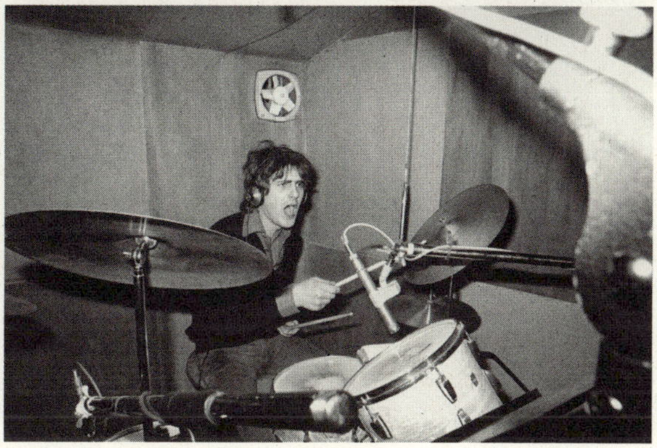

Esto lo dice todo. Luego se pensó en grabar. Un larga agonía de despacho. Maquetas por aquí, mierda por allá.

—Por lo menos, que nos pongan un equipo de sonido aceptable.

Sí, sí, la Belter y gracias. La Banda Trapera del Río tuvo que bailar con la más fea. Con unos medios técnicos y humanos difícilmente soportables. Tratados como bichos raros, de zoológico, sin entender nada de nada de lo que está pasando, con una condesdencia paternalista del carajo, La Belter y la Banda Trapera del Río se putearon mutuamente. Un single y un LP, hechos a contra reloj, mezclados en dos horas y prensados con la polla. Pero, ahí está, como un documento único en la historia discográfica.

Luego llegó el Canet Roc.

El de la virgen que descoñó Pau Riba. La Banda trapera del Río alucinó al personal, despertó a los dormidos y vivificó a los amuermados.

Un respeto impresionante, desde entonces, por la Banda Trapera del Río en todos los sectores más o menos enrollados. Llegó la hora del planteamiento definitivo. El Llobregat se tenía que ir a la mili. Rockhita quería dejar de ser el eterno segundón con la guitarra rítmica y cogió el bajo de Llobregat. Pero Rockhita era el único que vivía al margen de todo el rollo de La Banda. Por vivir fuera, vivía en Gavá. Por no aportar, pasaba de la mayoría de los ensayos.

Apareció el Montoya. Bueno, en realidad ya estaba. El Montoya Serrano estaba, como está el Silvio, como está La Banda del Metro. Como están todos los bienenrollados del mundo todo.

Y cogió el bajo. Y ahora La Banda Trapera del Río tiene una fuerza como sólo en sueños había querido tener. Y aquí está. Esta es.

Los que antes puteaban y marginaban a la Banda Trapera del Río quieren hoy comer en sus manos. La Banda Trapera del Río, hele sus huevos, está donde está por sus propios méritos. Sin ayuda de nadie. A pesar de todo.

Munster el 2007. L'escrit "Qué pasa con La Banda Trapera del Río" que es transcriu en aquestes pàgines és de la publicació *La Banda de los Traperos* —editada per ells mateixos— i explica clarament la trajectòria, l'actitud i les dificultats de la banda des dels seus inicis el novembre del 1976.

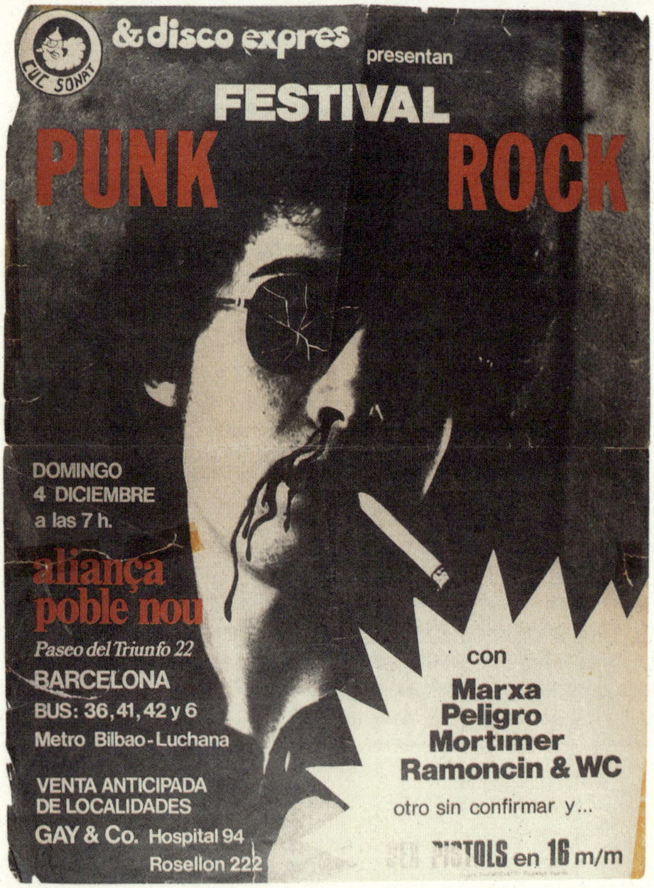

HISTÒRIA D'UN CARTELL

Per fer el cartell del Festival Punk Rock de l'Aliança del Poble Nou (4.12.77) vam dir als grups que aportessin idees. Finalment vam seleccionar una foto del cantant del grup Mortimer feta pel bateria del mateix grup. Vam afegir el text a la imatge i vam posar sang rajant del nas. El cartell s'imprimia a dues tintes (vermell i negre) i primer vem posar la sang en vermell. Quan vam veure el resultat vam pensar que ens portaria molts problemes i, a més, no reflexava la idea que teniem d'un festival punk; per això vem deixar la sang en negre. Quan els de la sala i els que havien de sonoritzar-la van veure el cartell es van espantar i es volien fer enrere, però els contractes ja estaven signats. També vam tenir problemes a l'hora de penjar-los, doncs a molts llocs no ens el deixaven posar, ja fos per la sang o per la paraula PUNK. Disco Exprés va fer diriem que d'espònsor; Gay & Co venia les entrades a la seva botiga de discos i CucSonat ho va organitzar. Quan es va imprimir el cartell encara no haviem confirmat si actuaria La Banda Trapera del Río, per la qual cosa no surt el seu nom al cartell i vam posar "otro sin confirmar". / Xavi Cot (CucSonat)

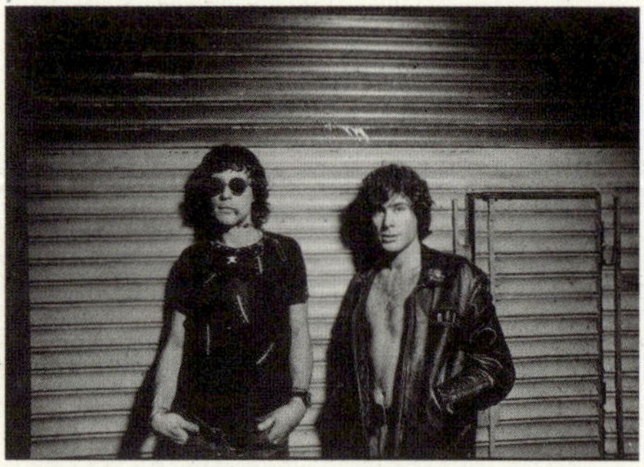

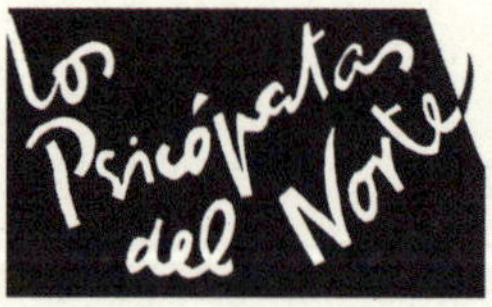

LOS PSICÓPATAS DEL NORTE, amb Carles Merseburguer a les guitarres i veu, Toni Pinar a la guitarra, Jordi Mustieles al baix i Jordi Carbó a la batería, va ser un dels nombrosos grups que van actuar a les Jornades Llibertàries, al Park Guell de Barna (22, 23 i 24 de juliol del 1977). Van pujar a l'escenari amb improvisació total i van tocar "Castigo". Posteriorment es va afegir al grup la genial Rosa Arruti.

Cartell del Festival Punk Rock de Barcelona, organitzat per CucSonat el desembre de 1977. | Jordi Valls i Salvador Costa de marxa per Barcelona, 1977. | Cartell de Los Psicópatas del Norte, 1978.

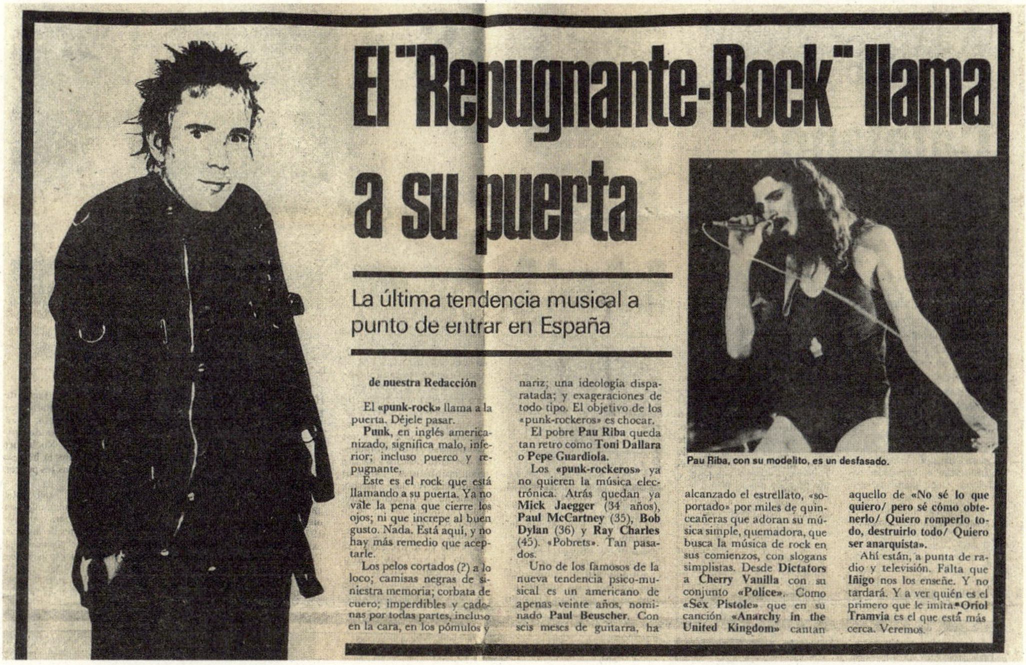

El "Repugnante-Rock" llama a su puerta

La última tendencia musical a punto de entrar en España

de nuestra Redacción

El **«punk-rock»** llama a la puerta. Déjele pasar.

Punk, en inglés americanizado, significa malo, inferior; incluso puerco y repugnante.

Este es el rock que está llamando a su puerta. Ya no vale la pena que cierre los ojos; ni que increpe al buen gusto. Nada. Está aquí, y no hay más remedio que aceptarle.

Los pelos cortados (?) a lo loco; camisas negras de siniestra memoria; corbata de cuero; imperdibles y cadenas por todas partes, incluso en la cara, en los pómulos y nariz; una ideología disparatada; y exageraciones de todo tipo. El objetivo de los «punk-rockeros» es chocar.

El pobre **Pau Riba** queda tan retro como **Toni Dallara** o **Pepe Guardiola.**

Los **«punk-rockeros»** ya no quieren la música electrónica. Atrás quedan ya **Mick Jaegger** (34 años), **Paul McCartney** (35), **Bob Dylan** (36) y **Ray Charles** (45). «Pobrets». Tan pasados.

Uno de los famosos de la nueva tendencia psico-musical es un americano de apenas veinte años, nominado **Paul Beuscher**. Con seis meses de guitarra, ha alcanzado el estrellato, «soportado» por miles de quinceañeras que adoran su música simple, quemadora, que busca la música de rock en sus comienzos, con slogans simplistas. Desde **Dictators** a **Cherry Vanilla** con su conjunto **«Police»**. Como **«Sex Pistole»** que en su canción **«Anarchy in the United Kingdom»** cantan aquello de **«No sé lo que quiero/ pero sé cómo obtenerlo/ Quiero romperlo todo, destruirlo todo/ Quiero ser anarquista».**

Ahí están, a punta de radio y televisión. Falta que **Iñigo** nos los enseñe. Y no tardará. Y a ver quién es el primero que le imita. **Oriol Tramvia** es el que está más cerca. Veremos.

Pau Riba, con su modelito, es un desfasado.

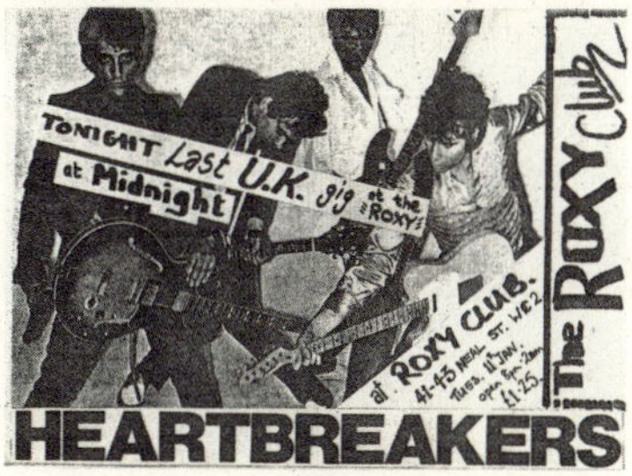

Dutch Tour
5.12.77 Eksit Club, Rotterdam, Holland
6.12.77 Maastricht, Holland
7.12.77 Pozjet Club, Tilburg, Holland
8.12.77 Stokuishal, Arnhem, Holland
9.12.77 De Effenaar, Eindhoven, Holland
10.12.77 Huize Maas, Groningen, Holland
11.12.77 Maf Centrum, Maasbree, Holland
13.12.77 De Klinker, Wimschoten, Holland - CANCELLED
14.12.77 Eksit Club, Rotterdam, Holland - CANCELLED

Never Mind The Bans Tour
16.12.77 Brunel University, Uxbridge
17.12.77 Mr George's, Coventry
19.12.77 Nikkers Club, Keighley
21.12.77 Lafayette Club, Wolverhampton
23.12.77 Stowaway Club, Newport
24.12.77 Links Pavilion, Cromer
25.12.77 Ivanhoes, Huddersfield (Afternoon Show For Kids)
25.12.77 Ivanhoes, Huddersfield (Evening Show)

US Tour 1978
28.12.77 Leona Theatre, Pittsburgh, USA - CANCELLED
5.1.78 Great South East Music Hall, Atlanta, Georgia, USA
6.1.78 Taliesyn Ballroom, Memphis, Tennessee, USA
8.1.78 Randy's Rodeo, San Antonio, Texas, USA
9.1.78 Kingfish Club, Baton Rouge, Louisiana, USA
10.1.78 Longhorn Ballroom, Dallas, Texas, USA
12.1.78 Cains Ballroom, Tulsa, Oklahoma, USA
14.1.78 Winterland Ballroom, San Francisco, California, USA

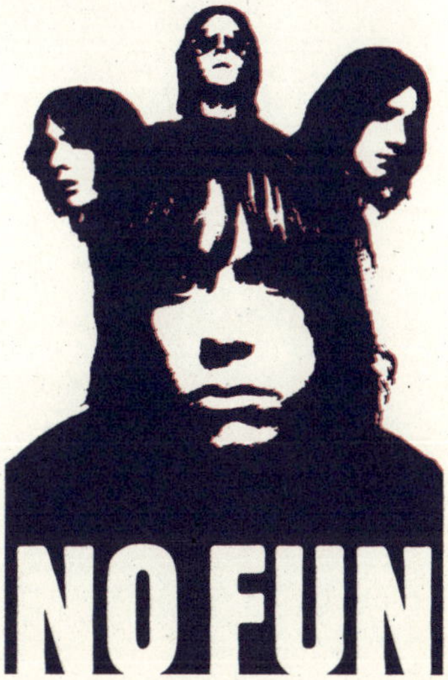

Article ranci i confús, amb fotos de Johnny Rotten i Pau Riba, publicat al diari *Catalunya Express*, 1.6.77. | Cartell de l'últim concert dels Heartbreakers a Anglaterra. | Darrers concerts dels Sex Pistols. | Iggy Pop & The Stooges, autors de la cançó "No Fun".

Sid and Nancy. Johnny Moped concert (1978)

"My name is Silvia Escario ... but people call me Silvia Resorte.

I was the singer in one of the first punk rock bands from Barcelona, called Ultimo Resorte.
We were the first punk band with a girl singer in Barcelona, and since then, I've been in other bands like Berlin 80... now I have a band called Algo Toxico.

I took these pictures of Sid and Nancy in London 1978. I don't remember the name of the club where I took them, it was like a big old dance hall, all I remember is that Johnny Moped was playing...

As I hardly knew any English, I'd used signs and looks to get to know a girl who had become famous as part of the London punk scene by her hair-style alone. She was called Soo Catwoman.

Me and Soo were on the dance floor, inventing ways how NOT to dance like punks, they were playing X-Ray Spex, and all of a sudden Soo stopped to tell me that Sid Vicious had just entered the club...

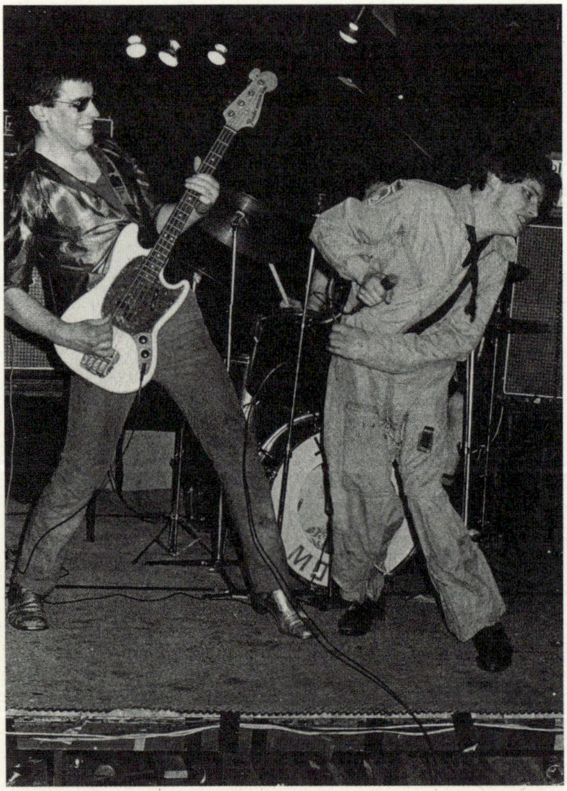

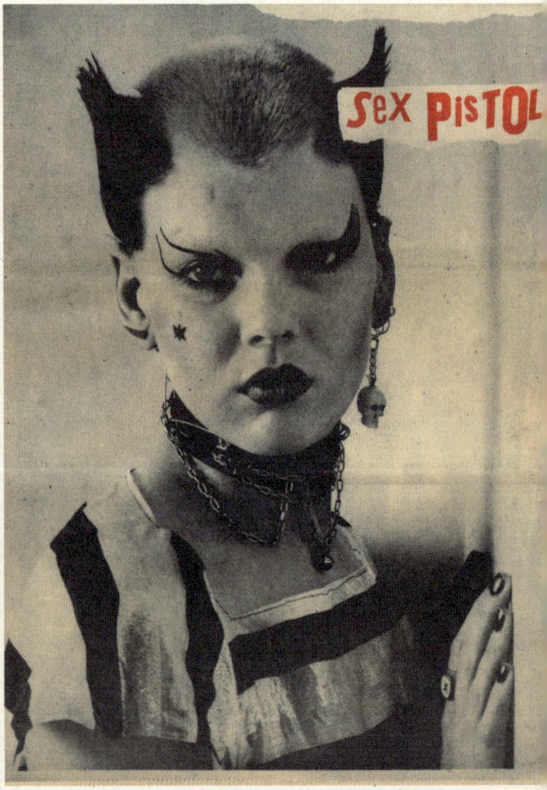

Johnny Moped fotografiat per Salvador Costa, 1977. | Soo Catwoman fotografiada per Ray Stevenson; portada del fanzine dels Sex Pistols *Anarchy in the U.K.*, 1976.

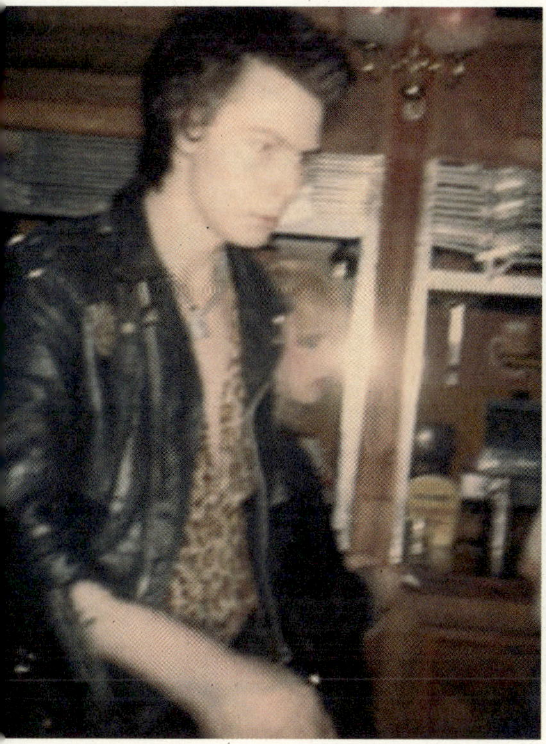

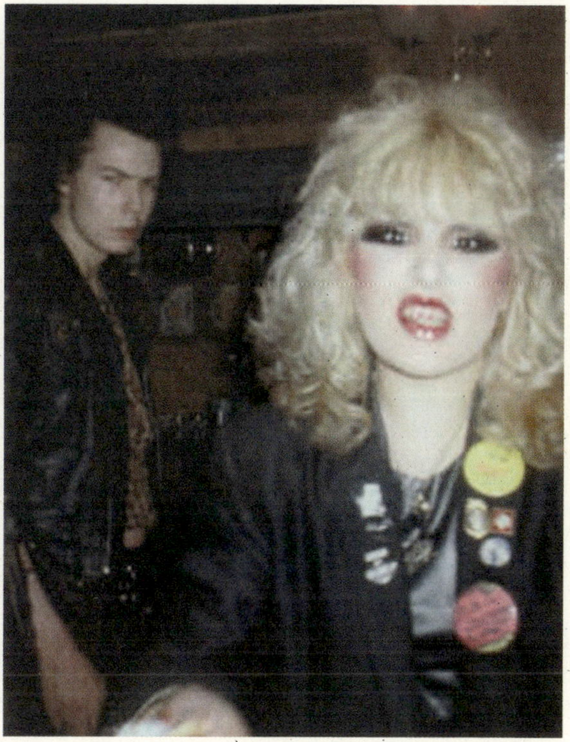

I got my camera, given to me by my grandmother (a former journalist during the Spanish civil war in the 1930's), and ran up to Sid.

I took my picture, but then I thought it wasn't very good, so I decided to take another one. I was preparing to take it, but just then Nancy appeared in the lens. She hit my camera and I dropped it to the floor.

I thought it was broken and picked it up, but it was fine. I turned to give Nancy an evil look... but she had already turned away, not worrying at all about me or my camera.

That really pissed me off, because the camera was from my grandmother, and she could have broken it. So I kicked her in the butt. Sid saw me doing it, and turned around and kicked me in my stomach.

Nancy came up to me again, went into my face and looked at me with RAGE, she grabbed my arms and almost scratched me with her long pink finger-nails (I had no nails to scratch her back), and we were just standing there staring at each other with hatred, until another punk girl came up to us telling us to not be angry, to drop it, it wasn't a big deal....

Sid Vicious i Nancy Spungen fotografiats per Silvia Resorte, 1978.

A few days later, I was returning to Barcelona, and I was only thinking of two things.
One, I felt real bad about the fight with Nancy, and regretted we couldn't have become friends instead of fighting, which by now, I felt just frustration and guilt about.
Second, I thought, I would never sell these photos or use them for profit. I didn't own them. Punk did.

In 1979 I formed a punk band with my then boyfriend. Our name was Ultimo Resorte, our first gig was at a psychiatric hospital. (Ultimo Resorte means Last Resort, but we had that name before the British OI band did).

Thinking back, I believe that Nancy, in those last days before her death, was truly trying to help Sid with his demons, but her own negative emotions and cravings were too hard to resist for her.

I always keep saying it wasn't Sid who killed Nancy. It was this world who killed both."

Silvia Resorte

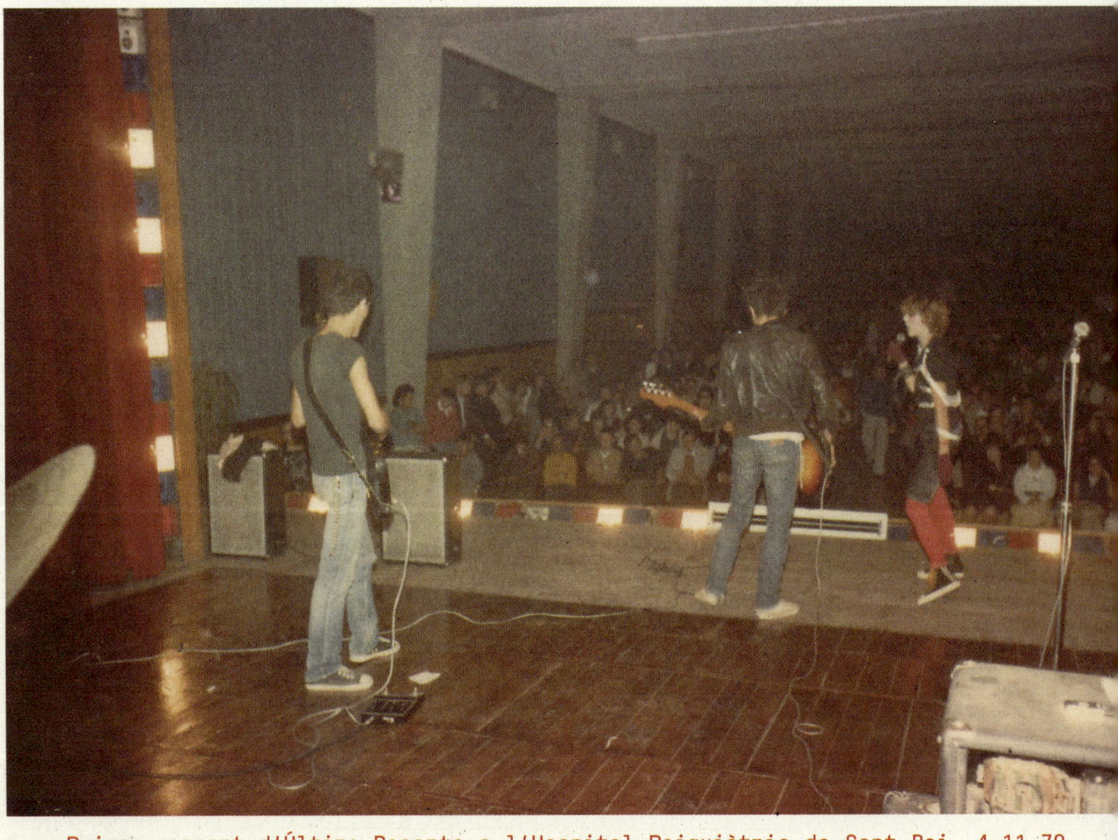

Primer concert d'Último Resorte a l'Hospital Psiquiàtric de Sant Boi, 4.11.79.

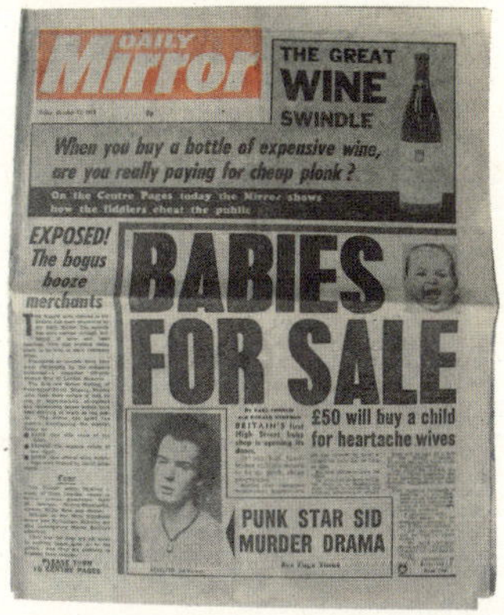

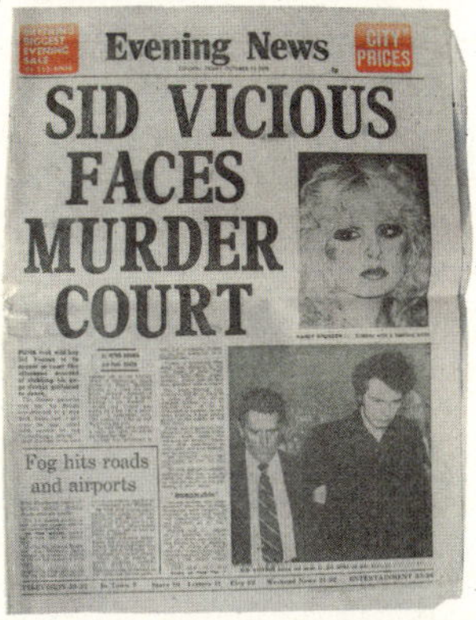

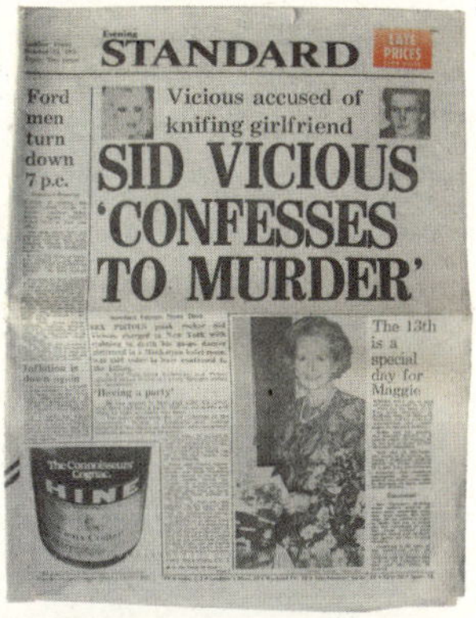

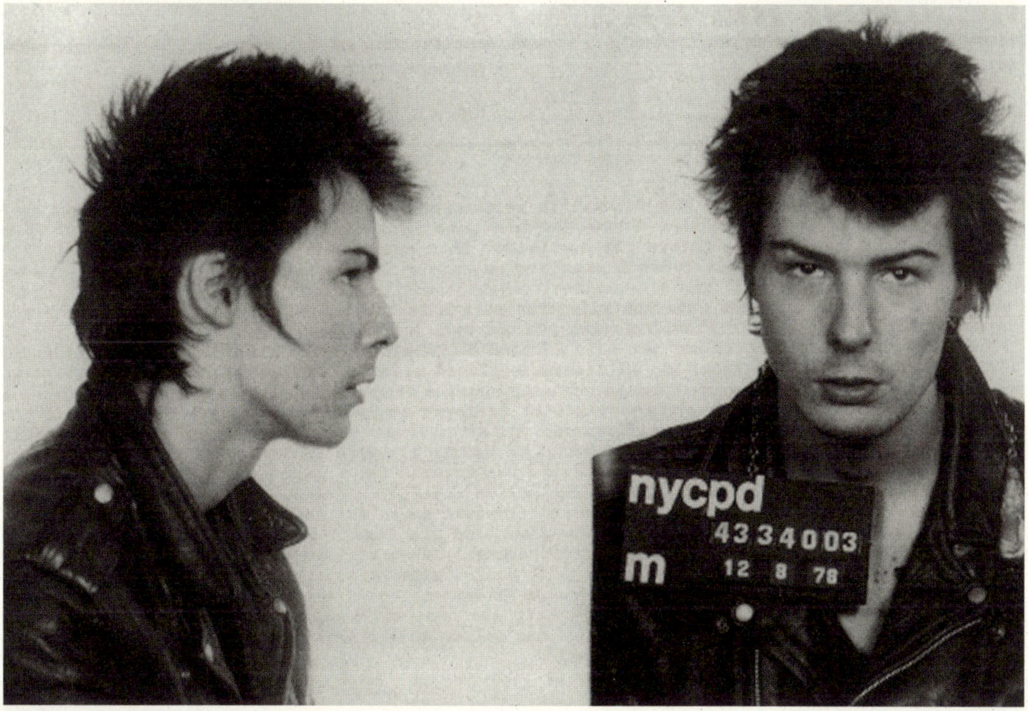

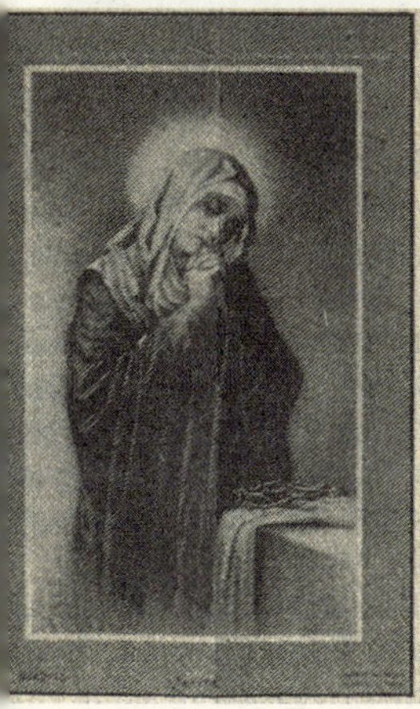

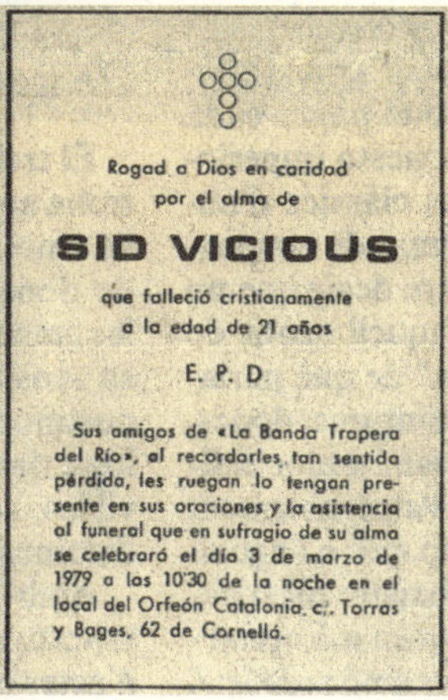
Rogad a Dios en caridad
por el alma de

SID VICIOUS

que falleció cristianamente
a la edad de 21 años

E. P. D

Sus amigos de «La Banda Trapera del Río», al recordarles tan sentida pérdida, les ruegan lo tengan presente en sus oraciones y la asistencia al funeral que en sufragio de su alma se celebrará el día 3 de marzo de 1979 a las 10'30 de la noche en el local del Orfeón Catalonia. c/. Torras y Bages, 62 de Cornellá.

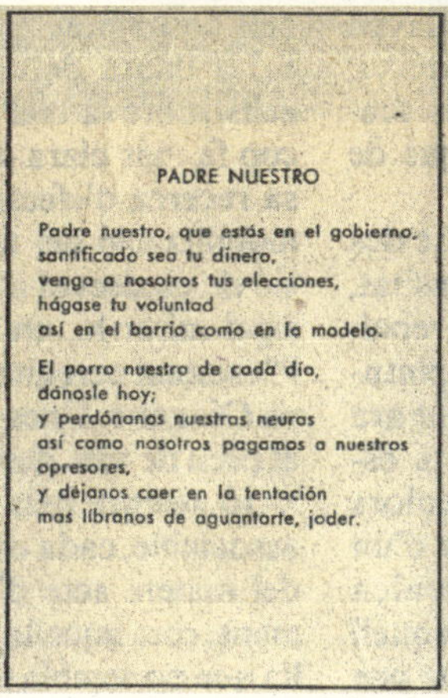
PADRE NUESTRO

Padre nuestro, que estás en el gobierno,
santificado sea tu dinero,
venga a nosotros tus elecciones,
hágase tu voluntad
así en el barrio como en la modelo.

El porro nuestro de cada día,
dánosle hoy;
y perdónanos nuestras neuras
así como nosotros pagamos a nuestros
opresores,
y déjanos caer en la tentación
mas líbranos de aguantarte, joder.

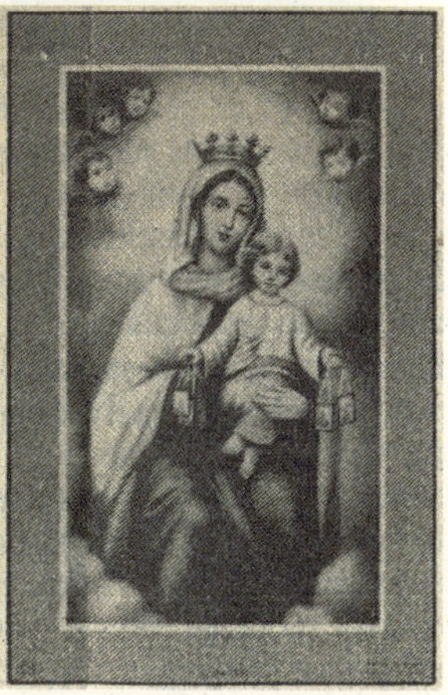

Premsa sensacionalista, 1978. | Sid Vicious fotografiat per la pasma de NYC, 1978. Michael Ochs Archives. | Recordatori de La Banda Trapera del Río convocant al concert funeral en honor de Sid Vicious, a Cornellà, un mes després de la seva mort, 1979.

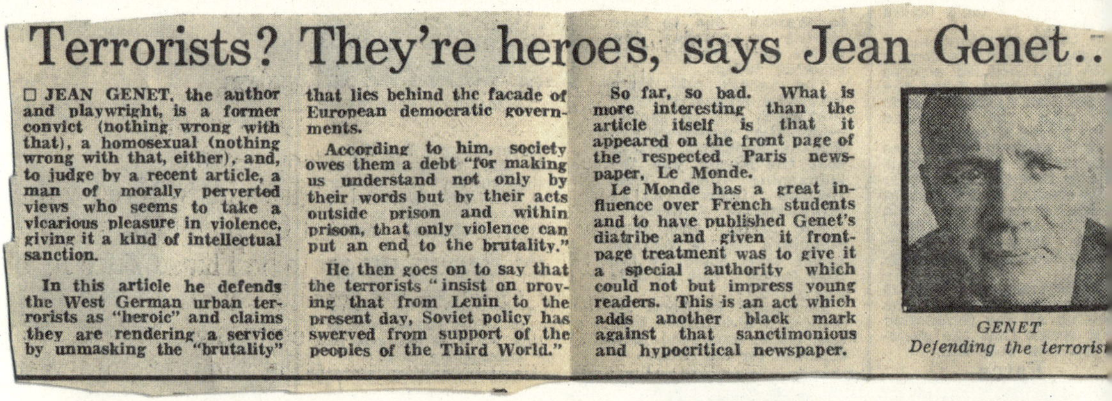

Terrorists? They're heroes, says Jean Genet..

☐ JEAN GENET, the author and playwright, is a former convict (nothing wrong with that), a homosexual (nothing wrong with that, either), and, to judge by a recent article, a man of morally perverted views who seems to take a vicarious pleasure in violence, giving it a kind of intellectual sanction.

In this article he defends the West German urban terrorists as "heroic" and claims they are rendering a service by unmasking the "brutality" that lies behind the facade of European democratic governments.

According to him, society owes them a debt "for making us understand not only by their words but by their acts outside prison and within prison, that only violence can put an end to the brutality."

He then goes on to say that the terrorists "insist on proving that from Lenin to the present day, Soviet policy has swerved from support of the peoples of the Third World."

So far, so bad. What is more interesting than the article itself is that it appeared on the front page of the respected Paris newspaper, Le Monde.

Le Monde has a great influence over French students and to have published Genet's diatribe and given it front-page treatment was to give it a special authority which could not but impress young readers. This is an act which adds another black mark against that sanctimonious and hypocritical newspaper.

GENET
Defending the terroris

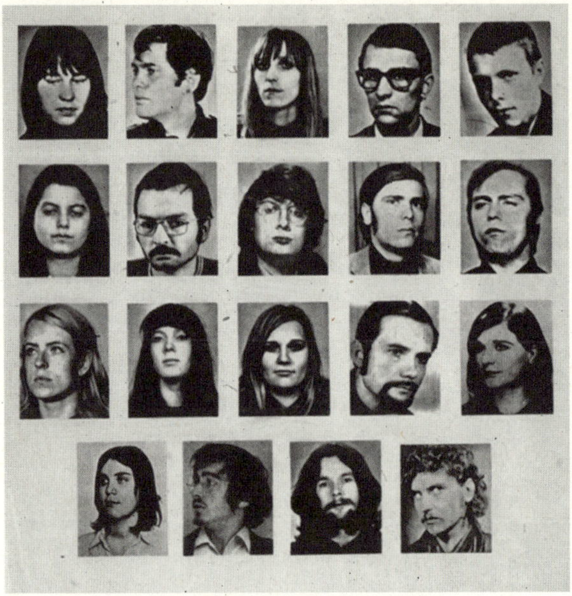

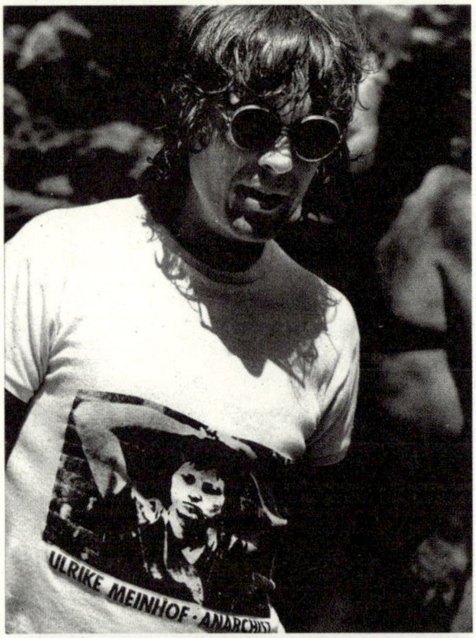

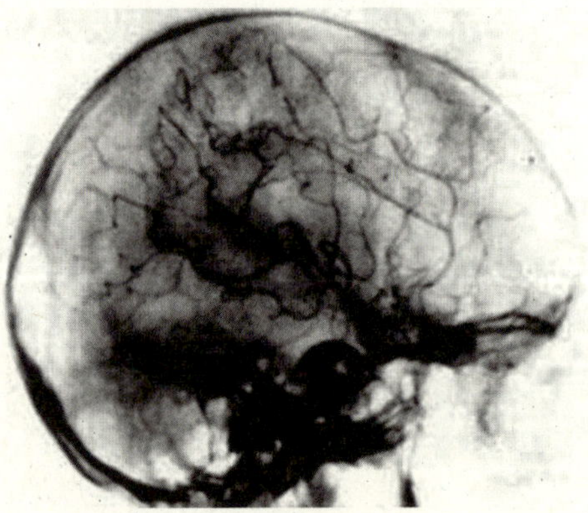

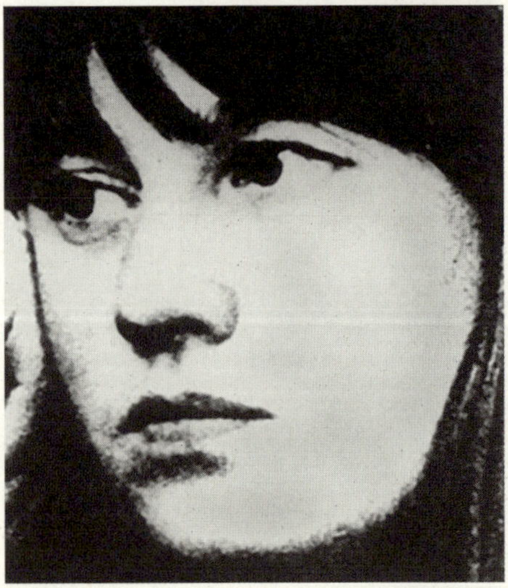

Notícia de premsa sobre l'assaig de Jean Genet "Violence et brutalité" publicat a *Le Monde* el 2 de setembre del 1977. | Fotografies de militants de la Rote Armee Fraktion, 1972. | Jordi Valls fotografiat per Salvador Costa, 1977. | Radiografia cranial d'Ulrike Meinhof. | Fotografies d'Ulrike Meinhof i Gudrun Ensslin. | Nota sobre el so dels concerts de Subway Sect i The Clash al Civic Hall de Guildford, 1.5.77.

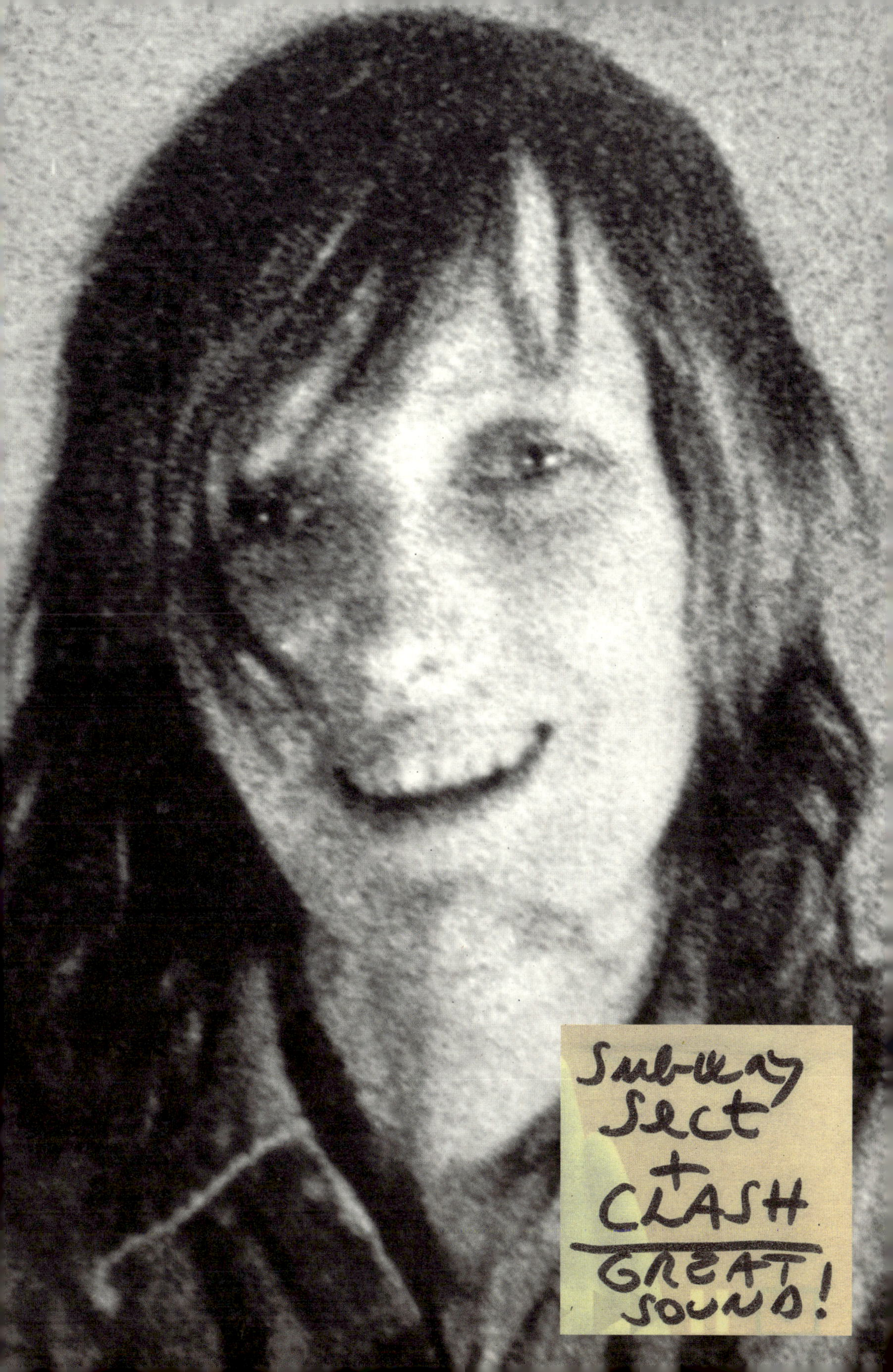
Subway
Sect
+
CLASH
GREAT
SOUND!

ABORTION

EUTHANASIA

MENSTRUAL

S NO RELIGION EX

ANARCHY

ENEMY OF

 Paraules de Jordi Valls, 2010.

TERRORISM

POLICE

KILLER

SUICIDE

HATE

THE STATE

FUCK MYSPACE

Nuestras maneras y nuestra afición a la historia habrán decidido a los más rápidos de nuestros lectores a calcularnos contrachapados a la antigua y a suponernos fósiles semiextintos del Pleistocenеté tardío, allí por 1977, período de deshielo de un movimiento anarquista tundido y apaleado, que reapareció por decreto y volvió a congelarse en diferentes facciones que dejaron bastante que cristalizar. Y es que ya no eran la megafauna de antaño.

Pues bien; es cierto, ahí estábamos, y algunos llegamos a correr delante de los grises (para luego jactarnos, en el patio del colegio, de las pelotas de goma que habíamos recogido en el campo de batalla), y algunos vimos en algún mitin la momia de Federica Montseny, pero aunque hubiéramos querido bailar con ella no se dejaba abrazar y se retiraba temprano, así que ¿qué hacer a partir de las diez? ¡Punk! éramos unos críos...

A finales de los 70, Crass y cía. tenían en España menos influencia que las Juventudes Libertarias de Burgos, y la ensalada tardó bastante en desplazar del menú a las anfetaminas y los barbitúricos. Algo se ganó, algo se perdió, pero no entraremos a discutir qués y porqués, que ya basta de marear la perdiz, aunque concederemos (aun sin acabar de entenderlo ni celebrarlo) que si el fenómeno punk pervive (si fenómeno alguna vez fue) debe de haber alguna razón.

El punk dispone hoy de más manuales, manifiestos y biblias que una biblioteca de ajedrez. Se puede practicar con sotana y hasta oír en una comisaria, aunque no es la norma. Igual que en la doctrina de la idea, hay una teoría para cada clase de anarquía, y menudean en él las aposiciones y los adjetivos, pero también quienes prefieren pasarse sin ellos.

No vamos a polemizar entonces sobre si el punk es compatible con la medicación para el Alzheimer o si caducó el mismo día que Sid Vicious. Comprendemos algunas cosas —o decimos que lo hacemos— y se nos escapan otras, como ¡que en MySpace las páginas punk se cuenten por millones y las anarco punk las haya a decenas de miles!

Imposible concebir que alguno de vosotros (si alguno hay), punks de línea dura y recta que devoráis burgueses y verdura y discrepáis de la dopa y del que vota, tenga relación con tal monstruosidad: lo sabemos, pero sabemos también que la asociación a un movimiento o tendencia que predica la rebelión pero fraterniza con el enemigo no es de recibo, así que sed buenos, empuñad las armas, aunque sean ceros y unos, y afeadle la conducta a vuestros consocios y conocidos, para que dejen de hacer el ridículo.

Alguien (más estupefacto que nosotros) nos ha hecho el trabajo, y ahí va nuestro compendio, traducido libremente, de argumentos e insultos contra MySpace. Quien quiera el documento completo y no se arredre ante el inglés, sólo tiene que buscar «the ABCs of Fuck MySpace» en la red.

MySpace pertenece a News Corporation, un conglomerado de doscientas empresas relacionadas con los medios de comunicación: 43 periódicos, 34 revistas, 29 estudios de cine o televisión y 72 canales de TV y varias editoriales. El dueño de todo eso es Rupert Murdoch, acérrimo patrocinador del Partido Republicano. La compañía se embolsa cerca de veinticinco mil millones de dólares al año. Fox News, una de las empresas, tuvo mucho que ver con el fraude electoral del 2000, cuando fue la primera en anunciar una muy dudosa victoria de Bush y logró crear una tendencia de opinión que fue decisiva para que... en lugar de un demonio tuviéramos a otro esta es nuestra .

MySpace ha amalgamado en un solo canal corporativo la mayoría de webs de grupos, homogeneizando así la imagen de internet y justificándose con la pobre excusa de una mayor comodidad.

No le faltan anunciantes y aumenta las tarifas basándose en la popularidad de su web.

Es hora de cortar con esto. ¿Qué carajo hace la escena punk en MySpace?

Es que es tan fácil...

También lo es Wal-Mart [una especie de Corte Inglés multinacional, que explota a casi dos millones de trabajadores] y cuenta con miles de tiendas y a nadie se le ocurriría incluir tal marca en la carátula de un CD punkarra.

Por otro lado, la web es una mierda: las páginas se hacen interminables y el diseño es infinitamente más pobre que el 99% de cualquier cosa que haya en la red. Por no decir que si soltáis una palabra más alta que la otra (lo que antes eran insultos al clero o tuteo a la autoridad) seréis reñidos o expulsados, y si no molestáis ni al carca de Murdoch es que los Crass tenían más razón que Dios y el punk murió en noviembre de 1978.

Las giras punk existían antes de MySpace, y si Black Flag pudo pasarse sin eso para dar conciertos por todo el país, tampoco te hace falta a ti. ¿O es que no tienes teléfono ni e-mail? ¿Qué banda existe sólo en MySpace, sin ninguna otra forma de contacto? ¿Quién anuncia sus conciertos exclusivamente en MySpace? ¿Qué grupo organiza sus giras solamente a través de MySpace?

¿Y qué pasó con el «Házlo Tú Mismo»? El punk se parió a base de fotocopias y de circuitos alternativos (que además funcionaron tan bien que fueron plagiados por el enemigo), así que no nos vengáis con que la comodidad es razón suficiente para aliarse con tipejos como Murdoch, a quien alimentáis con el solo hecho de aparecer en su web.

Más difusión no significa mejor difusión, sino generalmente lo contrario, a menos que aspiréis a ser conocidos por fans de Michael Jackson que ya no saben qué comprar o por renegados del country & western con distorsión.

Pensad en todo esto la próxima vez que actuéis ante cincuenta personas y un pollo (número y composición del público en el concierto de los Damned en el festival de Mont de Marsan), antes de anunciar: «Si habéis pasado un buen rato y queréis saber más del grupo, visitadnos en MySpace». O sed honestos y añadid: «Rupert Murdoch estará encantado de hacer negocio con vosotros».

Marc Viaplana

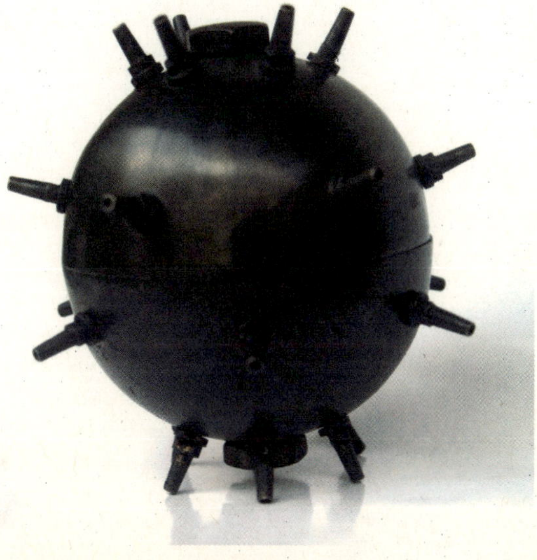

Text de Marc Viaplana publicat a la revista *BCN Week* l'octubre de 2009. | Orsini.

3 Foto: Big Stink. Nagasaki, 9.8.45. | Drugstore. | | Photo: Big Stink. Nagasaki, 9.8.1945. | Drugstore.

4–5 **«THE LONDON PUNK TAPES».** Arts Santa Mónica, por obra de Vagina Dentata Organ, presenta el original e inédito «The London Punk Tapes», el archivo de casetes con música original de los grupos punk Clash, Damned, Subway Sect, Sex Pistols, Generation X, Slits y Buzzcoks, que Jordi Valls grabó en directo, magnetófono en ristre –antes de que estos grupos entraran en un estudio–, en los antros urbanos y de los barrios suburbiales de Londres durante la explosión punk de 1976 y 1977. Al mismo tiempo, el archivo documental personal de aquella explosión (carteles, panfletos, programas, fanzines, revistas, recortes de prensa, fotografías, entradas de los conciertos, etc.) ha resultado, con la colaboración del artista multimedia Franc Aleu, en la producción de una pieza de videoarte, un collage de imágenes que se proyectará en siete pantallas simultáneamente, mientras suena la música grabada en directo con la calidad técnica de su momento. Con el mismo material documental se ha confeccionado, con el grafista Marc Valls, hermano del anterior, el libro catálogo del mismo título: THE LONDON PUNK TAPES.

El artista francotirador catalán Jordi Valls (1945), exiliado voluntario del franquismo, residió en Londres entre 1969 y 2007, y como muchos otros jóvenes del momento, vivió la revuelta a través de la música y el arte. A partir de la música electrónica e industrial de grupos como Throbbing Gristle y Whitehouse, se introdujo en el underground inglés y, en aplicación de la actitud punk del «Hazlo tú mismo» que propiciaba que todo el mundo se echara a la calle, empezó las ediciones de Vagina Dentata Organ con sonidos de no-música encontrada. Más que sonoras son obras audibles, en las que los sonidos se transforman en sonidos metafísicos y, al mismo tiempo, en esculturas u objetos-disco, con iconografías fetichistas reelaboradas visualmente por Marc Valls. Discos colgados de la pared o audiciones dirigidas al inconsciente automático irracional. La escasa producción de este artista nacido del punk se limita a impactantes cantos a los instintos básicos del sexo y la violencia en *Music for the Hashishins*; a las plegarias para el famoso suicidio colectivo de la secta del reverendo Jones en *The Last Supper*; al ejercicio físico rítmico de los tambores de Calanda en *The Triumph of the Flesh*; a los estertores y los gemidos de un orgasmo necrofílico con Marylin y Elvis en *Cold meat / Eros & Thanatos*; y el sonido de una Harley Davidson en *Un Chien Catalan*, entre otros. También expuso, una sola vez, en Grenoble el año 2000, en el marco de la exposición «Coup de grâce, la poésie comme connaisance objective», una serie de telas con retratos metamórficos de top models, pintados con la sangre del artista y esparcidos por el suelo de la galería. La obra de Valls, un nihilista fascinado por la destrucción por la destrucción, manifiesta con la realidad de la realidad un deseo de castrar una sociedad uniformada, aburrida y pedante.

Los punks, Vagina Dentata Organ y los dos hermanos Valls son el reverso del «Hay que ser radicalmente modernos» para una utopía ilustrada, cuando llegara el día (donde estamos) en que todos y cualquiera podría crear y editar en la cosmópolis. En el anverso de la *Iluminación* de los jóvenes *rimbaud*, el *infierno*; junto al *vidente* con rostro de *ángel en exilio* (de Verlaine), *mi contemporáneo, mi castrador* (de Pasolini). Drogas, sexo y violencia que escapaban de las sinestesias vocálicas de la bohemia simbolista en el siglo XIX para estallar de nuevo en la noche dadá, en la antipintura surrealista y en la respiración de la música punk.

La fatiga pre–postmoderna que cada revuelta acaba en «ismo», propiciarà un arte radical que en las postrimerías del arte mismo abandona el concepto para gemir e insultar sin proposición. El punk fue el «grado cero» de la música y el arte constituidos como una antimateria hecha de repulsión y podredumbre frente a los radicalismos formales seriados. El punk no abrió la politización ni a derecha ni a izquierda, sino en batallas campales contra la extrema derecha que es todo sistema. El dolor se exhibía en fotocopia quemada, un sadomasoquismo dolido por la estrechez del marxismo. Las letras punk son proclamas políticas de rabia.

En aquel marco de agonía de las ciudades postindustriales, de falta de expectativas para los jóvenes y de revuelta juvenil, los sintonizadores permitían la autonomía electropunk sin academia y corrían las carátulas de autoediciones y el intercambio de cintas sin mercado. La música no muere. Y la sociedad industrial fue tomada por independientes, autodidactas y amateurs, salvajes y perros callejeros, que en poco tiempo convirtieron la mierda y la podredumbre en oro, como Rimbaud. En Cataluña, el dictador acababa de morir, y los festivales de música (Canet Rock), más psicodélicos, layetanos y multitudinarios –con proclamas a favor de la amnistía, la autonomía y la libertad– contrastaban con el nihilismo político de los partidarios de la ruptura y los secuenciadores y audiogeneradores de primera generación de cambio de sistema. La mierda también se convirtió, sin alquimia, en oro. **/ Vicenç Altaió. Arts Santa Mònica | |**
"THE LONDON PUNK TAPES". Arts Santa Mònica, courtesy of Vagina Dentata Organ, presents the original, unreleased "London Punk Tapes", the cassette archive featuring original music by punk groups The Clash, The Damned, Subway Sect, The Sex Pistols, Generation X, The Slits and The Buzzcocks. They were recorded live by Jordi Valls, with his tape recorder round his neck, before these groups had made any studio recordings, in the venues in the city and the suburbs of London during the punk explosion of 1976-77. At the same time he has used the perso-

nal documentary archive of that explosion (posters, flyers, programmes, fanzines, magazines, newspaper cuttings, photographs, tickets for gigs, etc.) to produce, along with multimedia artist Franc Aleu, an art video, a collage of images, projected on 7 screens at once as the music is played, taped with the technical quality of live gigs at that time. Moreover, this documentary material has also been used for the eponymous book-catalogue, THE LONDON PUNK TAPES, which he has put together with his brother, graphic artist Marc Valls.

The unclassifiable Catalan artist Jordi Valls (1945), in voluntary exile from Francoism, lived in London from 1969 to 2007 and, like so many other young people at the time, he experienced the revolution via music and art. Through the industrial electronic music of groups like Throbbing Gristle and Whitehouse he got into the British underground and, following the punk do-it-yourself approach, which allowed anyone to get out on the street, he began releasing Vagina Dentata Organ with found non-musical sounds. They are audible rather than sonorous works, in which the sounds are transformed into metaphysical sounds and, at the same time, into sculptures or object-records with fetishist iconographies visually reworked by Marc Valls. Records hung on the walls or concerts aimed at the irrational automatic unconscious. This punk-inspired artist's sparse output is reduced to overpowering hymns to the basic instincts of sex and violence in "Music for the Hashishins"; the prayers for the famous collective suicide of the Reverend Jones's sect in "The Last Supper"; the physical rhythmic exercise of the drums of Calanda in "The Triumph of the Flesh"; the death rattle and the orgasmic groans for necrophilia towards Marilyn and Elvis in "Cold Meat / Eros & Thanatos", and the sound of a Harley Davidson in "Un chien Catalan", among others. He also exhibited once in Grenoble (2000) in the context of "Coup de grâce, la poésie comme connaissance objective", a series of canvases with metamorphous portraits of top models, painted in the artist's own blood and thrown on the floor in the middle of the gallery. The work of Valls, a nihilist fascinated by destruction for destruction's sake, manifests a desire to "castrate" a society uniform, boring and pedantic with the reality of the situation.

The punks, Vagina Dentata Organ and the two Valls brothers are the other side of "we've got to be radically modern" for an enlightened utopia when the day came (now) that anyone and everyone would be able to create and publish in the cosmopolis. On the flipside of the "enlightenment" of the young Rimbauds, "hell"; next to the "seer" with the face of "an angel in exile" (of Verlaine), "my contemporary, my castrator" (of Passolini). Drugs, sex and violence that escaped the vocalic synaesthesias of nineteenth-century symbolist bohemia to continue to explode again in the Dadaist night, Surrealist anti-painting and the roar of punk music.

The pre-post-modern fatigue that all revolts end in "ism" will bring about a radical art that, in the dying days of art itself, abandons the concept to groan and insult for no reason. Punk was the "degree zero" of the music and art that were established as anti-matter, made of disgust and putrefaction, in the face of the mass-produced formal radicalisms. Punk opened up politicization to neither the left nor the right, but in pitched battles against the far right that all systems are. The pain was exhibited in a burnt photocopy, a sadomasochism afflicted by the narrowness of Marxism. Punk lyrics are political manifestos of rage.

In that context of the death throes of post-industrial cities, of the young people's lack of prospects and of youth rebellion, tuners made possible electro-punk autonomy without an academy and self-produced covers and tape swapping without a market would be the norm. The music doesn't die. And moribund industrial society was occupied by independents, the self-taught and amateurs, wild men and city dogs, who after a while turned the shit and the putrefaction into gold, like Rimbaud. In Catalonia, the dictator had just died and the music festivals (Canet Rock), more psychedelic, Laietan and massive, with manifestos in favour of amnesty, autonomy and freedom, contrasted with the political nihilism of the supporters of rupture and the first-generation sequencers and audio generators of system change. The shit was also turned, without alchemy, into gold. **/ Vicenç Altaió. Arts Santa Mònica.**

THE LONDON PUNK TAPES. ¿Punk? «¡A la mierda con todo!», chillaban los jóvenes londineses en 1976, mientras 6–7
filósofos, sociólogos y psicólogos, siempre propensos a largas explicaciones intelectuales, buscaban con palabras sofisticadas, desde el confort y la seguridad de sus casas, un pretexto para definir el nuevo movimiento. Punk es la calle de los suburbios donde se mean y cagan los perros. Rostros sin futuro, guerrillas urbanas con guitarras y navajas. Tenía que ocurrir, para romper con el estado de apatía en que estaba sumido el rock, y coincidió con la violencia y la monotonía de toda metrópolis. La actitud y el sonido del punk son agresivos, anfetamínicos, más una masacre que una orgía, y se cambió la sierra mecánica por la guitarra eléctrica como instrumento de destrucción. La simbiosis entre los fans y los grupos musicales era perfecta, nihilista, con un deseo oculto de que la ciudad ardiera. El punk quiere escarbar con sus uñas el fondo de la llaga y arrancar y escupir sin escrúpulos su pus contra cualquier autoridad o institución estatal.

Entusiasmado por esta explosión urbana me lancé a la calle para grabar en directo las actuaciones de los siguientes grupos: The Sex Pistols, The Clash, The Damned, Subway Sect, Generation X, The Slits, Buzzcocks.

Estas grabaciones, inéditas hasta hoy, no habían sido nunca escuchadas en público.

Por otra parte, tratándose del añorado Malcolm McLaren y de Vivienne Westwood, era fácil predecir la gran campaña de marketing que en un futuro cercano se nos venía encima y que alcanzó la más extraordinaria *high fashion.*

Aun así, el fenómeno punk tuvo un impacto radical en el rock, con el resultado extremo de los Sex Pistols, un grupo cuyo nombre nos habla de sexo y violencia impregnados de anarquía. Eran los tiempos en que varios miembros de Baader-Meinhof fueron asesinados «por suicidio» en la cárcel.

En verano de 1976 estallan en Londres violentos disturbios urbanos *–riots–* contra la policía, durante el carnaval del barrio de Notting Hill. Un año después, los festejos públicos por todo el Reino Unido en celebración del vigesimoquinto aniversario de Isabel II, reina de Inglaterra, coinciden con las revueltas antifascistas del barrio negro de Lewisham, al sur de Londres, y con la inesperada muerte de Elvis Presley. Una gran metáfora.

Lo más enriquecedor del punk es su energía vital, visceral, y también su demostración de que cualquiera, con o sin talento ortodoxo, puede coger una guitarra, un pincel, un martillo, un escoplo, una cámara fotográfica o de cine y hacer cualquier cosa que se proponga. Sólo importa la intención, la fuerza de la imaginación. Nada más. Gracias, Malcolm McLaren. **/ Jordi Valls | | THE LONDON PUNK TAPES.** Punk? In 1976 the youth of London were shouting, "Fuck off!" The philosophers, sociologists and psychologists, who always seek a long intellectual explanation, were searching for a pretext to define a new movement with sophisticated words written from the safety and comfort of their own homes. Punk is the suburban streets full of dog shit and piss. Faces with no future, urban guerrillas with guitars and knives. It had to happen to smash the apathetic state in which rock found itself, together with the violence and monotony of any big city. The attitude and sound of punk is aggressive, amphetamine-fuelled, more of a massacre than an orgy. The chainsaw was exchanged for the electric guitar as an instrument of destruction. The symbiosis of the fans and the groups was perfect, nihilistic, with a hidden desire to burn down the city. Punk wants to scrape the bottom of the wound with fingernails and tear out and spit the pus to launch it unscrupulously against all authority and state institutions.

Out of fascination for this urban explosion I went out onto the streets myself to tape live shows of the following bands: The Sex Pistols, The Clash, The Damned, Subway Sect, Generation X, The Slits, Buzzcocks.

These unreleased recordings have never been heard in public before.

Also, through the sadly missed Malcolm McLaren and Vivienne Westwood, it was easy to predict the huge marketing campaign that would come our way in the near future, which is what happened, and end in the most extraordinary high fashion.

More than that, the punk phenomenon had a radical impact on rock music, the Sex Pistols being an extreme result of this. The name of this band speaks of sex and violence wrapped up in anarchy. It was the time when several members of the Baader-Meinhof group were murdered "by suicide" in prison.

In the summer of 1976, serious urban riots broke out in London against the police during the Notting Hill Carnival. A year later, the street parties all over the United Kingdom for the Queen's Silver Jubilee coincided with the anti-fascist uprisings in the black neighbourhood of Lewisham, in South London, and with Elvis Presley's unexpected death. A great metaphor.

The best thing about punk music is its vital, visceral energy, and the way it proves that anyone, even though they don't have orthodox talent, can grab a guitar, a paintbrush, a hammer, a chisel, a photo or movie camera and do whatever they set out to do. It only takes the intention, the power of your imagination. Just that. Thank you, Malcolm McLaren. **/ Jordi Valls**

8–9 Nota de Malcolm McLaren. | Tarjeta y fotografía promocional de la tienda SEX, 1976. | Palabras de Malcolm McLaren a Ray Stevenson, enero de 1976. | | Note by Malcolm McLaren. | Card and promotional photo for the shop 'SEX', 1976. | Malcolm McLaren's words to Ray Stevenson, January 1976.

10–11 Primeros conciertos de los Sex Pistols. * Primer concierto de Clash. Los Ramones actuan en el London Roundhouse con Flaming Groovies y The Stranglers. Imagen de los Ramones a partir de la foto de Roberta Bayley, 1976. ** Primer concierto de los Damned. *** Primer concierto de Buzzcocks. En Manchester, los Sex Pistols tocan «Anarchy in the U.K.» por primera vez. | El 13 de julio aparece el primer número del fanzine *Sniffin' Glue...* [50 ejemplares en fotocopias] publicado por Mark Perry. | Palabras de Paul Cook, 1976. | Notas de prensa, 1976. | Recorte de una fotografía de Ray Stevenson publicada en el periódico *Anarchy in the U.K.*, 1976. | No future: texto de la entrada de un concierto de los Sex Pistols, 1976. | | First Sex Pistols gigs. * The Clash's first show.

The Ramones play at London's Roundhouse with the Flaming Groovies and The Stranglers. The Ramones, from Roberta Bayley's photograph, 1976. ** The Damned, first show. *** The Buzzcocks' first show. In Manchester, the Sex Pistols play "Anarchy in the UK" for the first time. 13th July, first issue comes out of Mark Perry's *Sniffin' Glue...* fanzine [50 xeroxed copies]. | Words by Paul Cook, 1976. | Press notes, 1976. | Clip of a photo by Ray Stevenson published in newspaper *Anarchy in the UK*, 1976. | No future: written on a ticket for a Sex Pistols gig, 1976.

Cartel y panfletos diseñados por Hellen Wellington-Lloyd, Nils Stevenson y Jamie Reid, agosto del 76. | Un joven percusionista rastafari abuchea a un agente de policía durante la revuelta del carnaval de Notting Hill, el 30 de agosto de 1976. La revuelta se produjo al final del carnaval y acabó en una durísima represión policial. Entre los participantes en la revuelta estaban Joe Strummer y Paul Simonon de The Clash. Su canción «White Riot», escrita poco después, está inspirada en aquellos hechos. Fotografía de Homer Sykes. | Fotograma del film *Scorpio Rising*, de Kenneth Anger, 1964. | Conciertos de los Sex Pistols, en los meses de agosto y septiembre de 1976. | * Festival Punk de Mont-de-Marsan, Francia, con actuaciones de Eddie and the Hot Rods, Doctor Feelgood, Roogalator, The Damned, Bijou... | ** Primer concierto de Subway Sect; primer concierto de Siouxsie and the Banshees, con Sid Vicious —el inventor del «pogo»— en la batería. | | Poster and flyers by Helen Wellington-Lloyd, Nils Stevenson and Jamie Reid, August '76. | Young Rastafarian percussionist shouts at a policeman during the Notting Hill Carnival riots, 30th August 1976. Rioting broke out at the end of the Carnival and was severely put down by the police. Joe Strummer and Paul Simonon, of the Clash, took part in the riots. White Riot, written shortly after, is based on those events. Photo by Homer Sykes. | Still from Kenneth Anger's *Scorpio Rising*, 1964. | Sex Pistols gigs, during August and September 1976. | * Punk Festival in Mont-de-Marsan, France, with performances by Eddie and the Hot Rods, Doctor Feelgood, Roogalator, The Damned, Bijou...| ** Subway Sect's first gig; Siouxsie and the Banshees' first show, with Sid Vicious – the inventor of the pogo – on drums. 12-13

Cabecera y páginas del programa publicado por el 100 Club, en el que se anuncian los dos días del Punk Festival. | Nombres y sobrenombres. | Cubierta del K7 de las grabacions de los conciertos de Clash y Sex Pistols en el Punk Festival. Londres, 20.9.76. | Condón. | | Headline and pages from the 100 Club's programme for their two-day Punk Festival. | Names and aliases. | Cassette cover with live recordings: The Clash and the Sex Pistols at the Punk Festival. London, 20.9.76. | Condom. 14-15

Palabras de Malcolm McLaren. | *Orsini* de Marc Viaplana. | Escáner de un cóctel bomba y bomba orsini en suspensión. | K7 con la grabación de los conciertos de los Sex Pistols y The Clash en el 100 Club. Punk Rock Festival, Londres, 20.9.76. | | Words by Malcolm McLaren. | Orsini bomb by Marc Viaplana. | Scan of Molotov cocktail and Orsini in suspension. | Cassette with live recordings: Sex Pistols and The Clash at the 100 Club. Punk Rock Festival, London, 20.9.76. 16-17

Caras A i B del K7 con los conciertos de The Clash y Sex Pistols en el Punk Festival, septiembre del 76. | Recorte de periódico: Johnny Rotten fotografiado por Ray Stevenson en el Punk Festival. | La policía huye durante la revuelta del carnaval de Notting Hill, el 30 de agosto de 1976. *Evening Standard*. Hulton Archive. | | A and B sides of cassette with live recordings: The Clash and the Sex Pistols at the Punk Festival, September '76. | Newspaper clip: Johnny Rotten pictured by Ray Stevenson at the Punk Festival. | Bobbies on the run during Notting Hill Carnival riots, 30th August 1976. *Evening Standard*. Hulton Archive. 18-19

Steve Walsh (SW). Mark Perry (MP). *Sniffin' Glue...* 4, octubre 1976. | K7 con el concierto de Clash en la University of London, 16.10.76. | | Steve Walsh (SW). Mark Perry (MP). *Sniffin' Glue...* # 4, October 1976. | Cassette with The Clash's show at the University of London, 16.10.76. 20-21

Panfleto que anuncia una noche de pura energía en el ICA Theatre, octubre del 76. | | Leaflet announcing a pure energy night at the ICA Theatre, October '76. 22-23

Portada de *Sniffin' Glue...* 4, que publicó la entrevista a los Clash. | Cubierta de K7 con los conciertos de los Clash en la University of London, 16.10.76, y de los Damned en el Hope & Anchor Pub, 2.11.76. | | Cover of *Sniffin' Glue...* # 4, with The Clash interview. | Cover of cassette with live recordings: The Clash at the University of London, 16.10.76, and The Damned at the Hope & Anchor Pub, 2.11.76. 24-25

26-27 Páginas de la agenda de Jordi Valls, 1976. | Caras A i B de la cinta TDK con los conciertos de Clash i Damned en Fulham Old Town i en el Hope & Anchor Pub respectivamente. | | Jordi Valls' agenda pages, 1976. | A and B sides of cassette with live recordings: The Clash at Fulham Old Town and The Damned at the Hope & Anchor Pub.

28-29 Mark Perry (SG). *Sniffin' Glue...* 3, septiembre de 1976. | The Damned. Brian James (21), Rat Scabies (19), Ray Burns / Captain Sensible (22) y David Vanian (20). Fotocopias que ilustran la entrevista de Mark Perry. | | Mark Perry (SG). *Sniffin' Glue...* # 3, September 1976. | The Damned. Brian James (21), Rat Scabies (19), Ray Burns aka Captain Sensible (22) and Dave Vanian (20). Photocopies illustrating Mark Perry's interview.

30-31 Portada de *Sniffin' Glue...* 3, que publicó la entrevista a los Damned en septiembre de 1976. | Recorte de periódico con anuncios de conciertos de The Damned, 1976. | | Cover of *Sniffin' Glue...* # 3, includes interview with The Damned in September 1976. | Newspaper cutting with ads for shows by The Damned, 1976.

32-33 K7 con el concierto de The Damned en el Hope & Anchor Pub, Londres, 2.11.76. | Brian James, Rat Scabies, Ray Burns/Captain Sensible, David Vanian. | | Cassette with show: The Damned at the Hope & Anchor Pub, London, 2.11.76. | Brian James, Rat Scabies, Ray Burns aka Captain Sensible, Dave Vanian.

34-35 Steve Mick (SM). *Sniffin' Glue...* 5, noviembre de 1976. Fotografías de Subway Sect. | SUBWAY SECT. Vic Godard (19) y Paul Myers (19). | | Steve Mick (SM). *Sniffin' Glue...* # 5, November 1976. Photos by Subway Sect. | SUBWAY SECT. Vic Godard (19) and Paul Myers (19).

38-39 Recortes de prensa. | Portada de *Sniffin' Glue...* 5, que publicó la entrevista a Subway Sect, en noviembre de 1976. | Letra de la canción «Nobody's Scared» y K7 con los conciertos de Subway Sect y Clash en el Royal College of Art, en noviembre del 76. | | Newspaper clips. | Cover of *Sniffin' Glue...* # 5, with Subway Sect interview in November 1976. | Lyrics for "Nobody's Scared" and cassette with live recordings: Subway Sect and The Clash at the Royal College of Art, November 1976.

40-41 Panfleto que anuncia la exposición «Prostitution» de COUM Transmissions, sobre la cual el parlamentario conservador británico Nicholas Fairbairn declaró: «Estos son los aniquiladores de la civilización». Los miembros de COUM Transmissions integran el grupo Throbbing Gristle desde su debut, el 6 de julio de 1976, en la Air Gallery de Londres y marcaron el inicio de la era de la música industrial. | Conciertos de los Sex Pistols, en septiembre, octubre y noviembre de 1976. | Recorte de periódico: los Sex Pistols fotografiados por D. Muscroft en el Outlook Club de Doncaster, 27.9.76. | Titular sensacionalista de la revista *New Musical Express*, 6.11.76. | Título de una de las canciones de los Sex Pistols. | Entrada y panfleto de los conciertos de Patti Smith y The Stranglers en el Hammersmith's Odeon, 23.10.76. | K7 con el concierto de Sex Pistols en el Notre Dame Hall, en Leicester Place, Londres, 15.11.76. | | Flyer with ad for COUM Transmissions' art show Prostitution, about which conservative MP Nicholas Fairbairn said: "They are the wreckers of Western civilization". The members of COUM Transmissions formed the band Throbbing Gristle after their debut – 6th July 1976 – at the Air Gallery in London, when they introduced the era of industrial music. | Sex Pistols gigs, in September, October and November 1976. | Newspaper clip: the Sex Pistols in photos by D. Muscroft at the Outlook Club, Doncaster, 27.9.76. | Sensationalist headline from New Musical Express, 6.11.76. | Title of one of the Sex Pistols' songs. | Ticket and flyer for Patti Smith and The Stranglers at the Hammersmith Odeon, 23.10.76. | Cassette with the Sex Pistols gig at Notre Dame Hall, Leicester Square, London, 15.11.76.

42-43 Este cuadrado negro sobre fondo blanco es la funda del primer disco de los Sex Pistols. Cara A: «Anarchy in the UK». Cara B: «I Wanna Be Me». Cook/Jones/Matlock/Rotten. EMI Records, 26.11.76. Prohibido en la radio y con muchas críticas negativas en la prensa, «Anarchy in the UK» sonaba como nada que se hubiera escuchado antes. | Cara A del disco y letra de la canción «Anarchy in the UK». | | This black square on a white background is the sleeve for the Sex Pistols' first single. A side: "Anarchy in the UK". B side: "I Wanna Be Me". Cook/Jones/Matlock/Rotten. EMI Records, 26.11.76. Banned on radio stations and given bad reviews in the press, "Anarchy in the UK" sounded like nothing ever heard before. | A side and lyrics for "Anarchy in the UK".

44-45 SEX PISTOLS. Glen Matlock (20), Johnny Rotten (20), Paul Cook (20) y Steve Jones (21), fotografiados por Ben Browton en el Lanchester Polytechnic, Coventry, 29.11.76. | | SEX PISTOLS. Glen Matlock (20), Johnny Rotten (20), Paul Cook (20) and Steve Jones (21), photos by Ben Browton at Lanchester Polytechnic, Coventry, 29.11.76.

 Traducción al castellano. | | English translation.

Fotografías de Ben Browton. Steve Jones en el Lanchester Polytechnic, Coventry. | THE CLASH. Mick Jones (21) y Joe Strummer (25). Páginas siguientes: Joe Strummer, Terry Chimes (20) y Paul Simonon (20) en el Lanchester Polytechnic, Coventry, 29.11.76. | | Photographs by Ben Browton. Steve Jones at Lanchester Polytechnic, Coventry. | THE CLASH. Mick Jones (21) and Joe Strummer (25). On the following pages: Joe Strummer, Terry Chimes (20) and Paul Simonon (20) at Lanchester Polytechnic, Coventry, 29.11.76. 46–49

Insultos de Steve Jones a Bill Grundy, televisados en directo el 1.12.76. | Página y portada del fanzine *Bondage* 1, fotocopiado por Shane MacGowan, diciembre de 1976. | Televisor de los años setenta con la imagen de Bill Grundy, presentador de Thames Television, durante la entrevista con los Sex Pistols en el programa «Today», 1976. | Taza de té victoriana. | Mosca universal. | Palabras de Bill Grundy, 1976. | Reacciones de la prensa inglesa, diciembre de 1976. | | Steve Jones insults Bill Grundy, live on TV, on 1.12.76. | Pages and cover of *Bondage* fanzine # 1, xeroxed by Shane MacGowan, December 1976. | Seventies TV set showing Bill Grundy, a presenter on Thames Television, during the interview with the Sex Pistols on the 'Today' programme, 1976. | Victorian teacup. | Universal fly. | Words by Bill Grundy, 1976. | Reactions in the British press, December 1976. 50–51

Recorte de periódico con la noticia del concierto en el Leeds Polytechnic, primero de los pocos conciertos del Anarchy Tour que se pudieron celebrar. Convertidos en enemigo público tras la aparición televisiva en el programa de Bill Grundy, los Sex Pistols fueron criticados en el Parlamento y en toda la prensa. La censura y el temor de los responsables de las salas hizo que se cancelaran la mayoría de los conciertos programados en la gira. | Conciertos y cartel del Anarchy Tour. * Los Buzzcocks se unen al Anarchy Tour en sustitución de los Damned. ** Concierto contratado por segunda vez tras ser cancelada la fecha original. | Autobuses de Jamie Reid publicados en el fanzine de los Sex Pistols, *Anarchy in the U.K.*, 1976. | Cartel del primer concierto de los Heartbreakers en el Roxy Club: Billy Rath, Walter Lure, Johnny Thunders y Jerry Nolan, 15.12.76. | | Newspaper clip with ad for show at Leeds Polytechnic, the first of the few shows that managed to go ahead during the Anarchy Tour. Having become public enemies after their TV appearance on Bill Grundy's show, the Sex Pistols were criticized in Parliament and all over the press. The fear and the censorship of many venue owners and managers led them to cancel most of the shows in the tour. | Shows and poster for the Anarchy Tour. * The Buzzcocks join the Anarchy Tour, replacing The Damned. ** Gig rearranged at a later date after the original one was cancelled. | Buses by Jamie Reid in Sex Pistols fanzine, *Anarchy in the UK*, 1976. | Poster for Heartbreakers' first gig at the Roxy Club: Billy Rath, Walter Lure, Johnny Thunders and Jerry Nolan, 15.12.76. 52–53

Rich Defame. Fanzine *48 Thrills*, 2, enero de 1977. | Carnet del Roxy Club. Durante todo el año 1977 y hasta su cierre –en abril de 1978–, el Roxy ofreció una frenética programación de conciertos; Don Letts era el pinchadiscos y desempeñó un papel decisivo en la difusión de la música reggae. | Generation X, fotocopia de una foto de Harry T. Murlowsky publicada en *Sniffin' Glue...* 6, enero de 1977. | | Rich Defame. Fanzine *48 Thrills* # 2, January '77. | Roxy Club member's pass. All through 1977 and until it closed (April 1978), the Roxy offered a frenzied array of shows; Don Letts was the DJ there and played a major role in popularizing reggae music. | Generation X, xerox of photo by Harry T. Murlowsky for *Sniffin' Glue...* # 6, January 1977. 54–55

Portada del fanzine *48 Thrills*, 2, donde salió publicada la entrevista a Generation X. | Panfleto que anuncia una actuación de Generation X en el Roxy Club, 15.1.77. | K7 con la grabación del primer concierto de Generation X en el Roxy Club. | Billy Idol fotografiado por Ben Browton en el Lanchester Polytechnic de Coventry en 1977. Dice Ben Browton (para TrakMARX, 2005): «Me gustaba la música que hacían entonces: "Ready Steady Go" y todo aquello. Billy Idol era muy guapo, iba de rocker con pelo rubio oxigenado y una mueca fija en la cara, y los Generation X eran extremadamente buenos actuando sobre el escenario.» | | Cover for issue no. 2 of fanzine *48 Thrills*, which included an interview with Generation X. | Flyer with ad for Generation X at the Roxy Club, 15.1.77. | Cassette with live recording of Generation X's first show at the Roxy Club. | Billy Idol, picture taken by Ben Browton at Lanchester Polytechnic, Coventry, in 1977. Ben Browton says (for TrakMarx, 2005): "I liked their music at the time: all that 'Ready Steady Go' and stuff. I think that at the time Billy Idol was very cute with his rocker/peroxide quiff/snarly lip look, and Gen X were extremely slick onstage." 56–57

Disco, funda y créditos del single *Spiral Scratch*, disco autoeditado por los Buzzcocks en su sello independiente New Hormones. | Fragmento de la canción «Boredom». | Pete Shelley y Howard Devoto en una foto magnífica. | Cubierta de la cinta con el concierto de los Buzzcocks en el Coliseum de Harlesden, Londres, 11.3.77. | | 58–59

58-59 Record, sleeve and credits for Spiral Scratch single, Buzzcocks' record released by them on their independent label New Hormones. | Extract from "Boredom". | Pete Shelley and Howard Devoto in a great picture. | Cover for live tape of the Buzzcocks at the Coliseum in Harlesden, London, 11.3.77.

60-61 Conciertos de los Sex Pistols en los primeros meses del 77. * Primer concierto de Sid Vicious como bajista de los Sex Pistols. | Palabras de Don Letts, publicadas en *Sniffin' Glue...* 7, febrero del 77. | Vivienne Westwood con la camiseta «Destroy», que combina imágenes de un crucifijo invertido, una esvástica y una pequeña foto de la reina de Inglaterra. Malinterpretado por muchos, el grafismo es un ataque al gobierno, la religión y el fascismo. | Noticia del periódico *Evening News*, 1977. | Mark Perry fotografiado por Erica Echenberg, 1977. | Disco de vinilo flexible regalado a los lectores de *Sniffin' Glue...* | Escrito de Mark Perry en el quinto número de su fanzine. | Palmolive, batería de las Slits, fotografiada por Ben Browton en el Lanchester Polytechnic, Coventry, 29.11.76. | Letra de una canción de las Slits. | Cinta TDK con el primer concierto de las Slits en el Coliseum de Harlesden, Londres, 11.3.77. | Portadas del fanzine Jolt, fotocopiado por Lucy Toothpaste. | | Sex Pistols gigs during first months of '77. * First gig with Sid Vicious playing bass for the Sex Pistols. | Words by Don Letts, in *Sniffin' Glue...* # 7, February '77. | Vivienne Westwood with "Destroy" T-Shirt: inverted crucifix, swastika and tiny pic of the Queen. Misinterpreted by many, the graphics are an attack on government, religion and fascism. | *Evening News*. | Mark Perry photographed by Erica Echenberg, 1977. | Flexible vinyl gift to readers of *Sniffin' Glue...* | Words by Mark Perry in the fifth issue of his fanzine. | Palmolive, drummer of The Slits, photographed by Ben Browton at Lanchester Polytechnic, Coventry, 29.11.76. | Lyrics of one of the Slits' songs. | Live tape of The Slits first gig at the Coliseum in Harlesden, London, 11.3.77. | Covers of *Jolt* fanzine, xeroxed by Lucy Toothpaste.

62-63 Lucy Toothpaste. Fanzine *Jolt*, 2, marzo 1977. | THE SLITS. Ari Up (14), Tessa (18), Viv Albertine (22) y Palmolive (22). | | Lucy Toothpaste. Fanzine *Jolt* # 7, March '77. | THE SLITS. Ari Up (14), Tessa (18), Viv Albertine (22) and Palmolive (22).

64-65 The Slits fotografiadas por Ben Browton en el Tiffany's, Coventry, 1977. | | The Slits at Tiffany's, Coventry, 1977, photographed by Ben Browton.

66-67 «God Save The Queen», segundo disco de Sex Pistols, salió justo a tiempo para coincidir con el *Queen's Silver Jubilee*, los festejos de celebración del vigesimoquinto aniversario de la coronación de la reina Isabel II de Inglaterra. Nunca nadie se había atrevido antes a cuestionar la monarquía públicamente, lo cual no dejó de tener repercusiones: varios miembros de la banda sufrieron ataques en la calle; hubo incluso miembros del Parlamento que pidieron que los Pistols fueran ahorcados en el patíbulo de Traitor's Gate, la siniestra Puerta de los Traidores de Londres. Prohibido en la radio, en la televisión y en muchas tiendas de música, este single fue un éxito de ventas –150.000 en apenas una semana– y alcanzó el segundo puesto en las listas de éxitos [aunque por volumen de ventas le correspondía el primero] sin mención del nombre del grupo. Cara A: «God Save The Queen». Cara B: «Did You No Wrong». Cook/Jones/Matlock/Rotten. Virgin Records, 27.5.77. | Recorte de periódico del 8 de junio de 1977, con la noticia de la libertad bajo fianza impuesta a Malcolm McLaren y a nueve personas más por los hechos del dia anterior. El 7 de junio –en plena celebración nacional del *Queen's Silver Jubilee*–, los Sex Pistols desafían la prohibición de tocar en suelo británico y dan un concierto en un barco que navega por el río Támesis a la altura del edificio del Parlamento de Londres. La policía aborda el barco, se forma un caos monumental y varias personas son detenidas, entre ellas Malcolm McLaren, Vivienne Westwood y Jamie Reid. | Carteles del diario *Evening News* con la noticia «Sex Pistol apuñalado», que alude al ataque con arma blanca que sufrió Johnny Rotten en el brazo, el 18 de junio. Paul Cook y Jamie Reid también fueron atacados con barras de hierro. | | "God Save the Queen", the Sex Pistols' second single, came out just in time to coincide with the Queen's Silver Jubilee, the celebrations to mark the twenty-fifth anniversary of the coronation of Queen Elizabeth II of Great Britain. Up till then no one had dared to question the monarchy so publicly, and the reactions were not long in coming. The band members were attacked in the street, some members of parliament even demanded that the Sex Pistols be hanged at Traitors' Gate, the sinister gateway to the Tower of London. Banned on the radio, on television and in many music shops, this single was a smash hit – 150,000 copies sold in just over a week – and it reached number two in the charts [although by volume of sales it should have been number one] without, however, the band's name being mentioned. A side: "God Save The Queen". B side: "Did You No Wrong". Cook/Jones/Matlock/Rotten. Virgin Records, 25.5.77. | Newspaper cutting from 8th June 1977 talking about the bail imposed on Malcolm McLaren and nine others for the events of the previous day. On 7th June – at the height of the Queen's jubilee celebrations – the Sex Pistols defied the ban on playing in

Britain and gave a concert from a barge sailing on the Thames just by the Houses of Parliament in London. The police boarded the boat, creating major chaos, and proceeded to arrest several people, including Malcolm McLaren, Vivienne Westwood and Jamie Reid. | *Evening News* posters announcing "Sex Pistol stabbed", referring to the knife attack that wounded Johnny Rotten in the arm on 18th June. Paul Cook and Jamie Reid were also attacked with iron bars.

Giras de los Sex Pistols durante los meses de julio y agosto de 1977; en Inglaterra actúan con diferentes nombres 68–69
para eludir el veto. | Una gran concentración antirracista impide el paso a los manifestantes del National Front –custodiados por la policía– en Lewisham, barrio mayoritariamente emigrante, al sudeste de Londres, 13.8.77. Fotografía de Paul Trevor publicada en la revista *Camerawork*, 8. | Páginas del fanzine desplegable *Temporary Hoarding* publicado por Rock Against Racism y producido por Red Wedge Graphics y Lucy Toothpaste en 1977 y 1978. Durante los años setenta, la crisis y el paro en Inglaterra contribuyeron a fortalecer el partido ultraderechista National Front. Su discurso racista y sus acciones violentas contra los emigrantes fueron en aumento. Uno de los movimientos más combativos contra este ascenso del fascismo en Inglaterra fue Rock Against Racism, respaldado por músicos de punk y de reggae con conciertos de The Clash, X-Ray Spex, Buzzcocks, Tom Robinson Band, Steel Pulse, The Ruts, Sham 69, Generation X… | | Sex Pistols tours in July and August 1977; in England they played under different names to dodge the ban. | A huge anti-racist meeting bars the way of the National Front demonstrators – protected by the police – in Lewisham, a district of South-East London where many immigrants live, 13.8.77. Photo by Paul Trevor published in issue no. 8 of the magazine *Camerawork*. | Pages from the foldout fanzine *Temporary Hoarding* published by Rock Against Racism and produced by Red Wedge Graphics and Lucy Toothpaste in 1977 and 1978. During the 1970s, in Britain, the crisis and unemployment contributed to strengthening the far-right National Front. Its racist message and the violence against coloured immigrants were getting worse. One of the most combative movements against this rise of fascism in Britain was Rock Against Racism, which received support from punk and reggae musicians with concerts by The Clash, X-Ray Spex, Buzzcocks, Tom Robinson Band, Steel Pulse, The Ruts, Sham 69, Generation X, and others.

En 1977, Salvador Costa pasa una semana en Londres y fotografía la escena de allí. El mismo año publica sus foto- 70–71
grafías en el libro *PUNK*, uno de los primeros testimonios que vio la calle, editado por Star Books en Barcelona. En estas páginas: portada del libro –con grafismo y fotomontaje del mismo Salvador Costa– y fotografías de un concierto de The Jam, que capta toda la energía y proximidad entre músicos y público. | | In 1977 Salvador Costa spent a week in London and photographed what was going on there. That same year he published his photos in the book *PUNK*, published by Star Books in Barcelona, one of the first testimonies published anywhere. On these pages: cover of the book, with graphics and photomontage by Salvador Costa, and photos of a concert by The Jam, in which he captures all the energy and the close rapport between the musicians and the audience.

Salvador Costa se entusiasma por el ambiente que se vive en Londres y retrata con autenticidad la actitud de los 72–73
jóvenes que asisten a los conciertos y de los grupos en acción. Su mirada atenta se fija en los detalles y fotografía los conciertos de The Models, The Cortinas, Cherry Vanilla, The Police, The Jam, Lurkers, XTC, Stranglers, Johnny Moped y, tal como se ve en estas páginas, a Generation X y a Johnny Rotten. | | Salvador Costa was excited by the atmosphere he found in London and he authentically portrayed the attitudes of the young people at the concerts and the groups playing. His attentive gaze was drawn to the details and he took photos at gigs by The Models, The Cortinas, Cherry Vanilla, The Police, The Jam, The Lurkers, XTC, The Stranglers, Johnny Moped and, as we see on these pages, Generation X and Johnny Rotten.

En Barcelona, Salvador Costa conecta con La Banda Trapera del Río y se convierte en fotógrafo del grupo y autor 74–75
de las portadas de sus discos. Sus fotos son un tesoro documental y han sido publicadas en el libro de Jaime Gonzalo, *La Banda Trapera del Río. Escupidos de la boca de Dios*, editado por Munster en 2007. El texto «Qué pasa con La Banda Trapera del Río» reproducido en estas páginas está extraido de la publicación *La Banda de los Traperos* –editada por ellos mismos– y en él se cuenta la trayectoria, la actitud y las dificultades de la banda desde sus inicios en noviembre de 1976. | | In Barcelona, Salvador Costa got in touch with La Banda Trapera del Río and he became the group's photographer and designed the covers of their records. His photos are a documentary treasure and can be found published in the book by Jaime Gonzalo *La Banda Trapera del Río. Escupidos de la Boca de Dios*, published by Munster in 2007. The sentence "Qué pasa con La Banda Trapera del Río" transcribed on these pages is from the publication *La Banda de los Traperos* – published by them – and clearly shows the band's career, attitude and difficulties from their beginnings in November 1976.

76-77 Cartel del Festival Punk Rock de Barcelona, organizado por CucSonat en diciembre de 1977. | Jordi Valls y Salvador Costa, de marcha por Barcelona, 1977. | Cartel de Los Psicópatas del Norte, 1978. | Artículo rancio y confuso, con fotos de Johnny Rotten y Pau Riba, publicado en el diario *Catalunya Express*, 1.6.77. | Cartel del último concierto de The Heartbreakers en Inglaterra. | Últimos conciertos de los Sex Pistols. | Iggy Pop & the Stooges, autores de la canción «No Fun». | | Poster for the Punk Rock Festival, in Barcelona, organized by CucSonat in December 1977. | Jordi Valls and Salvador Costa on a night out in Barcelona, 1977. | Poster of Los Psicópatas del Norte, 1978. | Old-fashioned and confused article, with photos of Johnny Rotten and Pau Riba, published in the newspaper *Catalunya Express*, 1.6.77. | Poster of The Heartbreakers' last gig in England. | The Sex Pistols' last gigs. | Iggy Pop & The Stooges, composers of the song "No Fun".

78-79 Johnny Moped fotografiado por Salvador Costa, 1977. | Soo Catwoman fotografiada por Ray Stevenson; portada del fanzine de los Sex Pistols, *Anarchy in the U.K.*, 1976. | Sid Vicious y Nancy Spungen fotografiados por Silvia Resorte, 1978. | | Johnny Moped photographed by Salvador Costa, 1977. | Soo Catwoman photographed by Ray Stevenson: cover of the Sex Pistols fanzine Anarchy in the UK, 1976. | Sid Vicious and Nancy Spungen, photographed by Silvia Resorte, 1978.

80-81 Primer concierto de Último Resorte en el Hospital Psiquiátrico de Sant Boi, 4.11.79. | Prensa sensacionalista, 1978. | Sid Vicious fotografiado por la pasma de Nueva York, 1978. Michael Ochs Archives. | Recordatorio de La Banda Trapera del Río y convocatoria a un concierto funeral en Cornellá, en honor de Sid Vicious, un mes después de su muerte, 1979. || Último Resorte's first gig at the Hospital Psiquiàtric, Sant Boi, 4.11.79. | Tabloid press, 1978. | Sid Vicious photographed by the cops in New York, 1978. Michael Ochs Archives. | Card by La Banda Trapera del Río inviting people to the funeral gig in honour of Sid Vicious, in Cornellà, one month after his death, 1979.

82-83 Noticia de prensa sobre el ensayo de Jean Genet «Violence et brutalité» publicado en *Le Monde* el 2 de septiembre de 1977. | Fotografías de militantes de la Rote Armee Fraktion, 1972. | Jordi Valls en una fotografía de Salvador Costa, 1977. | Radiografía craneal de Ulrike Meinhof. | Fotografías de Ulrike Meinhof y Gudrun Ensslin. | Nota sobre el sonido de los conciertos de Subway Sect y The Clash en el Civic Hall de Guildford, 1.5.77. | | Press notice about Jean Genet's essay, "Violence et brutalité", published in *Le Monde* on 2nd September 1977. | Photos of members of the Red Army Faction, 1972. | Jordi Valls photographed by Salvador Costa, 1977. | Cranial x-ray of Ulrike Meinhof. | Photographs of Ulrike Meinhof and Gudrun Ensslin. | Note about the sound of the gigs by Subway Sect and The Clash at Guildford Civic Hall, 1.5.77.

84-85 Palabras de Jordi Valls, 2010. | | Words by Jordi Valls, 2010.

84-85 Texto de Marc Viaplana publicado en la revista *BCN Week*, octubre de 2009. | Orsini. | | Article by Marc Viaplana published in the weekly *BCN Week* in October 2009. | Orsini.

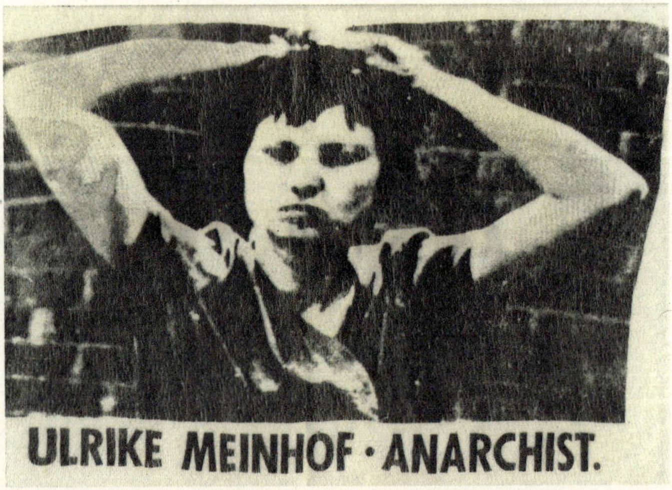